W9-AYT-821

MURDER

(AND BAKLAVA)

(A European Voyage Cozy Mystery —Book One)

BLAKE PIERCE

Blake Pierce

Blake Pierce is the USA Today bestselling author of the RILEY PAIGE mystery series, which includes seventeen books. Blake Pierce is also the author of the MACKENZIE WHITE mystery series, comprising fourteen books; of the AVERY BLACK mystery series, comprising six books; of the KERI LOCKE mystery series, comprising five books; of the MAKING OF RILEY PAIGE mystery series, comprising six books; of the KATE WISE mystery series, comprising seven books; of the CHLOE FINE psychological suspense mystery, comprising six books; of the JESSE HUNT psychological suspense thriller series, comprising fourteen books (and counting); of the AU PAIR psychological suspense thriller series, comprising three books; of the ZOE PRIME mystery series, comprising four books (and counting); of the new ADELE SHARP mystery series, comprising four six books (and counting); and of the new EUROPEAN VOYAGE cozy mystery series.

An avid reader and lifelong fan of the mystery and thriller genres, Blake loves to hear from you, so please feel free to visit www.blakepierceauthor.com to learn more and stay in touch.

Copyright © 2020 by Blake Pierce. All rights reserved. Except as permitted under the U.S. Copyright Act of 1976, no part of this publication may be reproduced, distributed or transmitted in any form or by any means, or stored in a database or retrieval system, without the prior permission of the author. This ebook is licensed for your personal enjoyment only. This ebook may not be re-sold or given away to other people. If you would like to share this book with another person, please purchase an additional copy for each recipient. If you're reading this book and did not purchase it, or it was not purchased for your use only, then please return it and purchase your own copy. Thank you for respecting the hard work of this author. This is a work of fiction. Names, characters, businesses, organizations, places, events, and incidents either are the product of the author's imagination or are used fictionally. Any resemblance to actual persons, living or dead, is entirely coincidental. Jacket image Copyright INTERPIXELS, used under license from Shutterstock.com.
ISBN: 978-1-0943-7357-7

BOOKS BY BLAKE PIERCE

EUROPEAN VOYAGE COZY MYSTERY SERIES
MURDER (AND BAKLAVA) (Book #1)
DEATH (AND APPLE STRUDEL) (Book #2)
CRIME (AND LAGER) (Book #3)

ADELE SHARP MYSTERY SERIES
LEFT TO DIE (Book #1)
LEFT TO RUN (Book #2)
LEFT TO HIDE (Book #3)
LEFT TO KILL (Book #4)
LEFT TO MURDER (Book #5)
LEFT TO ENVY (Book #6)
LEFT TO LAPSE (Book #7)

THE AU PAIR SERIES
ALMOST GONE (Book#1)
ALMOST LOST (Book #2)
ALMOST DEAD (Book #3)

ZOE PRIME MYSTERY SERIES
FACE OF DEATH (Book#1)
FACE OF MURDER (Book #2)
FACE OF FEAR (Book #3)
FACE OF MADNESS (Book #4)
FACE OF FURY (Book #5)
FACE OF DARKNESS (Book #6)

A JESSIE HUNT PSYCHOLOGICAL SUSPENSE SERIES
THE PERFECT WIFE (Book #1)
THE PERFECT BLOCK (Book #2)
THE PERFECT HOUSE (Book #3)
THE PERFECT SMILE (Book #4)

THE PERFECT LIE (Book #5)
THE PERFECT LOOK (Book #6)
THE PERFECT AFFAIR (Book #7)
THE PERFECT ALIBI (Book #8)
THE PERFECT NEIGHBOR (Book #9)
THE PERFECT DISGUISE (Book #10)
THE PERFECT SECRET (Book #11)
THE PERFECT FAÇADE (Book #12)
THE PERFECT IMPRESSION (Book #13)
THE PERFECT DECEIT (Book #14)
THE PERFECT MISTRESS (Book #15)

CHLOE FINE PSYCHOLOGICAL SUSPENSE SERIES
NEXT DOOR (Book #1)
A NEIGHBOR'S LIE (Book #2)
CUL DE SAC (Book #3)
SILENT NEIGHBOR (Book #4)
HOMECOMING (Book #5)
TINTED WINDOWS (Book #6)

KATE WISE MYSTERY SERIES
IF SHE KNEW (Book #1)
IF SHE SAW (Book #2)
IF SHE RAN (Book #3)
IF SHE HID (Book #4)
IF SHE FLED (Book #5)
IF SHE FEARED (Book #6)
IF SHE HEARD (Book #7)

THE MAKING OF RILEY PAIGE SERIES
WATCHING (Book #1)
WAITING (Book #2)
LURING (Book #3)
TAKING (Book #4)
STALKING (Book #5)
KILLING (Book #6)

RILEY PAIGE MYSTERY SERIES
ONCE GONE (Book #1)

CAUSE TO DREAD (Book #6)

KERI LOCKE MYSTERY SERIES
A TRACE OF DEATH (Book #1)
A TRACE OF MUDER (Book #2)
A TRACE OF VICE (Book #3)
A TRACE OF CRIME (Book #4)
A TRACE OF HOPE (Book #5)

CHAPTER ONE

London Rose felt a surge of air rising out of her lungs.

Don't yawn, she sternly told herself.

Whatever you do, don't yawn.

She didn't want to make her boredom any more obvious than she thought it already must be. But her boyfriend, Ian Mitchell, didn't seem to have noticed. He just kept talking endlessly—and nervously—about his accounting business.

"I'm talking about the future, London," Ian said. "And I think the future looks very good."

The yawn now started retreating, collapsing on its own weight.

The future, London thought.

She wished she had Ian's confidence in the future. She hadn't told him that she had every reason to believe she was about to become unemployed. She wished she didn't have to tell him eventually.

That might fit his plans perfectly, she thought as he kept talking.

"You know, I've been asked to prepare all the books for my corporation's acquisition and merger …"

She'd been dating Ian for about a year now, spending time with him whenever she was here in New Haven, and he didn't always drone on like this. She had an uncomfortable suspicion why tonight was different.

"All told," Ian continued, "our business looks very sound indeed for the foreseeable future …"

London was sure that this buildup was poor Ian's clumsy way of trying to get to a certain point. She had guessed his intentions when he told her he'd made reservations at Les Chambres, one of the finest and most expensive restaurants in New Haven. She'd been here a couple of times years ago, but she had never been ushered past the maze of rooms into a private nook like this before.

She and Ian even had their own small fireplace. In May, Connecticut evenings could be cool enough to enjoy a fire if you wanted the ambience.

The setting was perfect, with firelight and candlelight, a soft glow

1

from the wall sconces, warm brown-and-cream-colored walls, and comfortable upholstered chairs drawn up to a small, elegantly set table.

The meal had been spectacular—chilled English pea soup with mint-marinated goat cheese, followed by a wonderful lobster tortellini.

The conversation, however, left something to be desired.

Ian was still carrying on about business.

"… you see, I've been doing annual projections for the company …"

As London tried to listen, she poked her serving of *choux profiterole* with her fork. The dessert pastry crumbled exquisitely, revealing an airy puffiness inside. She took a small taste, and it melted sweetly in her mouth.

It's perfect, she thought.

As someone who'd traveled the world trying the most delicious foods of hundreds of different places, she knew she was a pretty good judge of fine cuisine.

In fact, the *choux profiterole* was so light and delicate that it seemed almost a wonder that it didn't float off into the air. Surely she could enjoy it despite the awkward circumstances, just as she had the rest of the meal.

She only wished the evening wasn't destined to end the way she expected.

"… and we are mapping out a ten-year plan and a twenty-year plan," Ian continued.

Suddenly he paused.

Is he going to ask me now?

It would certainly seem like a non sequitur after what he had said so far.

He looked at her intently and smiled the warmest smile he could muster.

"You see, our business is all about stability. Predictability."

He leaned toward her across the table and murmured, "And I think stability and predictability are important—not only in business but in life."

He paused again, then added in a significant tone, "Don't you?"

London swallowed hard and painfully.

What on earth am I supposed to say?

Fortunately, before she tried to say anything, their haughty French waiter approached their table.

"Is everything as you wish, *monsieur, madame?*" he said with a thick accent.

Before London could open her mouth to say everything had been perfect, Ian spoke up.

"*Madame* and I would each like a glass of your best cognac."

"Very well, *monsieur.*"

As the waiter left, Ian forced out a chuckle.

"The waiter called you *madame,*" he said.

So did you, London wanted to say.

"Yeah, well, I'm not getting any younger," she replied. "I guess the days when French men automatically called me *mademoiselle* are over."

Although thirty-four isn't exactly matronly, she almost added.

"Oh, I don't think it's an age thing," Ian said. "You're still young and beautiful. I'm sure the waiter thinks so too."

The compliment didn't make London feel any better. Unfortunately, she knew that the waiter had given Ian a near-perfect opportunity for a follow-up. If Ian had his way, French men would be calling her *madame* for the rest of her life. And a lot of other people would be referring to her as *Mrs.,* no matter how old-fashioned that had become.

Ian smiled at her knowingly and said, "If you ask me, Marcel called you *madame* because we look so much like a couple."

"Do you think so?" London asked.

"Oh, I *know* so."

It was probably true, London had to admit.

And was that such a bad thing, really?

Why couldn't she just accept a good thing when she found it? What could possibly be wrong with marrying a stable guy like Ian Mitchell? She knew she ought to appreciate how he was doing his inelegant best to make this evening really special. And the food really had been wonderful.

But all this talk about predictability was getting to her. Predictability had never been something she'd sought out in her life. She'd always been more inclined toward spontaneity and adventure. But tonight London found herself wondering if maybe her older sister's advice was right. Maybe she was reaching an age when she should be reining in her adventurous spirit.

Would that be so bad?

3

I'll always have memories—and stories.

She and Ian both fell quiet for a moment. London was starting to wish he'd ask and get it done with. She figured she'd somehow manage to let out an appropriately ecstatic if not entirely sincere yelp of surprise, then breathlessly say yes two or three or four times.

It seemed a shame there weren't any other customers around to applaud. That would complete the scene perfectly.

Why shouldn't I say yes?

She hadn't found Ian to be boring a year ago, when her sister, Tia, had fixed her up with him. That had been right after London's awful year of dating Albert, a charming, sophisticated, well-to-do ne'er-do-well—and an utterly self-centered narcissist. After that nasty breakup, she'd felt more than ready to date a square and stable sort of guy.

And maybe this wasn't such an inopportune time to tie the knot. She'd recently returned from her most recent assignment as a hostess on a Caribbean cruise tour. She was pretty sure that the eleven-day Yucatán trip was going to be her last with Epoch World Cruise Lines. Rumor had it that the once-thriving company was about to go under, finally succumbing to growing competition in the cruise tour industry.

In fact, she'd received a text message just a couple of hours ago from Jeremy Lapham, the cruise line's CEO, asking her to attend a video meeting with him tomorrow morning.

Probably to fire me, she thought.

It was going to be a sad milestone in what had so far been a pretty eventful life—the end of an "epoch," so to speak. And right now, London really wasn't sure what the future held for her.

Suddenly, the *choux profiterole* seemed less sweet.

But maybe it was time to welcome a little blandness into her life. Surely there was something to say for square and stable. Also, she was still taken by Ian's good looks. With his handsome, clean-shaven face, he projected a no-nonsense, down-to-basics quality—not like Albert, who had first attracted London through sheer smoothness. And Ian looked especially nice tonight, dressed in his best three-piece suit.

And at the moment, she figured they looked pretty good together. She'd put on one of her loveliest outfits, a chiffon maxi dress with a demure black top that burst into a colorful riot of printed flowers near the hemline. She had even wrangled her short auburn hair into a style that resembled intentionally tousled waves rather than simply looking windblown.

4

Meanwhile, London sensed a change in Ian's demeanor. The poor guy was sweating now, and he tucked his finger under his collar as if it suddenly felt too tight and he was getting dizzy.

Please, just get it over with, she thought.

"London, the point I'm trying to make is …"

His voice faded.

"I think I understand," London said as gently as she could. "Life and business are really just alike, aren't they?"

He let out a small, self-deprecating laugh.

"If only I could put it so succinctly," he said.

Succinct would be good, London thought.

But it quickly became apparent that still wasn't going to happen.

"London, when my parents were about our age, they made a … *merger,* not unlike the one I'm currently negotiating in my work."

A merger? London thought, trying to keep her jaw from dropping.

"And do you know what their secret always was?" Ian continued. "*Planning.* From the very beginning, they planned everything they were going to do with their lives down to the last detail. And that's what I'd like us to do, too, starting tonight—make plans."

London felt her face grow pale.

Make plans?

This was going to be worse than she'd expected.

She'd seldom planned anything serious during her whole life.

Ian added, "And you know what a productive, prosperous, and *happy* merger my parents' marriage has been."

London didn't know anything of the kind. During the few times when she'd met Ian's parents, she'd found them to be robotically distant—not just to her, but to everybody, including each other. To London, Ian's family home had felt like a scene from the original version of *Invasion of the Body Snatchers,* when everyone got turned into fake-human pod people.

Ian looked upward meditatively.

"I think, now that the second quarter is ending, and mortgage rates are at a historic low, it's a good time to put down a payment on a house …"

London shuddered deeply.

"We'll be frugal, especially at first," he said. "We'll live below our means, in the same neighborhood with Tia and Bernard. That's right near a good school. We'll buy a ranch-style house. No stairs, so we won't have to move again for fifty years. We'll have one child in two years, then another two years later, and another two years after that ..."

Three children? London thought.

She'd seldom given much thought to having children at all. They had always been a distant possibility, never a scheduled priority.

"We should seize this moment," he continued. "This is a great time to open college accounts and start layaway plans. We can also decide what schools the kids will go to, starting with kindergarten and continuing all the way through college."

He scratched his chin thoughtfully.

"We're both in excellent health, I'm sure we'll be able to enjoy life well into our nineties."

London shuddered as she tried to imagine all those decades of meticulously weighed and measured bliss. She hoped he hadn't already picked out a cemetery plot and a tombstone. Fortunately, his monologue faded away before he could start talking about what they might say on their deathbeds. He was sweating even more than before, and he looked like he'd just run a mile or so.

He spoke a little hoarsely now.

"London ... I guess what I'm trying to say is ... I'd be deeply honored if you accepted this ..."

"Merger?" London asked.

He smiled and shrugged and nodded, apparently speechless.

"Um, Ian ... what just happened? Did you just ... pop the question?"

Ian squinted thoughtfully.

"Why, yes. 'Pop the question' might be the right way to put it."

He reached into his jacket pocket and took out a little black box and opened it.

Inside, of course, was a diamond ring.

"London Rose, will you ... merge your life with mine?"

As London felt the world swimming around her, the waiter returned to their table with two crystal snifters of cognac. Ian started to raise his glass in a toast. But unable to help herself, London took an ungracefully large swallow. She figured she was going to need at least one more cognac before the evening was over.

Meanwhile ...

What on earth am I going to say?

CHAPTER TWO

The explosions nearly drowned out Tia's voice.

"You told him *what*?" London's sister demanded, almost yelling to be heard over the noise her kids were making.

"I told him I'd think about it." London raised her own voice in reply.

"What's there to think about? Ian is perfect for you!"

Arguing with her older sister often felt to London like arguing with a mirror, seeing a reflection not of herself but of how she might someday be. Tia's similar features carried just a bit more of a frown, her figure carried a few more pounds, and her darker hair fell stylishly straight.

London didn't bother to suppress an audible sigh of despair. It would never be heard over the racket going on in the nearby family room. Tia's two daughters, ten-year-old Stella and twelve-year-old Margie, were blowing things up in the war game they were playing on the TV.

At least they're not falling into gender stereotypes, London thought.

All the same, she had to admit that princess costumes and Barbie dolls and tea parties would keep things a whole lot quieter around here.

It was the morning after that awkward dinner with Ian. As she often did, London was staying with her sister during a break between ocean voyages. This time, she was already worrying about where she would live if there was no new assignment coming up. Would she have to give up hotels and her sister's guest room and find a place of her own?

Or will I ... ?

After all, the Ian option was still open.

In the midst of the household chaos, Tia had managed to make a huge plate of ragged-looking pancakes. A chaotic breakfast with the kids had just come to an end, and the two girls had stampeded into the family room.

This was the sisters' first real chance to talk this morning, and Tia was not taking the news of London's indecision at all well. Now as London picked at the remaining syrupy scraps on her plate, Tia popped up from her chair and started clattering around the kitchen.

"I'll do that for you," London called. "Just give me a minute." Through some feat of domestic black magic, the sink and countertops seemed to be full of more dirty dishes than the washer could possibly contain.

"Oh, I'm used to taking care of it," Tia chirped. "You just finish your breakfast. This all becomes automatic after a few years."

They were both trying to avoid noticing Tia's seven-year-old towheaded son, Bret, who was standing beside the table staring silently at London.

"What else did you tell him?" Tia asked as she whirled by, grabbing some dirty dishes that had somehow wound up on a kitchen chair.

What did *I tell him?* London wondered. She gazed around the room, still ignoring the silent boy.

It was hard to remember exactly. Last night seemed like kind of a blur. London wondered whether she'd actually gone into a state of shock after Ian had proposed to her.

"I think … I told him … I was very …"

Tia's eyes widened while London searched for the exact word she'd used.

"Oh, no, London. Do *not* tell me you said you were 'flattered.' That would be wrong on so many levels. 'Flattered' would suggest that you doubted Ian's sincerity. And on top of his many other virtues, Ian is sincerity itself."

London thought sincerity seemed an odd word for it but …

He was sincere, in his way.

Anyway, London agreed with Tia about the word "flattered." No matter how stunned she'd been at the time, surely she hadn't said she was "flattered."

"I think … I said … I was touched."

"'Touched'?" Tia said, snatching up some forks that seemed to have magically appeared on the floor. "You said you were 'touched'? What's that even supposed to mean, anyway? 'Touched in the head,' maybe?"

London shrugged.

"I don't know," she said. "Just 'touched,' that's all."

"What about thrilled? Delighted? Honored?"

The way London remembered it, "thrilled" and "delighted" were hardly the adjectives to describe how she'd actually felt. As far as "honored" was concerned, it wasn't completely inaccurate. She had actually taken it as compliment that a guy as thoroughly *solid* as Ian wanted to include her in his precise and elaborate plans. But "honored" would have sounded so … what, exactly?

Victorian, maybe.

The very idea of a proposal was too old-fashioned for London's disposition. But at least Ian hadn't gotten down on one knee and whipped out the expensive ring. After all the business talk, her nerves might not have been able to take that.

Tia opened her mouth to scold London some more, then winced at the sound of an especially loud bang.

She called out, "Girls, that's enough of whatever war you've been fighting."

Stella and Margie whined loudly in near unison.

"Awww, Mo-o-mmm …"

"Aunt London and I are trying to talk," Tia added. "And we can't even hear ourselves think."

The girls obediently shut down their game, but London knew better than to hope for any enduring peace and quiet. She felt a chill run up her spine, and realized that eerie wide-eyed stare from little Bret was getting to her. She couldn't help thinking he looked like a kid from another old science-fiction movie, *The Village of the Damned.*

In fact, all of Tia's children looked to her as though they, like the alien spawn in the movie, could make walls melt with their minds if they really tried. They had all inherited their father's bland blondness.

Abandoning the clutter that remained in the kitchen, Tia poured fresh coffee into their cups and sat down across from London.

"Adults are talking, sweetie," Tia said to Bret.

"OK," Bret said.

He didn't move.

"That means you're supposed to leave, sweetie," Tia said to him.

He looked at her as if she'd snatched away a favorite toy.

"But I hardly ever get to see Aunt London," he said. "She's always away, going somewhere really far off."

London felt a stab of guilt.

He really misses me, she thought.

The fact that the feeling wasn't exactly mutual added to her pangs of conscience.

"Aunt London comes around whenever she can, sweetie," Tia said, tossing London a look of disapproval. "She visits us several times a year."

Bret still didn't move.

Staring at London with rapt admiration, he said, "My friends think it's cool that my aunt is the captain of a ship."

Tia patted Bret on the head.

"Uh, Bret, Aunt London isn't exactly a captain," she said.

"What is she then? A sailor?"

London could tell from Tia's expression that she'd momentarily forgotten her actual job title.

"I'm what's called a 'hostess,' hon," London said to Bret.

"Like when Mom throws a party?"

London shrugged and said, "Well, yeah, kind of."

"With presents and everything?"

London had no idea what to say. How could she explain to a seven-year-old the intricacies of working as a hostess on a gigantic cruise ship? Every day involved scores of logistical challenges and almost nonstop one-on-one human contact. It was up to her to organize and oversee games of shuffleboard, table tennis, and bridge, as well as birthday parties, dining activities, concerts, and much, much more. Her job was to help make sure that everything went perfectly, and she was good at her job.

And then there's the fresh air, she thought with a twinge of melancholy.

On most mornings when she stepped out on deck, London enjoyed the ocean air. Although Connecticut could be pleasant this time of year, she hadn't even been able to get outside yet. She briefly wondered why the kids were still inside the house on what appeared to be a nice day. Hadn't her sister once said she'd chosen to live in the suburbs because they'd have big back yards and parks?

Tia patted her son on the head again. He still didn't move from the spot.

"Adults are talking, sweetie," she repeated.

"OK."

This time Bret turned around and wandered away. At that very moment, the two girls almost ran the little boy down as they came charging into the kitchen trying to cut each other to ribbons with Star Wars–style LED light sabers. Bret let out a yell and grabbed futilely at one of their weapons.

This time, Tia simply ignored all of them.

It was a lost cause, after all, London realized. As soon as Tia quelled any racket in this house, a louder racket would spring up right under both of their noses.

"What about the ring?" Tia asked over the renewed burst of noise.

"What *about* it?" London said, not exactly understanding the question.

"Is it nice?"

"I suppose. Pretty. Expensive. Diamonds and all."

"Well, show it to me," Tia said.

"I don't have it."

Tia shuddered from head to toe. She let out a little scream of sheer horror.

"Oh, no! You threw it away?"

Both girls stopped swinging their sabers long enough to demand, almost in unison, "You threw the ring away?"

"No eavesdropping," Tia snapped. "Back into the family room. Your aunt and I need a chance to talk."

When the girls didn't budge, she added, "I'll tell you all about it later."

Giggling, the girls trotted out of the kitchen with the boy close behind.

When they were gone, London explained, "I didn't accept it. I haven't decided whether to marry him."

Tia slapped the table with her palm.

"Then let me decide for you. We'll get him on the phone right now."

"Tia, no," London said.

But Tia kept talking as if she hadn't said a word.

"You'll tell him you were a dope last night, and you'll apologize profusely, and you'll explain that it was just a fit of temporary insanity, and tell him yes, yes, yes over and over again, and then you'll ask when is a convenient time for you to see him again and you'll give him a big kiss and presumably fall into bed with him. Let's get him on the phone."

"No."

Tia's lower lip began to jut ominously.

Oh, no. She's going to pout.

"I take this personally, London," she said.

Of course you do, London thought.

Tia continued, "And I'm sure Bernard is going to feel the same way. Have you forgotten we introduced you to Ian?"

No, I haven't forgotten.

Tia went on, "Don't you remember what a basket case you were after you broke up with that jerk Albert?"

Of course I remember.

And at the time, London had felt deeply grateful to Tia and her husband, Bernard, for fixing her up with such a regular, steady, pleasant guy. It had seemed like exactly what she'd needed after dating an unpredictable sociopath.

Bernard was a partner in Ian's CPA business. In fact, Bernard and Ian were best friends. Bernard had gone golfing this morning, and now it occurred to London that he and Ian might well be out on the course together. Would they be discussing Ian's plans for London?

No, she thought. *More likely long-term interest rates.*

Tia's lower lip was trembling now.

"This is hurtful, London," she said.

London wished she could shrivel up into a self-protective ball like an armadillo. Her older sister's capacity to put her on guilt trips had always been uncanny.

Tia continued, "All Bernard and I wanted was for you to have the same happiness that we did. I feel like we both deserve it, you and I, after the childhood you and I survived."

Oh, please don't go there, London thought.

"Our parents raised us just fine," London said.

"Well, it wasn't exactly stable."

London was relieved when the doorbell rang.

"I'll get that," Tia yelled as she jumped up and hurried off to answer it.

London sat staring at her coffee for a blissful moment while all the noise was in the background. She noticed that an assortment of toys seemed to have materialized out of nowhere on the tabletop, but she decided to ignore them.

Thinking about Tia's words, London had to admit that their childhood had not been stable. Being raised by two flight attendants meant living with a lot of disruption and moving around. But London had always had a greater tolerance for instability than her sister had—and a greater sense of adventure.

Even when she and Tia had been kids and their father had come out as gay, London had seen it as an exciting transition in all their lives. Her parents hadn't divorced, and the whole family had continued to live under one roof, as cheerfully as ever. And both Mom and Dad kept right on being good role models.

But their happy family hadn't lasted forever. When London and Tia were in their early teens, their mother had decided to go on a European tour on her own.

She'd never come back.

Nobody had any idea what had happened to her.

There had been no sign of foul play. She had apparently just walked away and taken off on her own. London had believed that something terrible must have happened to her, but Tia always said ...

"I guess she wasn't as happy as she made herself out to be."

That wasn't a question that London liked to think about. As an adult, she had avoided the whole issue by limiting her assignments to Caribbean cruise routes.

Tia came back and sat down across from her.

"It was just the yard man with a question," Tia informed her. "Now where were we?"

She was gazing at London with a hurt expression on her face, almost like she might start crying.

"I've always tried to be a good big sister, London," Tia said. "Haven't I succeeded at that?"

"Of course you have," London said.

"Then why can't you follow my example? Look around you. This is a *good life*, London. What Bernard and I have here with the kids and our friends and neighbors is good. It's *real*. You can't go escaping all over the world for the rest of your life. Life means responsibilities and commitment. And those are wonderful things. Those are *rewarding* things. Surely you can see that."

London flinched as the roar of a lawnmower started up outside the kitchen window.

Tia took a sip of coffee, then calmly continued her argument.

"The best thing," Tia was saying, "is that you and Ian can settle down right here in this neighborhood, maybe even just down the block."

London's felt a twinge of déjà vu at those words.

Then she remembered something Ian had said last night.

"We'll live below our means, in the same neighborhood with Tia and Bernard."

She almost gasped aloud.

Have Tia and Ian been conspiring together?

Is Bernard in on it too?

She cautioned herself not to get paranoid. Nevertheless, one thing seemed perfectly clear. Ian, Tia, and probably Bernard were on the same wavelength and had the same intentions toward her. If she married Ian, she would wind up *right here* in every sense.

Here, as in a version of her sister's life.

And the truth was, there were things about it that appealed to London.

It was a nice house.

Life here was stable—and safe.

Most of the time, London even liked her sister's kids.

And of course, she'd surely wind up enjoying her own kids.

Doesn't everybody?

So maybe Tia was right. Maybe London was just trying to run away from reality, from responsibilities and commitment. Maybe it was time to do what Mom and Dad had never quite done.

Maybe it's time to really grow up.

"London," Tia demanded a bit shrilly, "are you even listening to me?"

"Of course …"

A loud artificial whinny was followed by the squeaking and banging of Bret's toy rocking horse. The little boy had pushed his steed into the kitchen and climbed aboard the spring-mounted animal, rocking with all his might.

As Tia began to reprimand him, London's heard her cell phone ring.

It was a notification of an item on her schedule.

Meanwhile, the girls had started playing their video game again, filling the air anew with the sounds of explosions and gunfire.

London knew she'd never be able to carry on a conversation, much less deal with the setback she was expecting.

She said to Tia, "I've got a video conference scheduled for right now."

"Who with?"

"Jeremy Lapham. The CEO of Epoch World Cruise Lines."

"Wow, that sounds important."

Yeah, it sounds like I'm going to get fired, London thought.

Tia started to move some of the items on the kitchen table.

"I'll make some room for you right here," she said.

"Uh, Tia …"

London gestured toward Bret and the girls and the racket they were still making.

Getting the message, Tia said, "Go ahead and take it to the guest room."

London tucked the laptop under her arm and made her way through the bedlam.

She felt awfully jangled, but told herself that didn't much matter if all Jeremy Lapham was going to do was give her the ax. It might even be a relief to just get it over with.

Maybe, she thought, sudden unemployment would settle her argument with her sister. Maybe it would make Ian's marriage proposal seem a lot more attractive.

CHAPTER THREE

London felt apprehensive as she opened up her laptop in the guest room. She really wasn't looking forward to this video call. If she was going to get fired from Epoch World Cruise Lines, she didn't know why the company CEO felt that he had to give her the news personally. After all, she was just one among many middling employees, including cooks, cosmetologists, fitness directors, bartenders, and so forth. Surely he wasn't calling each and every one of them.

But Jeremy Lapham was known for his peculiar ways. London had never met him, but the eccentric, solitary, and shadowy CEO of Epoch World Cruise Lines was something of a legend in his way.

I guess I'm about to find out why, London thought.

With a sigh, London clicked open the videoconference program and waited.

She was startled by a sudden blast of sound, but it wasn't the signal for a call coming through. It was the computer-game warfare out in the family room blasting louder again. Before she could decide what to do about the noise, she heard her sister's voice call out sharply.

"Girls! Turn the volume down!"

Again came the familiar chorus, "Awww, Mo-o-mmm ..."

"I mean, it girls."

Then London found herself in relative quiet again—and also back in an unnerving state of suspense.

I just want to get this over with, she reminded herself firmly.

After this was done, she could decide what to do with the rest of her life. Not that there was necessarily much to decide, since Ian and Tia seemed to have plotted everything about her life in such excruciating detail. Probably all she really needed to do was take Ian up on his proposed "merger."

London's heart jumped as her computer beeped. She accepted the call and found herself face to face with Jeremy Lapham.

Well, not *exactly* face to face with him.

The CEO's webcam was tilted oddly. She had a clear view of his abdomen. He was wearing what seemed to be an elegantly patterned velvet smoking jacket. Stretched on his lap was an enormous, extremely fluffy black and white cat, which he was petting with long, slender fingers. The cat's purring made a slow, steady, rather ominous rumbling over the speakers.

She could see the man's neck and his cleft chin and a pair of thin lips. The top of the screen cut off the image just above his nostrils, so she couldn't even see his eyes. But it quickly occurred to her—maybe this was exactly how he wanted her to see him. It certainly lent him a certain mysterious aura.

Now those lips moved and Lapham spoke quietly.

"Hello, Ms. Rose. How are you today?"

London felt a brief impulse to just be honest and tell him exactly how she felt.

Kind of lousy.

I really want to get this over with.

But she didn't want to sabotage her chances of leaving Epoch World Cruise lines with the sterling job references she knew she deserved.

"I'm just fine, Mr. Lapham," she said instead. "How are you?"

"I'm well, thank you."

At that moment the bedroom door swung open. London turned and saw little Bret come into the room. He walked over near her chair and stood there silently, gazing up at her again.

Although Bret wasn't within range of her webcam, and she knew Jeremy Lapham couldn't see him, London knew it would be impossible to ignore the large-eyed boy staring at her.

She silently made a shooing movement with her hand, but he didn't seem to get the message and didn't move a muscle.

Then Stella and Margie rushed into the room, complaining in loud whispers.

"You're not supposed to be here!"

"Mom said you couldn't come in here!"

Their scolding didn't seem to make an impression on the boy, who didn't even look at them. What followed was a flurry of half-whispers and whined complaints as the girls took their little brother by the hand and escorted him out of the room.

When the door closed again, London saw that Lapham's cat was tilting his head luxuriously backward so that his master could scratch him under his chin.

"I wasn't aware that you had children," Lapham said.

"I don't," London said.

"No? I could swear that I just heard …"

"Those are my older sister's kids," London said. "I'm staying at their house for a few days."

"So you have no children of your own?"

"No."

"And you've never been married?"

"No."

London felt a bead of sweat break out on her forehead, and her palms felt suddenly clammy. Probably without meaning to, Lapham had touched on a topic that pushed her buttons, especially today.

"One of these days your biological clock alarm is going to go off," Tia often told her. *"Then you'll really be sorry."*

London didn't like being reminded of that.

"I was just having a look at your curriculum vitae," Lapham continued. "You're an interesting young lady, London Rose."

London squinted with surprise.

"Uh, thank you," she said.

The cat rolled over on his back and Lapham began to stroke his stomach.

"I've read your employee evaluations," he said. "Your supervisors have nothing but wonderful things to say about you. Which is all very remarkable, considering your modest beginnings. You don't even have a four-year college degree."

London felt a twitch of defensiveness. Her lack of much formal schooling was something of a sore spot for her.

But Lapham continued, "And yet you seem to be extremely well-rounded, with a rich understanding of culture, history, art, and music. You also have a keen business sense. In fact, your supervisors say you're as knowledgeable as many people with advanced degrees in liberal arts and languages and business. You're even fluent in several languages. How have you managed to make so much of yourself?"

London felt a little dizzy at this last question.

Just now her sister had criticized her for not wanting to grow up.

But this man was praising London for things that Tia couldn't possibly understand or appreciate.

It felt good, but puzzling.

What's going on? she wondered.

18

"Well," she answered cautiously, "I do have a two-year Associate of Science Degree in Hospitality and Restaurant Management from Ketchum Community College right here in New Haven."

"How were your grades?" Lapham asked.

"Good," London said.

"Oh, let's not have any false modesty. You graduated with a perfect GPA."

London tried to keep her mouth from falling open. Apparently, Lapham had taken more than a "look" at her curriculum vitae. He'd studied it in some detail. But if he knew so much about her, why was he asking her all these questions?

"What came next?" he asked.

"Well, as soon as I graduated, I started working in a variety of jobs in the hospitality industry. Finally I applied to work for Epoch World, and I got the job. I fell in love with hostessing and worked really hard. I learned how to fill in for this person or that, picking up a lot of skills along the way, from bartending to bookkeeping."

"Quite the jack-of-all-trades, weren't you?"

"I guess you could say that," London said, finally throwing modesty to the winds. "I could lead tours, pair the best wines with any meal. Once I was able to give directions in a city I'd never even been to before."

London still couldn't see Lapham's eyes, but his cat seemed to be gazing at her with approval.

"Excellent," Lapham said. "But where did you come by your skill with languages?"

London couldn't help but chuckle a little.

"When you're a little kid and your parents are flight attendants, and you're being yanked all over the world from one country to the next, you've got to learn some of the local lingo just to play hopscotch with other kids. You could drop me into any country in Europe and I'd manage to get by."

Lapham laughed aloud.

"You haven't told me anything I don't already know," he said. "But it gives me a lot of pleasure to hear it directly from you. You mustn't underestimate yourself, London Rose."

London felt a thrill from head to toe.

Only now did she realize how hard she'd been struggling with insecurity since last night's dinner with Ian.

19

She'd really, really needed to have this conversation.

But where is he going with this?

"You may have heard that Epoch World Cruise Lines is running into some financial difficulties," Lapham said. "It's a competitive business, and we've lagged behind in some ways. I'm afraid we're having to sell off our ocean-going fleet of liners."

London's spirits sagged. It sounded like his kind words were just to cushion the letdown after all.

Then Lapham said, "But we're not going to go belly-up, believe me. There's plenty of life in Epoch World yet."

He tilted his screen so that the cat disappeared, and his own warm, smiling eyes came into view.

"Tell me, Ms. Rose," he said. "Does this melody mean anything to you?"

He pushed a button, and a recording of a small string orchestra started to play. It was a delightful melody, as light and airy and perfect as last night's *choux profiterole.*

London felt a deep, emotional stab of nostalgia.

The music meant something to her, all right—more than Mr. Lapham could possibly know from having read her curriculum vitae.

Don't cry, she told herself.

But it was hard not to cry. She remembered her mother's glowing expression as she'd played this very melody on the piano. And now the sound of it flooded London with some of the most wonderful memories of her childhood.

"Well?" Lapham asked.

London gulped down a knot of emotion.

"It's by Mozart," she said, "and it's called *Eine Kleine Nachtmusik.*"

"Which means?"

"It can be translated as either 'a little night music,' or 'a little serenade.'"

"Very good," Lapham said. "As it happens, *Nachtmusik* is also the name of a new cruise boat I just purchased—not a huge ocean-going ship like you're used to, but a more modest vessel to travel the rivers of Europe."

"A tour boat?" London asked.

"More like a large luxurious yacht," Lapham said, "with only about a hundred passengers. I believe there's a great future in river tours. I'm

20

really hoping to launch a whole new *epoch* for Epoch World Cruise Lines. But there's a lot at stake in this new venture. I want to get things off to the best possible start. And to do that, I have to hire the best possible staff."

London's heart jumped up into her throat.

She suddenly realized that Jeremy Lapham was about to offer her a proposal—and a very different sort of proposal than the one Ian had made last night.

"I want you to be the *Nachtmusik*'s social director," Lapham said. "It will involve responsibilities and duties far beyond anything you've done for us before. But before you say yes or no, I should tell you—if you want the job, you must be in Hungary by tomorrow morning. That's where the *Nachtmusik* will begin her voyage on the Danube. I apologize for the short notice, but the position came open quite unexpectedly."

London's eyes widened. It finally made sense for Lapham to be calling her personally. He had an emergency on his hands, an essential slot to fill, and this phone call was an interview for the position.

"How …?" was the only word that she could get out right away.

He kept on talking. "I've already booked you on a flight tonight. I've checked it out, and there's a connection from New Haven to New York, and then it will be an overnighter to Budapest. But you have to let me know right now if you're willing to go. I'll email you the contract and details on the compensation package, which I think you'll find satisfactory."

Then Lapham was silent, waiting for her answer.

London's thoughts were racing.

It was Sunday morning now. If she did this she'd be in another country for breakfast tomorrow. A wonderful country, rich with history but also highly developed and comfortably modern.

Even so, this seemed like a staggering decision—especially after all the doubts that had troubled her since yesterday.

At that moment, as if on cue, Bret came charging into the room followed by his two sisters, who were attacking him with light sabers. Howling, he ducked under the covers of the bed and his sisters pounced, beating their plastic weapons at the living lump under the blankets.

Tia came sweeping into the room, scolding her children and tucking Bret under one arm. She gave London an apologetic look. Their eyes met for a moment, and London again had that feeling that she was looking into a mirror—or rather into a future in which she was living her sister's life down to the smallest detail.

She remembered what Ian had said last night.

"We'll have one child in two years, then another two years later, and another two years after that ..."

Something dawned on her.

That was exactly the schedule Tia and Bernard had stuck to at the beginning of their marriage—three children within the first six years. In that future reality London would not only have a mirror-image family, she'd have the same kids' toys, the same sink full of dishes, the same ...

Everything!

London felt her own future life becoming monotonous already as Tia herded her children out of the guest room and pulled the door shut again.

Something her sister had just said echoed through London's mind.

"You can't go escaping all over the world for the rest of your life."

But for the first time, it occurred to London—traveling was *not* escape, at least not for her.

For me, it's life itself.

"Yes," she said to Lapham. "Oh, yes. Thank you. I will take that job."

CHAPTER FOUR

London was dashing through JFK Airport when her phone rang.

Oh, please, let this be Ian, she thought as she took the phone out of her bag.

She'd been trying to reach him ever since she'd gotten off the phone with Jeremy Lapham this morning. But she knew he'd been out earlier today golfing with a client, and he never let himself be disturbed on the links. Although she didn't look forward to this conversation, she definitely didn't want to leave the country without resolving things with him.

She took the call, and sure enough, it was Ian.

"Ian, hi," she said breathlessly.

"Hello, London."

"Um … I've been thinking about your 'merger' and …"

"And?"

London was just picking her carry-on bags up after they'd passed through the metal detector.

"Like I said last night, I'm touched," she said. "But …"

A silence fell between them.

"I got an offer this morning," she said. "The CEO of Epoch World Cruise Lines called me and offered me … well, a job I just couldn't turn down."

She heard a grunt of impatience in Ian's voice.

"More traveling?" he asked sternly.

The question took her aback. Of course, the answer was yes—but it was also so much more than that. This job was important to her in ways she didn't know how to begin to explain to him.

"It's something different from what I've been doing," she said. "It's a river tour boat that's setting out on a trip on the Danube. The trip starts tomorrow in Budapest. And I won't be just a hostess anymore. I'll be the social director for the whole tour."

Another silence fell.

He's not impressed, she thought.

At the same time she wondered—why should he be? Those job

titles—hostess and social director—didn't mean a thing to him.

"Where does this leave us?" Ian asked.

London was gasping as she rushed through the concourse toward her departure gate.

"Ian, I'm … I'm afraid I'm just not ready for your—'merger.' I'm not saying I'll feel that way forever. Maybe after a couple more years of—"

"The deal is off," Ian interrupted.

Huh? London almost said aloud.

"I gave you my best offer," Ian added. "Now that offer is withdrawn. I'm afraid this matter is no longer up for negotiation."

London was dumbfounded.

Up for negotiation?

She certainly hadn't made that assumption …

Or did I?

Maybe she'd been too vague. Maybe he'd thought she was only stalling.

Or bargaining.

Meanwhile, Ian sounded almost spookily businesslike, and yet somehow very polite at the same time.

"I hope you understand, London. It's just that I'm a very busy man and I'm not sitting still. The train has left the station, so to speak—and you've missed it. I wish you the best, though, and I'll harbor no hard feelings."

"I—I'm glad to hear that," London said.

"I hope you don't regret this decision," Ian added. "Forgive me for saying so, but I don't think it sounds especially wise. But then, it's your choice, not mine. And I wish you good travels—although Hungary sounds like a very depressing place to me."

"Thank you for … understanding," London said.

They both said goodbye and ended the call.

London suddenly found herself breathing easier, as if some sort of load had been lifted. She felt unexpectedly relieved.

Although she'd told Ian that her choice might not be permanent, she realized now that she really couldn't ever live her sister's life, much less with someone as … it took a moment for the right word to come to her.

Someone as *managerial* as Ian.

It was hard to imagine that, just this morning, she'd still been struggling with whether to accept Ian's "merger."

In fact, maybe if Jeremy Lapham had actually fired her instead of offering her such a tantalizing job, she and Tia might be making wedding plans at this very moment.

A narrow escape, she realized as she showed her boarding pass to the attendant at the flight gate, then joined the line of passengers to board the plane.

*

London's eyes snapped open at the sound of the pilot's voice.

"We have just arrived at the Budapest Ferenc Liszt International Airport, named for the virtuoso pianist, conductor, organist, and composer, Franz Liszt ..."

She smiled as the same announcement was repeated in French, German, Italian, and of course Hungarian. It felt wonderful to wake up to the sounds of all those languages.

I'm really in Europe again, she realized.

It was now just after eight in the morning here in Budapest, although London knew that her body would keep trying to convince her that it was hours earlier. But as a seasoned traveler, she had tricks for diminishing jetlag from her transatlantic trip. For one thing, she'd slept as much as she possibly could during the eight-and-a-half-hour flight. At the moment she felt quite refreshed.

She got up from her seat and opened the luggage compartment and took down her carry-on bags, then squeezed her way off the plane with the other passengers. She felt exhilarated even by the crush of bodies as she made her way toward the immigration desks and presented the form she'd filled out during the flight.

"Enjoy your stay in Budapest," the smiling immigration official said to her in accented English.

London summoned up the courage to try a Hungarian word.

"Köszönöm," she replied, smiling back at him.

His amused nod told her that she might not have pronounced "thanks" perfectly, but that he appreciated the effort.

Then she went to the baggage pickup area, where her bags quickly arrived on the carousel. Since she had no goods to declare, she didn't have to make a stop at customs. A porter put her bags onto a handcart, and she followed him into the main terminal.

She gasped aloud as the vast, modern "Sky Court" spread all around her with its soaring ceiling and overhanging gallery and newspaper and gift stalls.

London suddenly felt freer than she had in a long time. She took special delight in the crowds of people darting about everywhere, some of them speaking languages of which she didn't know a single word. It was chaotic, certainly—but it was the kind of chaos that suited her, nothing like the chaos of her sister's home.

She followed the porter outside, where he quickly flagged down a little yellow cab and loaded her bags into its trunk.

The driver drove her into the heart of the part of the city known as *Pest*, where shiny glass office buildings gradually gave way to older brick buildings, and the city revealed more and more of its ancient character.

Finally, London Rose gasped with delight as the little yellow cab turned onto Soroksári Road. A familiar melody lilted through her mind—"The Blue Danube."

The magnificent river had just come fully into view, and the breathtaking scene proved that the famous waltz was aptly titled. The Danube was a luscious shade of blue in the morning light, and it was flanked on either side by one of the most beautiful cities in the world.

Budapest was spread out around her like some sort of half-forgotten dream. The grand sights of this ancient city fairly shimmered with her pleasant memories of wide brick buildings, domes and towers, parks, shops, and street performers.

London smiled at what Ian had said to her before her departure.

"Hungary sounds like a very depressing place to me."

She wondered where on earth he had gotten such an idea. There was nothing the least bit depressing about this gorgeous city.

She rolled down the cab window and breathed the fresh, clean air. It was promising to be a cool, lovely day, and Budapest sparkled all around her, truly living up to its nickname, the "Pearl of the Danube."

And now here she was on a riverfront drive, looking out her taxi window at the lovely Danube with its beautiful bridges. All kinds of boats were docked along the waterfront, ranging from private yachts to long, low river tour ships, some of which could hold nearly two hundred passengers. Across the river was the part of the city known as *Buda*, hilly and wooded with old, red-roofed buildings.

This seemed like a good time to give her small Hungarian

vocabulary another bit of exercise.

"I haven't been to Budapest in a while," she said to the driver in Hungarian.

"When was your last visit?" the driver asked, sounding pleased that a foreigner was going to the trouble to speak with him in his own language.

"It's hard to say," London said as the years seemed to gape behind her. "Not since the last century, I guess."

The driver chuckled.

"That narrows it down to about a hundred years," he said.

London chuckled as well.

"Well then, I guess it was sometime during the 1990s," she said.

"That's not as long ago as it sounds. And Budapest never changes much, at least not in its heart."

The driver pointed to a large modern building near the riverbank. It had enormous windows fronted by straight, simple columns and angular shapes on the roof.

"You wouldn't have seen that building before," he said. "It's the Müpa Budapest, a cultural center that opened in 2005."

As they drove past the Müpa, the driver pointed to another large, eccentrically shaped building with a rounded entrance. "And that's the Hungarian National Theatre. It opened in 2002. Odd to look at, isn't it? At least many people who live here think so."

The dates made London feel just a little queasy.

Has it really been that long since I was here? she thought.

She suddenly felt older than she usually thought of herself as being. But at least she was still able to ask some questions in Hungarian—and even better, she could understand most of the replies.

And she could see that much of the city really hadn't changed. Most of it was too rooted and monumental to ever give way to time. Across the river she could see the Citadella, a mighty stone fortress that had been built on that hilltop in the nineteenth century. Farther along the opposite bank was the breathtaking Buda Castle, more than a mile across with a magnificent dome rising in its center. It loomed ever larger as they continued along the riverfront.

The sight of the castle gave her a pang as she remembered visiting it with her parents when she'd been just a little girl. Her mom and dad had taken her there for several days on end to explore the endless wonders of the castle—its galleries, crown jewels, sculptures,

27

fountains, and historical rooms.

It seems like just yesterday, she thought.

But many years had passed, and for a moment London felt sharply how much she missed her mother. She refused to let herself slip into a state of melancholy, though. There were simply too many wonderful things to see.

Just beyond the castle, the massive Szécheny Chain Bridge stretched over the Danube. London knew that the historic bridge had been built in 1849 to bring together three cities—Buda, Pest, and Obuda—into the single city of Budapest.

The driver slowed as they neared the bridge. London felt a tingle of excitement as she spotted the name *Nachtmusik* on the hull of a ship docked there.

There it is! she realized.

The boat was sleek and somewhat smaller than the other cruise-line riverboats docked along the bank, but it was built in the same low, elongated style. Like the others, it was some twenty yards out on the water, and a long, canopied gangway connected it to the stone embankment.

The driver parked the cab, got London's luggage out of the trunk, and set it down at the end of the gangway. London paid him and thanked him, then stood amid her suitcases staring at the boat as he drove away.

Such a cozy little vessel was a startling sight after years of having worked on massive ocean-going cruise ships that could hold literally thousands of passengers. As much as she'd always loved her work, she'd grown tired of the sheer vastness of those larger ships.

She immediately felt a burst of affection for this sleek, friendly-looking vessel. It was going to be her new home for the near future, and she felt good about that.

Just as London stepped toward the gangway, she heard a voice call out from the other end of the gangway.

"London Rose! As I live and breathe!"

London laughed with delight as she recognized the Bronx accent that had reached her across the water. The tall blond woman dashing across the gangway toward her was her old friend Elsie Sloan.

"Elsie!" London cried. "What are you doing here?"

"I could ask you the same thing! The last I heard you were cruising the Caribbean."

"And the last I heard, you were sailing all around Eastern Asia."

"Well, times change."

"They do at that," London said, struck by how true those words seemed right at the moment. As they hugged and greeted each other, London realized that Elsie hadn't actually changed since they'd worked a year and a half together on a ship along the coast of Australia. They'd been inseparable workmates for several years until they'd been separated geographically by tour assignments.

Elsie's ruddy complexion still almost rivaled the bleached brightness of her hair, and both contrasted sharply with the familiar Epoch World Cruise Lines uniform—dark blue slacks with a blouse and vest.

A deckhand trotted after Elsie down the gangway, and Elsie told him to take London's bags to stateroom 110. He piled them onto a handcart and scurried back to the ship with them.

Elsie said, "I didn't believe it when the concierge told me you'd be arriving this morning to work on this cruise. But I kept a sharp lookout, and here you are! I insisted on being the first person to greet you and show you around the good ship *Nachtmusik*, so come on, away we go! You'll love it, I'm sure."

"We've got a lot of catching up to do," London said, as they walked together along the gangway.

"I'll say," Elsie said. Then she added with a wink, "But I can tell by your radiant expression that you've been having a wild and exciting love life lately."

"Not exactly," London said. "But a guy did propose to me the night before last."

"A rich guy?"

"Well, stable, at least."

"You said no, I take it. Otherwise you wouldn't be here."

"That's right."

Elsie let out an uncharacteristically anxious sigh.

"Well, you know me—I'm not one for settling down. Like you, I enjoy a life of freedom and adventure. Even so, I hope you didn't make a mistake."

"What do you mean?" London asked.

"I'm sure you've heard that Epoch World Cruise Lines is in financial trouble. From what I've heard, European river cruises are the company's last resort. And this Danube trip will be its first cruise. If it doesn't go well …"

Elsie's voice faded away, but London sensed she knew what she was leaving unsaid. She remembered how Jeremy Lapham had assured her during their conference that Epoch World wasn't about to go "belly-up," and there was "plenty of life" in the company.

But what else did I expect him to say?

He'd been trying to sell her on a new job, after all.

Besides, he'd also said, *"There's a lot at stake in this new venture."*

No doubt the whole future of Epoch World was hanging on this first European tour—and on London and Elsie and the rest of the crew doing their very best at their jobs.

"What's your job here on the *Nachtmusik?*" London asked.

"Bartender. In the main lounge. And you? Nobody's told me yet."

"Social director," London said.

Elsie's eyes widened.

"Social director! Oh, dear. So it's *you* …"

Her voice faded away.

"Is there going to be a problem?" London asked.

"I hope not," Elsie said with a shrug. "I'll tell you about it when we get you settled in."

London felt her first pang of unease since she'd arrived in Budapest.

As excited as she was about this new job, she sensed that she might be in for some rough going.

There could be trouble in paradise, she thought.

CHAPTER FIVE

London and Elsie followed the gangway into the reception area, which looked like the lobby of a small but luxurious hotel.

"We're on the Menuetto deck," Elsie said as London signed her name in the register. "The decks are named after the movements in *Eine Kleine Nachtmusik.*"

London felt a slight jolt at the mention of the piece her mother had played so often when she'd been little.

Better get used to hearing about it, she thought.

The ship was named after that piece, after all.

"We'll start at the top and work our way down," Elsie said as they stepped into an elevator.

The elevator took them up one floor to the ship's top deck—the Rondo deck, Elsie said it was called. It was one huge sun deck with lounging chairs spread out around a small plunge pool. The view took London's breath all over again, and she turned around to take it all in. It was the best view of the city she'd gotten so far.

Elsie led London toward the front of the ship, where the glass-enclosed bridge towered over everything else.

Elsie waved to the bridge and called out.

"Yoo-hoo! Oh, Captain Hays!"

A portly, middle-aged man with a walrus-style mustache poked his head out the door. He appeared to have been conferring with some of his staff.

"Yes?" he said.

"I've brought our newest crew member to see you," Elsie called. "This is our social director, London Rose. London, this is our intrepid captain, Spencer Hays."

The captain's eyebrows wiggled a bit flirtatiously.

"'London Rose,' is it?" he said in a pronounced English accent. "So glad you could make it. A lovely name for a lovely lady. Charmed, I'm sure."

London said, "I'm honored to be aboard, Captain Hays."

"Jolly good!" the captain said. "We'll have more time to get to know each other during the voyage. I'll do everything in my power to make your stay here a happy one."

He ducked back inside the bridge to continue conferring with his staff.

"Come on, let's take the stairs," Elsie said.

London followed Elsie down spiraling steps back to the Menuetto deck. They took a quick look at the lounge in the bow of the ship, which had plush furniture and huge windows with a wonderful view of the river. A familiar melody wafted through the lounge speakers. Elsie couldn't name the piece, but she was sure that it was by Mozart.

"This is the Amadeus Lounge," Elsie told her. "I'm the chief bartender here," she added proudly. "I've got a staff of four—or is it five? Anyway, it'll be enough to make me drunk with power. I'm really going to enjoy bossing people around."

"I'm sure you will," London replied with a grin.

They passed back through the reception area into a passageway lined with staterooms. Pointing to the signs on the stateroom doors, Elsie said, "You can see we've got a theme for the higher-class rooms and suites—music of the Danube."

London saw that the rooms had names on them: Liszt, Haydn, Schubert, and other composers of the Danube region. Elsie used a keycard to open the "Beethoven" grand suite. London immediately heard a lovely piano tune that she recognized from childhood—*"Für Elise,"* she thought it was.

The suite was large and luxurious, with a separate seating area and a balcony. It was decorated with hints of early nineteenth-century Vienna, including pages from music scores.

"I've never seen a suite this large on a boat," London said.

"Yeah, but I'm not sure I'd want to honeymoon here," Elsie said, pointing to a large portrait of Beethoven over the bed.

London gazed at the composer looking down with crossed arms and a frown of seeming disapproval. He didn't look like he was in any mood for romance.

"I guess he was known for being cross and cantankerous," she said.

"Yeah, well, there aren't any pictures of Beethoven smiling and winking as if he's purring 'ooh-la-la.'"

As they went back into the hallway, Elsie said, "There are just two of those grand suites. Also some smaller suites and very elegant staterooms on this deck."

London followed Elsie down more spiraling stairs to the next level—the Romanze deck. It had mid-sized staterooms that were named after other musical legends—Brahms, Bartok, Johann Strauss II, and even the Trapp Family Singers.

They looked into the lavish Habsburg Restaurant, where tables were perfectly set in preparation for the next meal, then back to the stairs and down another flight to the lowest level—the Allegro level.

The rooms here didn't have any special names, and Elsie escorted London to a door with the number 110 on it. But when Elsie opened that door, London was startled to see where her own baggage had been left there for her.

"Oh, my!" London gasped. "The deckhand must have brought my bags to the wrong room!"

It was a single room, small but only slightly less luxurious than the suite she had viewed two decks above. It actually more impressive than some of the cheaper passenger quarters she'd seen on her ocean voyages.

Elsie took London by the arm with mock concern.

"London, sit down. I've got something to tell you that might cause you some alarm."

She nudged London over to the bed and helped her sit there.

"I know this is going to come as a shock," she said, "but the deckhand didn't make a mistake, and you mustn't faint or pass out or anything like that. This is *your* room. Yours and no one else's."

On the pillow beside her, London saw an information folder with her name on it, a room keycard, and an ID badge that read:

LONDON ROSE
SOCIAL DIRECTOR

"Oh, my!" London said again.

"Not quite like the old days, is it?"

"No, it's certainly not," London said, catching her breath.

Back when she and Elsie had worked together on cruise ships, they'd often been quartered in windowless rooms with bunk beds and two or three other hostesses.

This room had a queen bed and was decorated in shades of soft gray and blue. The narrow, high window gave her a very nice view.

"You've even got a private bath," Elsie informed her. "With a shower." She walked over to a closet and opened it. Several crew uniforms were hanging inside, with plenty of room left for all the clothes London had packed and any she might buy in European shops.

"You'd better get into these duds," Elsie said, pointing to a uniform. "Passengers will be boarding in a half hour, and you're supposed to be there to greet them."

London went into the bathroom, washed up quickly, and changed into her own uniform—dark blue slacks with a blouse and vest. She fixed her makeup and combed her hair.

Elsie applauded when London emerged.

"Excellent!" she said. "You do that outfit proud!"

Before London could reply, there was a sharp knock at the door. Elsie opened it and a uniformed, dark-haired woman strode in.

Elsie sputtered, "London, this is Amy Blassingame, our concierge and—"

The woman interrupted, looking at her watch.

"I wish I could say it was a pleasure to meet you, Ms. Rose. But I'm afraid you're already running late. Our passengers are ready to board right now. You'd better get up there and greet them—that is, if you hope to keep this job."

Amy Blassingame held out a folder.

"You'll need this," she snapped. "Jot down everybody's individual needs and demands next to their names, then leave the list in my box at the reception desk. I'll take care of things from there."

London took the folder and tried to utter a thank-you, but the woman whirled and left without another word.

For a moment, London just watched her go, stunned by the hostility she felt emanating from a complete stranger. A quick look at the folder revealed that it was a list of passenger names.

"Let's go," London said to Elsie. When they dashed into the hallway, Amy Blassingame was nowhere in sight.

"I thought you said I had a half hour," London said as they as they got into the elevator.

"That's what Amy said to tell you," Elsie replied breathlessly. "Oh, London, I'd been meaning to warn you about Amy the River Troll. How did you get this job?"

"Jeremy Lapham called me personally. Just yesterday."

"And what did he say?"

"That the position had opened unexpectedly."

"That's right," Elsie said. "The woman they had signed up dropped out. I think she decided to elope with her Italian lover. Anyhow, Amy was expecting to get the job herself. She's been fuming about it—and about *you*—all morning. Messing around with the boarding time is just her way …"

"But I didn't—"

"I know, you didn't mean to ruffle any feathers. But I'm afraid that Amy the River Troll has it in for you anyway. Just remember—you're her boss, not the other way around. You might have trouble getting her to accept that, though."

London's heart sank a little. Wielding actual authority over resentful staff members was not something she'd learned how to do when she'd been a mere cruise ship hostess.

There sure are lots of new things to get used to, she realized.

Anyway, she was determined not to let a little river troll issue dampen her spirits.

When they arrived at the boarding area, London could see a line of passengers standing behind a chain on the far end of the covered gangway that led into the boat. She opened the glass doors of the reception room and waved at the deckhand who was in charge of that chain. At the sight of her signal, he lifted the barrier so the newcomers could board.

"Good luck," Elsie whispered as she headed away.

London took a deep breath as the first passengers moved toward her.

Leading the group was a tiny, grim-looking, elderly woman. She was wearing unnecessary furs and enough jewelry to topple such a small person over. She was only carrying a large leather handbag, but an impressive pile of luggage followed her in the care of a deckhand.

Despite the woman's dour expression, London smiled brightly and opened her mouth to welcome the very first guest to step into the *Nachtmusik*'s cheerful reception area.

Then London's attention was captured by something strange about that handbag.

Long brown hair streamed down outside of it, as though the woman had rather carelessly stuffed a wig into it.

As London stared at that wig, she suddenly saw a pair of dark brown eyes pop open.

The wig was looking back at her.

35

CHAPTER SIX

The brown eyes blinked at London a couple of times. Then the bundle of hair lifted a little, revealing a shiny black nose. A set of bared teeth appeared below that, accompanied by a low growl.

Some kind of mechanical toy? London wondered.

Then the bundle of hair let out a sassy, yapping bark, confirming once and for all that the bundle of hair was neither a wig nor a toy. The tiny, elderly woman was carrying a very small dog in her handbag.

Is this going to be a problem? London wondered.

In the whirlwind of events that had brought her here overnight, nobody had told her anything about the policy for pets for this tour. She'd seen passengers with service animals while working on ocean-going lines, but it had never been her job to determine whether to allow them aboard.

London managed to smile in her best professional manner.

"Welcome to Epoch World Cruise Lines' very first tour of the beautiful Danube," she said. "May I have your name?"

The woman glared at her grimly. Her face was extremely thin and extremely pale, but the irises of her spectacled eyes appeared to be solid black—much darker than the dog's eyes.

"Surely you know that already," she snapped, pointing to the folder in London's hand. "You've got a passenger list right there."

London was bewildered by the woman's rather nonsensical logic.

"I still need you to tell me—" she began.

"And I'm telling you, you've got it right in front of you. I've got a reservation right here in the Menuetto deck in one of your finest staterooms—the Beethoven Grand Suite."

I just looked at that suite, London realized.

She almost giggled at the memory of Beethoven's portrait hanging over the bed. The great composer and this angry woman had much the same scowl. London thought the two might hit it off just fine.

Maybe they'll spend the whole trip happily scowling at each other.

Anyway, this bit of information made it easier to find the woman's name, which was Lillis Klimowski.

"We're glad to have you joining us on the *Nachtmusik*, Ms.—"

"That's *Mrs.* I'm tragically widowed, if you must know."

"Mrs. Klimowski," London said with a nod.

Before she could decide how to broach the question of the woman's pet, an angry voice brought that subject up.

"You can't bring a dog on board," a man right behind Mrs. Klimowski complained loudly.

The middle-aged man was much bigger than Mrs. Klimowski. He was wearing plaid pants and was standing next to a buxom, gum-chewing woman with heavily dyed red hair.

"I beg your pardon," Mrs. Klimowski replied sharply.

"You heard what I said," the man said.

Mrs. Klimowski turned her nose up at him.

"I'll have you know that Champion Sir Reginald Taft is no ordinary animal. He was a show champion in his youth—or so I was told when I purchased him. He's officially my emotional support dog. We're quite inseparable. Sometimes I think, if it weren't for Sir Reginald, I'd go quite mad—especially when dealing with uncouth boors such as yourself, Mr. ... what *is* your name, presumptuous fellow?"

The man linked his arms with the gum-chewing woman.

"We're *Mr.* and *Mrs.* Gus Jarrett, and we're on our honeymoon."

London glanced at her list and saw that Gus and Honey Jarrett were booked into Trapp Family Singers room on the Romanze deck, one level down. They looked to London as though this was far from the first honeymoon either of them had been on. She guessed that they both might have gone through a fair number of spouses by now.

Then another couple stepped out of line to have a look at the dog. They were a kindly-looking pair of pudgy elderly people. The woman was allowing the dog to sniff her hand.

"Oh, but look at this adorable creature, Walter!" she said.

"He's very cute indeed, Agnes," her husband said.

London glanced down the list and found the names of Walter and Agnes Shick, who were booked into the Johann Strauss II suite on the Menuetto deck.

The couple's admiration seemed to improve the dog's mood a little. Still held tightly in the leather handbag, Sir Reginald Taft actually allowed Agnes Shick to scratch him under the chin without snapping her finger off.

But Gus Jarrett was seething now.

"I'll have you know that my lovely bride is allergic to dogs!" he said.

His gum-chewing wife gave him an odd look, as if this was news to her. London felt sure that Gus was inventing Honey's allergy just to make trouble. Anyway, they were quartered a deck below Mrs. Klimowski's suite, so surely allergies didn't have to be an issue. All they had to do was maintain a reasonable distance from the dog.

Still scratching Sir Reginald, Agnes Shick looked at Gus and Honey with a smile.

"You needn't worry about allergies," she said.

"Indeed you don't," Walter Shick added. "This is a Yorkshire Terrier. The breed is hypoallergenic."

"Hypo-what?" demanded Gus Jarrett.

"Hypoallergenic," Agnes repeated. "This lovely mane of his is more like human hair than animal fur. He won't cause your wife any more allergic problems than … well, than I would, or Walter, or any other person here."

Agnes had stopped scratching the dog, and the animal growled again in London's direction, looking as irritable as before.

Why does that dog keep growling at me? she wondered.

At least London was relieved that Sir Reginald wasn't going to be a health hazard to any passengers who might have allergies.

Meanwhile, the boarding line was getting longer by the minute, and passengers were beginning to look impatient that things were stalled. And London still didn't know how to handle the unexpected animal. She tried to remember what she'd been told about support animals by people she'd known in other parts of the travel industry.

"Do you have any paperwork on Sir Reginald?" she asked Mrs. Klimowski.

"Paperwork? Why on earth would he require any paperwork?"

"My understanding is that passengers are usually expected to have a letter from a therapist or a medical professional, something to certify the need for an emotional support animal. Do you have a letter like that?"

"Do I have it? Of course I have it! I already filed it with your company!"

London glanced at the passenger list again to make absolutely sure that there was no mention of a support animal by Mrs. Klimowski's name.

"Perhaps you could show it to me again," London said with a polite smile.

"Show it to you again! I think not! I'm through dealing with an underling like yourself. I demand to see the social director for this tour."

"That would be me," London replied firmly.

Mrs. Klimowski's eyes widened.

"I find that very hard to believe!" she said.

London realized that her own smile was getting a bit stiff as she displayed the badge on her uniform—the one that identified her as "London Rose, Social Director."

"I'm sorry if I'm not quite the person you expected," she said with exaggerated courtesy. "But I promise to fix this problem right away, and to do my very best to make the rest of your voyage a happy one."

Mrs. Klimowski looked thoroughly unappeased.

"I must be on my way before I lose my temper," she said. "You may speak to me when you've resolved this issue. You will find me in my grand suite."

She turned and stalked away, with the deckhand lugging her luggage along behind her. As the woman disappeared into the corridor that led to the staterooms, the dog looked back at London and growled again.

Again she wondered why that dog seemed to dislike her so.

But Sir Reginald was probably here to stay. London really couldn't imagine that anybody was going to pry Mrs. Klimowski and Sir Reginald Taft out of the Beethoven suite.

Meanwhile, the line of passengers waiting to board had gotten dauntingly long. Most of the one hundred or so booked for the trip seemed to be arriving right now. But Agnes Shick was still standing close to London with an expression of concern.

"Surely there's no reason not to let that adorable dog on board," she said.

"I hope not," London admitted.

Walter Shick gestured toward London's passenger list.

"Does the list say where Mrs. Klimowski is from?" he asked.

It hadn't occurred to London to check.

"She's from Port Mather, in Long Island," London said.

"Well, that makes things simpler, doesn't it?" Agnes said.

"She must have flown with the dog when she came over," Walter added. "If so, she surely really must have a certification letter, or it wouldn't have been allowed on the plane. Does it really matter if she can't produce it just this minute?"

London smiled with relief at the suggestion. She wouldn't have to challenge Mrs. Klimowski after all. She could just ask the woman to produce the letter sometime later.

"Welcome aboard," she said to Walter and Agnes Shick. "And thanks so much for your help."

"I'm glad if we've fixed things for the dog," Walter said. "Too bad we have to let that woman aboard though …"

Agnes poked her husband in the ribs.

"Now, Walter, is that a nice thing to say? Without Mrs. Klimowski along, who would be here to take care of Sir Reginald?"

London thanked the couple again, and they headed up the gangway.

The next passenger in line was a tall, black-clad man with thick black hair and an icy expression. London felt a chill just from looking at him. It was easy to imagine him as a young undertaker.

"Welcome to Epoch World Cruise Lines' very first tour of the beautiful Danube," she said. "May I have your name?"

"Cyrus Bannister," he said. "I believe you'll find me booked into the Schoenberg Suite."

Then with a smirk he added, "I'm sure I'm the only person who wanted it."

It took London a second to get the joke. She'd never listened to much Schoenberg, but she hadn't liked what she'd heard. It was too strange and dissonant for her tastes. She figured many other people probably felt the same way.

But maybe Cyrus Bannister liked things to be strange and dissonant.

He said to London, "I couldn't help noticing your altercation with that woman. I'm afraid she's going to be, shall we say, high maintenance. I hope she won't give you too much trouble."

"Oh, no trouble at all," London said diplomatically.

Then, glancing toward the boat, she added, "I don't know what to think of her dog, though."

"Why is that?"

"Well, he doesn't seem to like me. He keeps growling at me."

Cyrus Bannister's lips twisted into a peculiar grin.

"I happen to know a few things about dogs," he said. "And I can tell you for a fact—he wasn't growling at *you*." Peering closely at London, he added, "He was growling at *her*. Every time she bumped him around in that bag, he let out a growl. He doesn't like being in there."

London didn't know quite what to say in reply. She finished her greeting, and Cyrus Bannister headed up the gangway, followed by his luggage.

As London got ready to greet the next passenger, she thought about the woman and her dog and how Mr. Bannister had just described her as "high maintenance."

Sounds about right, London thought. She hoped the maintenance was taken care of for now.

But somewhere in her gut, she sensed that this wasn't the end of complications involving Lillis Klimowski and Sir Reginald Taft.

*

London soon felt positively besieged.

She kept smiling and repeating her greeting over and over again:

"Welcome to Epoch World Cruise Lines' first tour of the beautiful Danube."

But she often barely got the words out before a boarding passenger made some sort of request, complaint, or demand.

"Your porter is getting our luggage mixed ..."

"I'll need a folded international newspaper waiting outside my stateroom door every morning promptly before ..."

"I'll need coffee delivered at ..."

"I'll need brandy delivered at ..."

"I'll need ..."

The demands came in a seemingly endless litany. It didn't help that most of the one hundred passengers booked for this tour had shown up as soon as boarding had opened. Things might have been easier for London if they'd straggled in at various times during the afternoon.

She was beginning to feel a bit dizzy. What had that last one asked for? London wasn't completely sure what she had just promised a young man for his single stateroom. Additional pillows, or was he the one who wanted ...? Well, she'd check her notes later.

Most of the passengers' demands weren't unreasonable and weren't even unusual. She couldn't blame them for wanting to have things their way. After all, her job was to make them happy.

But there are just so many of them, she kept thinking.

She'd never faced this kind of an onslaught as a cruise ship hostess. In those days, she'd only had to organize activities for specific groups after everybody was settled in. But she reminded herself that Amy Blassingame had said she'd take care of all these specific demands. At least London wasn't going to have to follow up on every detail.

Still, London hadn't felt this harried since many years ago, when she'd worked as a waitress while going to community college. She only hoped she didn't look as frantic as she had back then during lunch and dinner rushes.

The afternoon flashed by like a series of jerky movie scenes, with smash cuts from one to the next. She felt relieved to get the final passenger in the line on board, but there was still more work to do.

She hurried around the ship alerting various crew members to their new duties concerning luggage, newspapers, coffee, and a host of other demands the passengers had made. Finally she looked at her to-do list and saw that everything was checked off—at least for the moment. She took the list to the front desk and told the receptionist to put it in Amy Blassingame's box.

I did it! she thought.

At least she hoped she had. It had all gone so fast that it seemed like a blur.

London shook off her concerns and headed up to the open Rondo deck for a welcome breath of fresh, late afternoon air. Some passengers were chatting happily as they wandered the sundeck, and a couple of others had plunged into the pool. To her relief, none of them approached her with new problems to take care of.

She stopped at the rail and looked out over the river. The *Nachtmusik* wouldn't be leaving for its next destination until late tonight. Even while they were still here in the dock, the guests seemed to be already settling in nicely and enjoying themselves.

Maybe the pressure will let up for a while, she thought hopefully.

As she stood at the rail and gazed at the Danube flowing peacefully past the boat, she remembered Mom and Dad taking her on boat rides on that lovely river. And there, up ahead of the boat's mooring, was the Szécheny Chain Bridge. They had carried her across that bridge on their shoulders and then through the mighty Citadella and the wonders of Buda Castle.

She'd been trying not to think about Mom since she'd been in Budapest.

But now she couldn't seem to help it.

What happened to her? she wondered, as she so often had over the intervening years.

She remembered Tia's words: *"I guess she wasn't as happy as she made herself out to be."*

As London looked around at the cheerful pearl of a city, she wondered whether Tia might be right. Maybe marriage and family hadn't been enough for Mom. Maybe their mother hadn't met with some terrible fate. Maybe she'd simply left her New World life for a much more exciting life in the Old World.

Maybe she was more like me than I knew, London thought.

After all, London herself couldn't imagine living her sister's life.

But at least she hadn't spent years trying to live that way. Her mother had been married with two daughters when she'd disappeared.

London felt a sudden ache in her throat.

Didn't she care about us? she wondered.

Her thoughts were interrupted by a nearby male voice.

"Enjoying the view, I see."

She turned and saw a tall and rather handsome man walking toward her. He was wearing the ship's official dark blue suit, but she was sure she hadn't seen him before.

And yet somehow, she was immediately intrigued by him.

CHAPTER SEVEN

London tried not to gawk at the good-looking stranger. Although his black-rimmed glasses made him appear bookish, he was elegant and stylish in an Old World manner. She hadn't quite caught the words on his small, dignified nameplate when he stepped to the rail right next to her.

Who is he? she wondered, a bit surprised at her own reaction. She also had to wonder if she was blushing. During the year that Ian had been her boyfriend, London hadn't given much thought to other men.

He was obviously an official on the staff, but which one?

"It's a beautiful city," she replied to his comment, pleased to begin a casual conversation.

"I cannot think of a city more beautiful," the man replied. He turned toward her, extended his hand, and added, "I am Emil Waldmüller, resident historian on the *Nachtmusik.*"

London shook his hand and was impressed by his firm yet gentle grip. She guessed that he was in his forties, and she recognized his accent as German.

"I'm pleased to meet you, *Herr* Waldmüller. I'm London Rose."

"Call me Emil, please," the man said. "May I call you London?"

"Please do."

"I saw you greeting passengers. You handled it well. You must be our new social director."

"I am," London said. She felt relieved that someone thought she had managed the boarding rush all right.

From Emil's slight smile, London guessed that he'd gotten wind of Amy Blassingame's fury at someone else getting that job. Perhaps he'd even witnessed one of her outbursts.

"Yours is a demanding task," he continued. "Passengers are not always easy to please."

"No, but I've been doing my best to serve people for years. I learned a motto during my years as an ocean cruise hostess. 'The customer may not always be right, but the customer is always the customer.'"

"A wise saying," Emil said with a nod. "Right or wrong, one must always err on the side of the customer's wishes."

Emil leaned on the rail and looked at London.

"I am sorry to add to your workload," he said. "But I just met with a group of passengers who have a request."

"What is it?" she asked.

"Well, our passengers have the rest of the day free, and of course many will be sightseeing on their own. But this small group is less familiar with the city, and they would at least like to go out to a nice restaurant before we leave—and so would I."

London wasn't sure whether Emil was asking her permission to take the guests out or whether he wanted her to go with them.

"There's plenty of time for a dinner in Budapest," she said. "It's up to the passengers whether they eat in the ship's restaurant or go ashore."

Emil continued, "Although I myself have been here many times and could show them about, they expressly asked for you to join us."

He shrugged a little.

"I understand," London said with a smile. "Actually, an outing would be good for me too. I've been kind of envying our passengers. At least they've had some time to explore. I just got here in time to go right to work, and I haven't had a moment go anywhere. I was afraid I wouldn't get to see anything more of Budapest than the view through my cab window and from right here on this deck."

"So you will lead our group?" Emil asked.

"I'll be glad to," she said shyly. "But would you come along to give me a hand? I'm sure your knowledge of Budapest is much more up-to-date than mine, especially when it comes to choosing a place for dinner."

Emil smiled, looking a bit shy himself.

"I was hoping you would ask," he told her.

London felt a twinge of interest. Did she detect a hint of attraction from him?

She realized that her uniform felt rumpled and even a bit sweaty. She'd been wearing it all afternoon as she'd dashed about helping passengers get settled. There were several fresh uniforms in her closet, but she knew that Epoch company directives actually encouraged her to dress normally for social occasions ashore. Suddenly she looked forward to getting into something less severe.

"Give me a few minutes," she said. "I'd like to freshen up. I can meet you and the group at the gangway."

"I look forward to it," Emil agreed. "I shall gather the company."

Feeling a bit giddy about the coming evening, London took the elevator down to the Allegro deck. In her cabin, she changed out of her uniform into a more appropriate outfit for an evening in the city—a midi-length skirt, a brightly patterned tunic, a long lightweight sweater, and some shoes with sensible heels. She brushed her bright auburn hair and made a final check in the full-length mirror.

You'll do, she decided.

Then London took the elevator up to the Menuetto deck, where she found Emil and the group of about ten passengers waiting for her in the reception area. She recognized all their faces, of course, having greeted each of them a while earlier. Walter and Agnes Shick were here, along with Gus and Honey Jarrett.

Then she was startled by a familiar growl. London turned and saw that Mrs. Klimowski had arrived—and she was carrying that bundle of long hair in her leather handbag. Sir Reginald Taft was staring at London, still looking quite unhappy.

The woman was again weighed down with furs and overloaded with jewelry, including a pair of massive earrings that made her look positively top heavy. Most conspicuous was what was surely a valuable pendant hanging at her throat by a gold chain. It consisted of a large ruby decorated around the edges with small diamonds, all mounted in a gold setting.

London stifled a sigh. She clearly saw that she had a problem on her hands.

But she knew that she had to choose her words carefully.

"Mrs. Klimowski, I'm afraid I can't recommend that you go out this evening like ..."

Her voice faded.

"Like what?" Mrs. Klimowski replied.

"Well, with so much jewelry, and ..."

"And?"

London couldn't help but hesitate.

Surely she knows what I mean, she thought.

Then another familiar voice spoke up.

"I believe she is referring to your dog, madam."

The speaker this time was the mysterious, black-clad Cyrus

Bannister, who was gazing at Mrs. Klimowski dourly.

"I can't imagine why," Mrs. Klimowski snapped.

As if in agreement, the dog bared his teeth and growled.

Bannister's lips twisted into a very subtle sneer.

"Madam, if you don't mind my saying so, those valuables make you a veritable moving target for thieves. And your dog won't be welcome in many of the places we might choose to visit."

"Nonsense!" Mrs. Klimowski said. "I've been here for two whole days now, and I've come and gone exactly as I've pleased, dressed just as I am and with my precious Sir Reginald cradled in my arms."

Bannister inhaled sharply.

He was clearly about to escalate his criticism of Mrs. Klimowski. The last thing London wanted right now was an altercation.

"It's all right, Mrs. Klimowski," she said hastily, before Bannister could speak. "I'm sure we'll manage somehow."

"Well!" Mrs. Klimowski snorted. "I would think that goes without saying! This very discussion has left me most unsettled."

Emil spoke up before the argument could take off again.

"What do you say we all get going?"

There was a murmur of happy agreement from almost everybody.

"Well, then," Emil added, "I suggest we eat at the Duna Étterem, my own favorite restaurant here in Budapest. It is just a short walk from here."

The members of the group were all agreeable—except Mrs. Klimowski.

"I'm afraid I must announce a change of plans," the elderly woman said resolutely.

London stifled a sigh.

Now what? she wondered.

CHAPTER EIGHT

Several other passengers were beginning to look annoyed. London struggled to think of some way to turn an impending calamity into a pleasant evening.

"Can't we just go to dinner?" Agnes Shick asked the formidable little woman.

"Not yet," Mrs. Klimowski replied firmly.

"Why ever not?" Walter Shick demanded.

But Mrs. Klimowski was looking quite resolute.

"We must go first to St. Stephen's Basilica," she said. "After all this unpleasantness, I'm in need of spiritual solace. Mine has been a tragic life. I have a greater need than most people for the comfort of prayer."

She was glaring almost accusingly at London right now, as if she were personally responsible for her lifetime of hardships.

Before anybody could object, Emil spoke up with a smile.

"I think that is an excellent suggestion. It is just a ten-minute walk from here, and it is practically right on the way to the Duna Étterem."

"Very good," London agreed, again relieved at his smooth intervention. "Let's be on our way, shall we?"

As they all filed through the reception area doors and across the gangway, she jotted down a list of the people so she wouldn't lose track of them. Then, as she and Emil steered the group away from the docked boat, London heard murmurs of discontent from a few others.

"Didn't we visit St. Stephen's just yesterday on that city tour?"

"I hadn't planned to go there again."

"I hadn't planned to go there at all."

"I'm hungry right now."

Looking markedly less frail now, Mrs. Klimowski had plunged on ahead of them all, with her dog still tucked inside her leather bag. She led the group with determination, apparently unable to hear what was being said behind her back.

Not that it would matter if she did *hear,* London thought.

Mrs. Klimowski didn't seem to be the kind of person who worried about what other people thought about her.

Emil leaned toward London as they walked and spoke to her in a whisper.

"They are not exactly—what is that English idiom? 'Happy settlers'?"

London smiled as she gently corrected her German companion.

"You're close. It's 'happy campers.' No, I'm afraid they're not. I hope we don't have a mutiny before the night's over. Thank you for helping me out."

"I am glad to oblige," Emil replied. "But you seem to be worried."

London hesitated, unsure of whether she should unload her anxieties to a man she'd met just a little while ago. But Emil seemed genuinely concerned—and besides, London was starting to genuinely like him.

"I'm afraid I'm off to a rocky start at this job," she said. "I've never done anything quite like this before. Hostessing on a cruise ship is … well, more narrowly focused than this."

"It seems to me you are doing fine."

Emil's reassurances helped London relax a little. When they left the docking area, they rounded the end of a city park and headed along a narrow street.

London was relieved that Emil spoke to the group. She hoped his casual chatter would distract them from their annoyance with Mrs. Klimowski.

"Here we must walk in the street," he told them. "Everyone does, so the vehicle traffic takes other routes whenever possible."

The shops, greenery in large planters, and outdoor cafés left little sidewalk area, so they stepped into the patterned stone street. London was glad that she knew enough about touring to wear shoes with wide heels. Most of the other women in her group had also chosen sensible footwear.

"And there is St Stephen's, just ahead of us," Emil announced.

The basilica's magnificent dome was in full view between the shops and offices along the way. Even from this far end of the street, it was an impressive sight.

As they walked toward the massive dome, Emil continued, "I am sure you have heard the name of St. Stephen many times since you arrived in Budapest. He is Hungary's patron saint, and a thousand years ago he was the country's first Christian king. This basilica was built in his honor, completed about a hundred years ago."

When they reached the end of the street, they entered an enormous square of swirling orange and brown mosaic designs. St. Stephen's dome and twin towers now loomed high before them.

"Have you been to the Basilica before?" Emil asked London.

"Not since I was a little girl. I'd forgotten how tall it was!"

"Yes, even taller than Buda Castle," Emil said with a nod. "Exactly the same height as the Hungarian Parliament Building, making them the two tallest structures in Budapest. The two buildings are said to represent how spiritual and worldly concerns are of equal importance."

Then Emil laughed a little.

"I do not mean to come across as—what is the idiom?—a 'know-everything'?"

London laughed a little as well.

"Close again," she said. "It's a 'know-it-all.' And I don't think you come across that way at all. Anyway, knowing this kind of thing is your job, after all. And right now I could use a bit of your expertise. Since I've had no time to prepare, I'm afraid I won't be much use as a guide. Would you very much mind …?"

"Leading a little tour? I'd be delighted."

London breathed a bit easier. She felt lucky to have met Emil just when she'd needed him.

As the group gathered together, Lillis Klimowski stood apart from them staring at the mighty facade. Her dog was peering crossly out of his leather bag.

As he began to talk, Emil took on an authoritative, Old World, professorial sort of air. But far from it making him seem to London like a "know-it-all," she found him to be more impressive—and also more than a bit attractive.

"Ladies and gentlemen," he said, "as we make our visit, I'm sure you will find St. Stephen to be a palpable presence inside the Basilica. And St. Stephen holds a firm protective hand over this great city—quite literally, as you will soon see."

London felt a strange chill at those words, "a palpable presence."

The words "protective hand" also triggered some distant memory.

What was it that had held her in awe when she had visited here as a child with Mom and Dad? She couldn't remember now exactly what it was that had touched her so deeply.

As they stepped onto the porch, Emil pointed out a bas-relief of the Virgin Mary on the massive pediment that towered above them. The passengers dutifully put money into the donation box and continued on through the main portal and into the sanctuary, where London joined the others in a collective gasp of amazement. Some genuflected and made the sign of the cross, while others simply stood in stunned reverence.

The interior of the basilica was staggering, with walls of dark marble, mighty columns, and great sculptures. The light was dim, but even so, London felt almost blinded by the elaborate gold leaf decorations, the countless paintings and mosaics, and the gigantic stained glass windows.

And the sheer size of the place made her positively light-headed.

Just like when I was little, she thought.

Now she could remember how it had felt to walk in here all those years ago, with her parents right beside her. She remembered how glad she'd been that Mom and Dad were each holding her by the hand— because otherwise, she might have fallen down from dizziness.

If only Mom and Dad were here right now to hold her hands again, to make sure she didn't fall.

But I'm grown up, she reminded herself.

I can stand on my own.

Meanwhile, Mrs. Klimowski's dog wasn't proving to be a problem. Perhaps more than a little awe-stricken himself, Sir Reginald Taft's face wasn't even visible, and he looked like nothing more than a wig again.

Mrs. Klimowski stopped at the baptismal font, touched the water with her fingers, and then made the sign of the cross and whispered in prayer before she continued on into the sanctuary and sat down in silence. London remembered what the woman had said before the group had left the ship.

"Mine has been a tragic life. I have a greater need than most people for the comfort of prayer."

London had no idea what kinds of tragedies Mrs. Klimowski might have suffered.

Maybe she just overdramatizes things.

She also seemed to have a disagreeable tendency to blame others for whatever happened to displease her in life. Even so, for a moment London felt able to overlook the woman's self-centeredness and sympathize with whatever was troubling her.

Emil led the rest of the group on through the basilica. After they'd

51

made a full circuit of the sanctuary, they took an elevator ride up inside the dome and stepped outside to see a panorama of the entire city spread out below them. The sun was descending toward the faraway hills on the other side of the river, painting the sky with brilliant colors and filling the city with a golden glow.

When the group descended into the sanctuary again, Emil led them into a smaller side chapel where a glass cabinet held an elaborately decorated golden shrine.

"This is a reliquary," Emil explained in a reverent voice. "A while ago, I mentioned that St. Stephen still held a protective hand over this great city. Let me show you what I meant."

He slipped a coin into a slot, and a light came on inside the reliquary.

London joined the others in a collective gasp of amazement.

That was it, London remembered.

In a smaller glass container was a man's right hand, cracked and withered with extreme age. It was clenched into a mighty fist and encrusted with pearls and other precious gems.

That was the object that had struck her with such awe when she was a little girl.

Emil said quietly, "This is the 'Holy Right' of St. Stephen himself, the founder of Christian Hungary. It is said that, when he died in 1038 AD, St. Stephen's whole body decayed and crumbled except for his right hand, which has been preserved ever since—a symbol to all Hungarians of his guardian spirit."

When the group returned to the sanctuary. Mrs. Klimowski was still in her pew, making the sign of the cross as she finished praying. She finally got up and rejoined the others, and they all walked out of St. Stephen's.

Before they headed out to the restaurant, London gathered the group together in the broad stone square in front of the Basilica, where she called out their names from the list she'd made before they'd left the ship. Then they headed away into the twilit city, where lights were coming on everywhere, adding a new level of enchantment to their surroundings.

As they entered a lively, well-lighted pedestrian street where practically everybody seemed to be happy and smiling, London again remembered something that Ian had said to her before her flight.

"Hungary sounds like a very depressing place to me."

London let out a small chuckle as she walked along with a spring in her step.

How wrong you were, Ian! she thought.

She breathed a sigh of relief at the sheer chance that had brought her here—a last-minute vacancy for a job that Jeremy Lapham considered her to be well-suited for. If this job hadn't come along, she might be engaged to Ian by now. Flashing back to the chaos of her sister's home, it occurred to her yet again that she'd narrowly escaped living exactly that kind of life.

I really got lucky, she thought.

At that moment, Mrs. Klimowski put her hand to her forehead and swayed a little.

"Oh, I don't feel well. I must sit down! I must take my medicine!"

Emil stepped forward and offered her his arm with a gallant smile.

"Do not worry, madam," he said. "The restaurant is only a few steps away. We'll make sure you are comfortable then."

"Thank goodness," Mrs. Klimowski said to Emil, taking his arm. "You are most kind."

As the group followed after Emil and Mrs. Klimowski, London heard the elderly woman grumble to Emil, "Are you sure this is the right place?"

They had arrived at a most unpromising edifice that bore the sign "Duna Étterem." The brick facade had once been fairly elegant, with a jutting balcony and stone architectural motifs. But what appeared to be several layers of paint were peeling away, and the brick and stonework were positively crumbling in places. London couldn't help but worry—had Emil led them to a condemned building by mistake?

Still escorting Mrs. Klimowski by the arm, Emil turned to London and smiled, as if to reassure her that this was indeed the right place.

"Well," Mrs. Klimowski grumbled. "I'm hungry enough, anyhow."

London thought the group looked rather glum as they entered, but inside, the restaurant was inviting and spacious, with low arching ceilings and candlelight everywhere. The tables were set with white tablecloths and perfectly folded napkins.

"This will do," Gus commented.

"Very well indeed," Bannister added.

Fortunately, the Duna Étterem wasn't busy at the moment, so the host was able to arrange three tables where the group could sit together. Once seated, they were handed menus by a waiter named János, who began to greet them in excellent English.

Just then, Sir Reginald let out a sharp growl and poked his head out of the leather bag.

János stepped back, startled.

"Madam," he said, "I'm afraid you can't keep that dog in here."

London braced herself for the ugly scene she knew was coming.

CHAPTER NINE

Mrs. Klimowski drew herself up, looking markedly less frail than she had a few moments ago.

"I'll have you know that Sir Reginald Taft is my emotional support animal," she said in a growl not unlike her dog's. "He is essential to my mental and physical health. Wherever I go, he goes too. If he leaves, I leave."

Mrs. Klimowski and János stared grimly at each other.

London glanced around the table. The others in the group were looking intently at their menus, although she could detect a slight smirk on Cyrus Bannister's features.

"Well?" Mrs. Klimowski snapped. "It's entirely up to you."

János seemed unimpressed by the woman's furs and jewels and imperious manner. His expression darkened.

"Very well, madam," he replied in a clenched voice. "I'm afraid you must leave our establishment."

"Then you must force me to me leave," Mrs. Klimowski replied.

London had to admire the woman's sheer stubbornness, but it was clear they had reached an ugly impasse. What if János bodily lifted Mrs. Klimowski out of her chair and hauled her away, perhaps with help from others in the restaurant staff?

"No one is going to force anybody to do anything," London said sharply, standing up and confronting the waiter directly.

The man didn't budge.

Just then another customer stepped up and spoke to János quietly in rapid Hungarian. London had trouble catching much of what he said, but the gist of it seemed to be that the animal was hardly making any trouble, and the lady obviously needed its companionship, so why not let her and the dog stay?

London breathed a sigh of relief when the waiter finally nodded in sullen agreement.

She used her best Hungarian to thank the stranger who had intervened on behalf of the dog. She thought he cut an authoritative figure, with his jutting push-broom mustache, wavy gray hair, and kindly but intense expression.

As János took everyone's drink orders and went away to let them look at their menus, London sat down again. The stranger smiled graciously at the group and spoke in somewhat stilted English with a thick Hungarian accent.

"I am Vilmos Kallay, and I am at your service. I am a poet, although I'm sure you wouldn't have heard of me even if you were Hungarian. My 'day job,' so to speak, is as a university professor."

"Indeed?" Emil asked, looking pleased to meet another scholar. "What is your area of expertise?"

"It is what some Scotsman once called, if I remember correctly, 'the dismal science.' I forget the man's name."

Emil nodded with a chuckle.

"Ah, economics, then," he said. "The Scotsman was Thomas Carlyle, by the way."

"Thank you for refreshing my memory," Professor Kallay replied.

Emil introduced himself to the professor. Then the professor added to the whole group, "If you haven't decided what to order for dinner, I highly recommend the *paprikácsirke*. It's a traditional Magyar recipe— diced chicken prepared with sour cream and dumplings. It is by far the finest dish on the menu."

At that moment, János the waiter returned with everybody's drinks. As he served them to the group, he eyed Mrs. Klimowski with scarcely concealed hostility.

She ignored the man completely.

"I thought that awful waiter was really going to throw me out," she said to London. "It's just been one crisis after another this evening. I don't know how much more I can take. I should never have left the ship tonight."

"Fortunately, the kind Professor Kallay has settled one crisis for us," London replied. She watched as Mrs. Klimowski pulled a brightly colored little box out of her bag and snapped it open. As she did so, she leaned forward so that her ruby pendant with its setting of diamonds and gold fell fully into view—not just to the people nearby, but to many others in the restaurant. London felt another spasm of worry.

It's like trying to keep a walking jewelry store safe, she thought.

And she's all dressed in furs.

And she's got a dog.

London found it hard to imagine how the woman could be "higher maintenance."

Mrs. Klimowski took a couple of pills out of the box, swallowed them with water, and put the box away. Whatever medicine she was taking, London hoped it would settle the woman's nerves.

Still a bit sulky, János began to take their orders. Although Gus and Honey decided to order goulash, everybody else took Professor Kallay's advice and chose the *paprikácsirke*. János nodded with approval as he jotted the orders down.

"An excellent choice," he said. "Ours is the best *paprikácsirke* in Budapest. You won't find its equal outside of Hungary. Of course, we use only the best, authentic Hungarian paprika. There is nothing else like it."

Professor Kallay chuckled as the waiter left. He leaned over the table and winked at the tourists.

"I'll tell you a little secret about *paprikácsirke*," he said. "It plays a certain modest role in literary history. In the first chapter of Bram Stoker's *Dracula*, Jonathan Harker orders it at a hotel on his way to his ill-fated visit to the count—only there it is called *paprika hendl*, or roasted paprika chicken. Mr. Harker quite liked it, as I remember, and even asked for the recipe, which is included in some editions of the book. Alas, he didn't take the same pleasure in Dracula's hospitality."

As everybody at the table laughed at this amusing anecdote, London was glad to see that they seemed to be relaxing and enjoying themselves. She noticed that Emil was using his phone to snap photos of the cheerful group.

"Do pull up a chair and join us," London invited Professor Kallay.

Looking at his watch, the professor shook his head.

"It is kind of you, but I've already dined, and I have a pressing appointment this evening."

"A pity," Emil chimed in. "I would have liked to have heard your scholarly views on post–Cold War economics in Hungary."

"And I would enjoy hearing your thoughts on German reunification," Professor Kallay said. "Perhaps another time. How long will your group be here in Budapest?"

Emil glanced at his own watch.

"I am afraid our tour boat is setting sail quite shortly," he said. "We are leaving tonight for Gyor."

"Ah, Gyor!" Professor Kallay exclaimed, his bushy eyebrows rising with approval. "A lovely city! I know it very well."

"Do you have any suggestions for our visit there?" London asked.

The professor scratched his chin.

"As a matter of fact, I do," he said. "There is an excellent restaurant that is not to be missed—the Magyar Öröm, I believe it's called. I hope it's still there. Alas, I haven't been to Gyor for years, myself. I wish you all a splendid voyage. And thank you for indulging my faltering English. It was a pleasure to have a bit of practice."

The group thanked the professor and wished him well, and he left the restaurant.

As the evening continued, János performed his duties efficiently and politely, but without a lot of warmth or enthusiasm. He kept glaring at Mrs. Klimowski resentfully and said as little to her as possible.

But there was no cause for complaint when the meals arrived. The *paprikácsirke* was every bit as delicious as Professor Kallay and János had said it would be. London enjoyed every bite of it. As the rich, creamy, slightly spicy dish rolled across her tongue, London realized János was right. Hungarian paprika was extraordinarily rich in flavor, but without overwhelming the chicken in the dish.

However, the medicine that Mrs. Klimowski had taken didn't seem to make her feel any better. She ate listlessly, saying almost nothing to anybody.

London made a decision to try and give special attention to the crotchety elderly woman. But right now she had to get everyone back to the *Nachtmusik* in time for its departure. The group's detour to St. Stephen's Basilica had been enjoyable but had put them behind schedule. By the time everyone finished a leisurely dinner and settled their checks, she knew she had to keep them moving.

But as they walked back along the way they had come, Sir Reginald Taft seemed to be trying to wriggle his way up and out of the bag that held him. Apparently oblivious to the dog's discomfort, Mrs. Klimowski patted him admiringly on the head.

"Yes, you *were* a fine little gentleman, Sir Reginald."

Frowning at the others, she added, "Now don't you feel ashamed for thinking so little of him? He's no mere animal, I tell you. I do believe Sir Reginald has more genuine humanity than some of you people."

Still wiggling, Sir Reginald growled at everybody, which rather contradicted Mrs. Klimowski's observation as far as London was concerned.

"I think your dog needs a little break," Cyrus Bannister remarked.

Mrs. Klimowski looked at him with a forced smile.

"For once we agree, Mr. Bannister," she said.

Then she added to the dog, "Why don't you stretch your legs and relax a bit, Sir Reginald?"

She lowered the bag to the pavement, and the little Yorkshire Terrier crawled out. He moved a bit stiffly after his long confinement, but London sensed that he was relieved to have at least a few moments of freedom.

She tried to keep the group moving toward the ship, but their progress was suddenly interrupted by a shrill outcry.

"Sir Reginald Taft! He's gone!"

CHAPTER TEN

London was swept by a sudden wave of alarm.

Mrs. Klimowski's dog had gone missing!

The woman's eyes were wide with terror. She kept calling out in a shaky voice.

"Sir Reginald! Sir Reginald! Where have you gone?"

In addition to her own alarm, London felt a spasm of guilt. This wouldn't have happened if she'd insisted that the woman leave her little dog behind in her stateroom.

They were on a brightly lit street, well within sight of the basilica. Like others in this area, the street was narrow and almost entirely used by pedestrians. At least Sir Reginald Taft wasn't likely to get hit by a car. But there were plenty of people on foot, coming and going amid the shops and cafés, and there was still the danger that the tiny animal would get stepped on …

Or get kidnapped.

Or maybe bite somebody.

Which, when she thought about it, seemed likely if a stranger did try to pick up the grouchy creature.

Meanwhile, Mrs. Klimowski kept calling out frantically.

"Sir Reginald! Sir Reginald Taft!"

Then London caught a flash of movement on the street's patterned stones. She stepped to one side to get a better look, and then breathed a sigh of relief.

Sir Reginald Taft was standing directly behind Mrs. Klimowski, looking up at his owner with apparent indifference as she kept calling out his name.

London had to stop herself from laughing. She saw that some of the other passengers weren't even trying to hide their amusement.

She pointed and spoke to the distraught woman.

"He's right there, Mrs. Klimowski."

"Where?"

"Right behind you."

"Is he, now? He's being a very naughty creature, then."

Mrs. Klimowski turned around to look for her dog. But in perfect synchronization with her turning, Sir Reginald moved to stay in position right behind her.

Mrs. Klimowski scowled at London.

"He's not there," she snapped.

Before London could try to explain, Gus Jarrett spoke up.

"Yes, he is, lady. He's right behind you."

Mrs. Klimowski turned around again, and again the dog deftly stayed behind her, moving in a full circle on the pavement.

Mrs. Klimowski put her hands on her hips and scowled at London and Mr. Jarrett.

"I think I can trust my own eyes. He's not there, I tell you."

The mysterious Cyrus Bannister was watching with crossed arms and an expression of sardonic amusement.

"Madam, you clearly don't know how to call your dog," he said.

Mrs. Klimowski let out a gasp of outrage.

"Whatever do you mean?" she demanded.

"You just keep saying his entire lengthy name over and over again."

Agnes Shick spoke to Mrs. Klimowski in a more kindly voice.

"The gentleman is right, dear. Just speaking his name could mean anything to him."

"It's his name!" Mrs. Klimowski said. "And I can assure all of you, he's exceptionally intelligent, with an IQ that's higher than any of yours, I imagine."

Bannister scoffed aloud.

"If you say so, madam," he told her.

London realized that this dog might indeed be plenty smart. He certainly seemed to be hiding behind his owner intentionally. She'd had few pets in her life and didn't know whether or not animals ever had a sense of humor.

Meanwhile, she had to figure out what to do. Should she simply walk over and try to pick the creature up? Might he run away with alarm and disappear among all the pedestrians?

Or might he just bite me?

The dog was small and mostly hair—just seven or eight pounds in all, she guessed. But he had pointy teeth and didn't hesitate to display them.

Suddenly, Honey, Gus Jarrett's red-headed, gum-chewing wife, came trotting forward on precarious heels in her super-tight skirt, speaking the first words London had ever heard her say.

"Oh, for crying out loud!"

She stooped down and called out to the dog pleasantly.

"Sir Reggie, Come here!"

Sure enough, Sir Reginald Taft trotted toward her.

"Good dog," Honey said.

To everyone's shock, Sir Reginald Taft jumped up into Honey Jarrett's arms. She stood up, triumphantly holding the little creature.

"Yes, that's a good boy!" she cooed, kissing and petting him. "Aren't you a little darling?"

Meanwhile, Cyrus Bannister sneered at Gus Jarrett.

"So your lovely bride is allergic to dogs, eh?"

Gus Jarrett's face was red with rage and embarrassment at how Honey had contradicted what he'd said earlier when they'd boarded. It was now pretty obvious that he'd only made that fuss about the dog just to make trouble, not because Honey had any real trouble with dogs.

"The dog's hypoallergenic," Gus snapped at Cyrus.

"Oh, yeah, I'd forgotten that," Cyrus said, still sneering. "Anyway, she sure seems to like dogs a lot."

Then Gus stared daggers at Honey, causing London to worry.

Mrs. Klimowski descended on Honey Jarrett with a look of horror and anger.

"Now, see here!" she said to Honey. "What on earth are you doing with my dear Sir Reginald?"

Honey stammered with understandable shock.

"I—I was only trying to—"

Snatching the dog back, Mrs. Klimowski snapped back at her.

"You took my dog away from me! What an unspeakably mean thing to do!"

As Honey kept trying to explain, her husband tugged her aside. London heard him whisper to her angrily.

"You've got a lot of nerve, making a fool out of me like that."

Honey snapped her gum defiantly.

"Gosh, I was just trying to be nice!" she said.

"There's no point trying to be nice to a worthless old bat like that," Gus whispered, holding her arm a little tightly. "And you sure as hell shouldn't have made such a scene. You humiliated me."

Mrs. Klimowski held her dog in her outstretched hands and tilted him jerkily about as she examined him. Sir Reginald bared his teeth and growled.

"Oh, my sweet creature, are you all right?" Mrs. Klimowski asked, almost tearfully. "That awful woman didn't hurt you, I hope."

Meanwhile, Sir Reginald wiggled uncomfortably for a moment. Then he went limp, apparently resigned to being restored to his former situation. Mrs. Klimowski stuffed him into the leather bag head first. The bag itself writhed as the dog managed to turn himself around so that he could breathe properly.

"I said it before," Cyrus Bannister murmured. "That is a very unhappy dog, and he doesn't belong in that bag. In fact, that woman has no business owning a dog at all."

Then he added, "Someone should do something about it."

London's eyes met his for a moment, and she felt a chill at his grim, purposeful expression.

She shook off the eerie feeling. She had to get her group back to the boat right now.

"We have to hurry," she told them. "If we're late, the *Nachtmusik* could leave without us."

"They wouldn't dare," Bannister said.

"They could," Honey replied. "Have you even read the rules? It says that Epoch World Cruise Lines is under no obligation to hold a ship for passengers who are tardy."

Hearing that, most of the others hurried toward the dock. Emil offered an arm to Mrs. Klimowski and got her headed in the right direction.

"If that ridiculous excuse for a dog has made us miss our boat ..." Bannister growled as he strode ahead.

London had a terrible feeling that might have already happened.

CHAPTER ELEVEN

Only when they rounded the final turn and saw the *Nachtmusik* still docked did London draw a breath of relief.

We made it.

The elegant ship was still in place, illuminated by an array of lights that reflected in the water around it. This was the first time she'd observed the yacht-like riverboat at night, and she felt privileged to have been chosen for a position aboard such a handsome vessel.

A crew was puttering about the gangway, so she trotted the final yards and signaled them to hold everything in place. Now she just had to be sure everyone got settled in for the night without any further drama.

London stood by the gangway and watched her charges board. They were all here, including the dog. As Emil gallantly escorted the tired, tottering Mrs. Klimowski up the gangway, she was grateful for his help.

She followed the passengers into the reception area and smiled and exchanged pleasantries with those who were inclined to be pleasant.

"Lovely evening," one said.

"Fantastic meal," said another.

"Most interesting," said another.

She managed a bright smile at Mrs. Klimowski, who seemed anything but happy. Emil took care of getting the dour lady and her dog back to their quarters. In a short time, London was alone.

She still felt daunted by all the work that lay ahead for the rest of the cruise—especially dealing with Mrs. Klimowski and her dog. But the truth was, she felt pretty good about how she'd handled the group this evening.

The meal had been excellent, especially the rich and generous serving of *paprikácsirke.* London remembered Professor Kallay mentioning that the recipe could be found in some editions of *Dracula.* She thought that maybe she'd look that up and try it herself. Although she'd felt too nervous to eat dessert herself, the others had partaken of the most scrumptious traditional items on the menu—jam-filled sponge cakes, cream puffs, plum dumplings, and the like. Even that unpleasant waiter, János, hadn't dampened the group's enthusiasm.

Now London took the spiral stairs up to the open Rondo deck, where other passengers were gathering to witness the boat's departure. She spotted her friend Elsie leaning against the port rail, looking out over the Danube and the hilly western part of the city glittering in the night.

London walked over and nudged her and said hello.

"Hey, where have you been all evening?" Elsie replied with a smile. "I thought maybe you'd show up at the bar."

"I had to take a group on a little impromptu tour," London explained.

"I guess you'll be doing a lot of that kind of thing. How did it go?"

"OK, I think. Aren't you supposed to be at the bar?"

"One of my assistants is giving me a break so I could come up and watch us pull out of Budapest. Nice of him, wasn't it? Things had slowed down because everybody was coming up here."

"You're looking pretty happy with yourself," London observed.

"It's been a while since I worked as a bartender," Elsie replied "I'd forgotten how much I enjoyed it. Sure, it gets pretty hectic. But the more the merrier, as far as I'm concerned. I guess I'm just a people person."

London smiled.

"I guess I'm a people person too," she said.

She could hear the crew working busily now, separating the boat from the gangway. London felt a bit melancholy at having to leave Budapest so soon after she'd gotten here. But she looked forward to seeing Gyor. She couldn't remember ever visiting it as a child.

Looking along the deck, London saw that Amy Blassingame was also leaning on the rail, looking out over the city.

Nodding in Amy's direction, London said to Elsie, "I think maybe it's time for me to make nice with her."

"Why?" Elsie said with a shrug. "What did you do wrong to the River Troll?"

"Oh, let's not call her that."

"You don't have to call her that if you don't want to. Answer my question."

"Well, I took her job, for one thing."

"That wasn't your fault. Jeremy Lapham just knew who'd be better for the job. He made the right call. Anyway, *I'm* sure glad he made the choice he did."

"Even so ..."

London's voice faded. Then she silently made up her mind and began to walk toward the concierge.

"Good luck," Elsie called after her. "I've got to get back down to my bar people." With that, the bartender headed back down the staircase.

Amy glanced up at London as she approached, then turned her eyes away again.

"Lovely view," London said.

Amy looked at her as if she hadn't already noticed her.

"Oh, it's you. Yes, it is nice up here this evening."

Amy turned her view back to the city.

London swallowed hard and gathered up her nerve to speak.

"Amy, I thought maybe we should clear just a few things up. I really didn't mean to step on any toes."

Amy looked at her with feigned incomprehension.

"What do you mean?"

"What I mean to say is ... I got a call from Jeremy Lapham just yesterday, when I was back in Connecticut ..."

With a half-smile, Amy locked eyes with London, waiting for whatever she was going to say next.

"I didn't mean to—" London began.

"Step on any toes?" Amy said, repeating London's phrase.

"Right."

"Whose toes would you mean?"

London winced a little.

Then Amy's smile broadened with mock realization.

"Ohhh, you mean *my* toes. I guess you may have heard that I was hoping to be the social director. Well, *c'est la vie*, as they say in France. You can't win them all."

Then Amy let out an exaggerated yawn.

"I'm exhausted," she said. "I'd better turn in so I can get to work bright and early tomorrow. My, that was quite a list of passenger demands you put together. It's going to keep me very busy!"

As if to punctuate the end of their conversation, the boat's whistle went off, and the *Nachtmusik* jerked as it began to pull away from the dock. The deck was suddenly moving under everybody's feet.

Without another word, Amy stalked away toward the elevator.

London gazed around and saw that the passengers scattered about the open Rondo deck seemed engaged with the view. She was about go and talk with some of them, when Emil Waldmüller approached her.

"I'm glad to see you," London said. "I wanted to thank you for all your help this evening, especially with Mrs. Klimowski."

"Oh, yes—Mrs. Klimowski. She is proving to be—what is an idiom in English?"

London chuckled again.

"'High maintenance' is one way of putting it," she said.

Emil's smile faded.

"'High maintenance,' yes," he said. "I am afraid that woman may test my patience—she and her bothersome dog both."

London was startled by his sullen tone. Because of his gallant behavior, she had begun to think of him as different from some of the others, sincerely more tolerant and accepting of other people's faults and foibles.

Was she spotting a touch of insincerity in this attractive man?

Emil must have noticed her surprise, because he hastened to add, "Nevertheless, I do try to accommodate the passengers as best I can."

With a slight bow, he turned away and also went toward the elevator.

As London watched him go, she was still a little disturbed by his tone. And she was well aware that her issues with Amy Blassingame were not over.

She silently scolded herself for letting any of it bother her.

Nobody's perfect, she told herself. *When you work with people, you have to deal with all kinds.*

And she had a perfectly pleasant job to do here on the *Nachtmusik*'s beautiful open deck. As the ship moved out into the river, dazzling lights of the ancient city were spellbinding.

She hurried to a group of passengers at the railing and pointed out the Buda Castle on the shore. It was brilliantly lit and looked even more impressive than it had by day. So did the massive Szécheny Chain Bridge, which cast shimmering reflections on the water as they passed under it.

Then she realized that an important sight was coming up on the opposite shore.

"We're passing the Hungarian Parliament Building," she said.

"Come, let's have a look."

The group followed London toward the opposite railing. Sure enough, a vast Gothic-style building came into view, its lighted edifice reflected and glistening on the water.

Remembering what the historian had said that afternoon, London told them, "It's exactly the same height as St. Stephen's Basilica, making them the two tallest structures in Budapest. They represent the city's worldly and spiritual life."

The passengers murmured their appreciation and London felt a glow of contentment. She knew she was exactly where she should be as she and this pleasant company stood together watching one of the world's most beautiful cities slip behind them into the night.

*

By the time London made her final rounds to check on the ship's passengers, most of them had turned in for the night. The few who were still up seemed happily occupied. Finally feeling the strain of a long day—one that had begun many hours ago on a different continent—she headed to her own stateroom.

When she opened the door and switched on the light, a reflection immediately caught her eye. A silver compote cover was right in the center of her little table. It definitely hadn't been there before.

She hurried over and lifted the shiny cover.

There on a china plate was an oddly shaped piece of pastry.

Baklava, she immediately realized.

It was a dessert of Turkish origin, popular in Eastern Europe and much of Asia, especially in the Middle East.

And it had been London's favorite pastry since …

Since when?

Since she was a small child, anyway. She couldn't remember when she'd first tasted it, but for all she knew, it might have been here in Hungary.

But who had delivered it here?

And why?

There wasn't so much as a card or message with it.

Had Emil ordered it for her?

She didn't think she'd mentioned to him or anybody else how much she liked baklava.

Is there a mind reader aboard?

She smiled at the unlikely idea. She remembered that she hadn't had any dessert back at the Duna Étterem, and now she felt hungry enough to enjoy it.

Beside the dish was some silverware wrapped in a cloth napkin. She sat down and cut off a small bite of the dessert.

Um-m-m.

The delicate, tissue-thin layers of filo layered with chopped nuts literally melted in her mouth. The honeyed syrup that saturated the dish seemed sweeter and more satisfying than any she'd tasted before. She felt positively light-headed at how delicious it was.

By the time she finished the baklava, London Rose felt that everything was right with the world. Whoever had sent her this gift had made a perfect ending to her first day on a new job.

A great way to start a new life.

When she finished the delicacy, she stood up and opened the curtains over her narrow window, revealing a lovely view of the river and the stars silhouetting the distant hills.

But who brought me such a nice treat?

She really had no idea.

CHAPTER TWELVE

Early the next morning, London opened her curtains upon a very different view from the one she'd had yesterday. They were in a narrow river and a line of people was standing on the shore, staring curiously at the *Nachtmusik*.

The sight took her aback for a few moments, then she realized that a boat like this must be a rare sight here. Although the little town was easily accessible by bus or rail, the people must be surprised that such a ship had ventured all this way into the heart of Gyor.

She knew that most tour boats wouldn't even attempt to make it up this tributary of the Danube to the place where the river narrowed and converged with the Rába and Rábca. Even though the modest-sized *Nachtmusik* was well-designed to reach unusual destinations, the pilot had to be exceptionally skilled to manage that passageway through the *Moson Danube,* or Small Danube.

Beyond the curious crowd, the other side of the river was a fanciful, densely packed assortment of quaint buildings with tiled roofs. London could see by the angles of their walls that the streets must be twisty and irregular. It was a less majestic city than Budapest—but if anything, it seemed more charming and fairytale-like.

Gyor's Old Town, she realized. She had never been here before, not even with Mom and Dad.

As she turned away from the window, London glanced at the silver compote on her table. Only a few crumbs and a few drops of sticky syrup remained there beneath it. She closed her eyes and felt as though she could taste that delicious baklava all over again.

Who left it there for me?

Maybe today she could solve the mystery of the baklava's origin.

Meanwhile, she had a busy day ahead. She put on her uniform and got ready for work. But as soon as she stepped outside her room, her spirits sank. Amy Blassingame was striding down the hallway toward her.

"London, I was just coming down to see you!" Amy cried out. She kept chattering as she came to a halt, blocking London's way. "I've been simply frantic all morning, going from room to room to take care of all those things on that enormous list of yours. And I'm afraid I've run into a problem. A passenger came to me with a small complaint—well, not a small complaint as far as he's concerned."

"What is it?" London asked.

"He said his room temperature wasn't absolutely perfect. Something about it having to stay exactly at seventy-eight degrees. He said it was wrong, I can't remember whether he said it was too high or too low. I told him I'd bring it up with you. I said I was sure you would make sure it got fixed."

London winced a little. Then she thought back to what Elsie had told her yesterday.

"Just remember—you're her boss, not the other way around."

And after all, this was an issue for a concierge to take care of, not a social director.

The time had come for her to exert her authority.

But how could she do that without making unnecessary waves?

Politely, she decided.

She smiled pleasantly.

"Well, please check in with the maintenance manager, will you? Tell him about the complaint. Maybe he can figure out some way to fix this. Or maybe he'll tell you that the temperature just can't be set any more precisely than it is. Either way, kindly talk to the passenger and explain to him how things are. I'll leave it up to you."

Amy's smile faded.

"But I've got so many other things to do," she grumbled.

"And so do I," London replied. "But I have confidence in you. I'm sure you can take care of it."

Amy stood glaring for a moment, as if about to protest. But of course, she couldn't very well complain about being asked to do her job—especially when she'd been asked nicely.

"All right, then," Amy said. "What else is on the agenda?"

"I've got a large tour group for today," London said. "We'll be leaving after breakfast."

"Really?" Amy said with a wistful sigh. "And I suppose I'll be spending the whole day aboard while you're out … well, never mind."

London had to admit that it didn't seem quite fair.

"I'll tell you what," she said. "I'll take them out for the morning and through lunch. Then we'll take a break and you can take over."

Amy smiled.

"Oh, that would be nice," she said.

"I'll need some help before we leave this morning, taking names of who will be on the tour. You can help me with that after breakfast on the gangway."

"Very good," Amy said. "I'll be there."

As Amy went away, London breathed a sigh of relief. Giving orders was still new to her, but she knew Elsie would be proud of how she'd asserted herself over the so-called River Troll.

She took the elevator up to the Romanze deck's Habsburg Restaurant. Servers were already busy setting the tables and generally getting things ready. Standing to one side, a man wearing a white chef's uniform was overseeing their progress.

London walked toward him and extended her hand.

"You're the head chef, I believe."

"That's right—Bryce Yeaton," the chef replied as he shook her hand. "And I do double duty as the ship's medic. And you're London Rose, our social director. I'm pleased to make your acquaintance."

"Likewise," London said. She noted that his accent was Australian, and that his face was … very pleasant, with a dimpled chin and flawlessly maintained stubble of beard.

Just then a harried-looking server came by with a request, and Bryce dashed off to solve a problem. London went to a side table and poured herself a cup of coffee, then Bryce came back her way.

"Sorry, London," he said. Then he asked with a grin, "Is it OK for us to call each other by our first names?"

"I'd certainly prefer it, Bryce."

"Glad to hear that, London."

They both chuckled. London found herself thinking that this man's cheerful features didn't look capable of frowning. He seemed to be quite likeable in an unremarkable sort of way. She did wonder why he was looking at her with an expression of curiosity.

"I thought I'd greet your breakfast customers this morning," she said, to explain her presence here.

"That's kind of you, but I've already got a hostess," Bryce said, nodding toward a woman who was helping set up the tables.

"I know you do," London said. "But I'm responsible for keeping about a hundred people happy, and it's a bigger challenge than I'm used to. I'd better spend some extra time dealing with them face to face."

A few passengers were arriving now, so London put down her coffee and started toward them, but Bryce's next words stopped her in her tracks.

"Did you enjoy your baklava?" he asked.

London's eyes widened.

"So—that was *you*?"

Bryce shrugged.

"I wanted to introduce myself to you yesterday, but you always seemed to be on the run whenever you weren't ashore. You seemed to be having a hectic day, so I thought maybe you'd like to end it with a nice dessert."

"It was a very nice dessert indeed," London said. "One of my very favorites, in fact. But why didn't you leave a note or something to …?"

"Let you know who it was from?" Bryce said. "Well, I guess I figured it would be kind of obvious …"

He shrugged, and London understood what he meant.

"*Of course* I should have realized …" she said. "How silly of me. It's a good thing I'm not a detective. I wouldn't be much good at it."

Then he said, "Here comes your lady with the dog. Though there's hardly enough there to be called a dog. But I don't think that kind of terrier will grow any bigger."

London saw that Mrs. Klimowski was entering the dining room with a grouchy-looking Sir Reginald peering out of her bag.

"The little thing doesn't seem to like being lugged around in that bag," she observed.

"Who would?" he replied. "Dogs are meant to run about, aren't they? Wonder if that one even can."

London laughed at the memory of Sir Reginald's nimble antics yesterday evening as he'd avoided his owner.

"You'd be surprised," she told Bryce.

With a grin, the chef rushed away to the kitchen.

London hurried to greet Mrs. Klimowski.

The woman hadn't looked well yesterday, and she didn't seem any better today. Of course, she was again laden with diamonds and that ruby pendant, and the haughty expression on her face hadn't changed either.

"Good morning, Mrs. Klimowski," London said. "Did you sleep well last night?"

She had a feeling she knew the answer, but it was her job to ask the question anyway.

"Not at all well, if you must know," Mrs. Klimowski said with a slight whine. "I got desperately seasick, and so did Sir Reginald, the poor dear. Isn't there anything that can be done to stop this boat from rocking so much?"

Rocking? London thought.

To the best of her knowledge, the *Nachtmusik* never rocked at all. It was a riverboat, after all, and not at the mercy of waves and tides and such. Perhaps Mrs. Klimowski had been disturbed by the boat's halting progress as it had approached Gyor through the Small Danube.

"I'm sorry you had a rough night," London said. "But when we get back onto the main Danube, the sailing should be easier."

"I should hope so. What's for breakfast this morning?"

London recited a few choice items from the menu.

"Oh, those won't do at all," Mrs. Klimowski huffed. "Not after that indigestible 'Dracula dish' last night. I'll just have to order something bland—a slice or two of dry toast, perhaps. Maybe I'll have something richer later on."

London took the woman by the elbow and escorted her toward a table.

"I hope you've planned an excellent tour for today," Mrs. Klimowski said.

London felt a twinge of worry. Mrs. Klimowski seemed rather frail as she guided her along. She wondered—should she make a firm suggestion that the woman stay on board and rest for today? Should she insist that the ship's medic take a look at her?

Then London remembered what she had learned earlier from reading the crew list. Since this was a smaller ship than most cruise vessels, many of the crew doubled up on their jobs. She herself had way more responsibilities than she'd ever had before. And as Bryce had mentioned, he was the boat's medic as well as the chef, available to treat minor ailments and to route passengers to onshore hospitals in emergencies. And she knew that the chef was quite busy right now.

As London helped the elderly woman into her chair, she assured her that the tour ought to be quite stimulating.

Then London went back to greeting other guests, pleased by how many of their names she could remember. When she finished, she looked for a place to sit down and have breakfast herself. Emil

Waldmüller was sitting alone, and he gestured for her to join him. She still felt strange after their uncomfortable exchange on the Rondo deck, and she wasn't sure whether to feel pleased or not.

But as she sat down with him, she immediately felt charmed again by his Old World bearing and his sophisticated smile. When a server hurried over to them. Emil ordered breakfast scones, and London decided on Eggs Benedict.

"I understand that we will be taking a tour group out this morning." Emil said.

"That's right," London said, feeling a flash of anxiety at the task ahead of her. "We're scheduled right after breakfast."

Although she knew that it was part of Emil's job to assist on scheduled tours, she wondered if it was going to be comfortable working with him today.

Apparently Emil noticed her hesitation, because his smile turned just a little shy and sheepish.

"Eh, I promise to be perfectly polite to all of the passengers. Even the dog."

London felt reassured. Perhaps he'd realized that he'd put her off a little last night, and wanted to do better.

*

After breakfast, London returned to her room and changed into a nice pair of slacks and a lightweight blouse. Sitting on the edge of her bed, she looked over the notes she'd prepared last night and loaded into her cell phone for today's walking tour.

Last night she'd used the Internet to review details about Gyor—its sights, its history, and its people. Now she had an impressive ongoing lecture prepared to deliver as she led her tourists through the city. She felt confident that she could recite it all by heart if she needed to.

She took the elevator up to the Menuetto deck and the reception room. Emil and Amy were already there, and some forty people soon arrived for the tour. The other passengers had either chosen to wander about on their own or to stay on the ship. Before they left the reception area, she and Amy took down the names of the people in the tour group.

Then London, Emil, and Amy led the group out onto the simple railed gangway, which extended over a small raft to the riverside. At the end of the gangway, a group of townspeople stood staring in fascination at the boat. London understood why. The *Nachtmusik* was a truly startling sight for this stretch of the Small Danube.

They were a friendly group, and many of them greeted the tourists as they set foot on the riverbank, some of them by saying "Hello," "Good morning," or "Welcome" in English. As London led the tour group away from the boat, she turned to wave goodbye to Amy. But she saw that Amy was talking to one of the townspeople—a rather ordinary-looking man who looked about London's age. London quickly realized what was going on.

Amy's flirting with him.

Or he's flirting with her.

Or they're flirting with each other.

It was a bit of a surprise. Until now, Amy had struck London as too stiff and officious for this kind of thing. And now London wasn't sure what to think about it. She was pretty sure that fraternization was against the ship's rules.

But she quickly assured herself that it hardly mattered. The *Nachtmusik* was scheduled to leave Gyor this evening—too soon for any kind of a romance to develop. As long as Amy kept doing her job, London had no reason to complain.

London and Emil led the group along the bank to the arched bridge and across the river toward Old Town.

As the town loomed larger in front of her, a strange sensation was rising up in her—a sensation she couldn't remember feeling before. This didn't feel like an ordinary tourist town.

At the end of the bridge, she and the group stepped into Old Town, with its plazas and twisting streets and its variety of quaint and lovely rooftops, spires, and edifices. Then that sensation swept over her completely. For a moment she wondered what was making her feel this way.

She suddenly realized what it was.

History.

Gyor was fairly alive with it, more so than any other city she'd ever visited.

Her group had gathered in a circle around her, expecting her to say a few words before starting their tour. London looked at the notes she'd prepared on her cell phone. Suddenly, they seemed incredibly dull, just a lifeless list of dates, names, and historical facts.

This won't do, she realized.

The lecture she'd prepared couldn't possibly convey the feelings she had right now.

It was all perfectly useless.

What am I going to say?

CHAPTER THIRTEEN

Abundant thoughts were crowding London's mind, but she couldn't seem to put any of them into appropriate words. She knew she had to say something. The passengers were standing there, waiting for her to introduce them to a city she had never seen before.

Of course, she had studied up on Gyor last night, but now that she had actually set foot in the city, what she had planned to say felt so … inadequate.

She glanced over at Emil, wondering for a moment if she should swallow her pride and ask him to help her out.

He was smiling at her in an oddly sympathetic way.

As if he knows how I feel.

As if he's felt this way himself.

And she realized—as a trained historian who had spent his life exploring and studying Europe, surely he *had* felt this way, probably on many occasions.

With a slight nod, Emil seemed to be reassuring her, encouraging her to let herself find the words she needed as she spoke them.

London began haltingly.

"I've never been to Gyor before but … I can already feel something about this city. I feel like I can learn something from it, and not just about history, but something about …"

London's voice faded and she paused.

Finally she said, "Let's just take a moment to imagine this place as it must have looked some eleven hundred years ago. None of these houses, buildings, streets were here. The warlike Magyars, whose Hungarian descendants live here now, swept into this area from the mountains, putting up tents to live in, right where we are standing."

She breathed deeply, feeling as if the city's past was filling her very lungs.

"The Magyars were the last of many peoples who had settled here since the Stone Age, since the dawn of civilization—the Celts, the Romans, the Slavs, and the Lombards. The Magyars gave it the name it has now—Gyor. And their village of tents would be the beginning of the city you see before you today."

She glanced among the tourists and saw that they were listening raptly.

"This city," she said in a voice that became quieter with awe, "this city has been built and destroyed over and over again. It was raided by the Mongols, destroyed by invading Czechs, then burned to the ground by the Magyars themselves to keep it from falling into the hands of invading Turks, who crept away in defeat. Then those who remained here began centuries of building and rebuilding that continues to this very day."

She turned around and took in the scene again.

"I think we've got something special to learn from this city, something important to our everyday lives. I think it has something to with … well, endurance and perseverance and tenacity and …"

Then she couldn't help but laugh a little at how her words were starting to border on the grandiose.

"But how would I know?" she finally said. "I just got here myself."

Most of her listeners laughed as well, then gave her a little burst of applause for her introductory remarks.

"Come on, let's have a look around," she said.

As London began to lead the group among the twisting and irregular streets, Emil touched her on the elbow.

"Well done," he said. "Very well done indeed."

London smiled at how sincere he seemed. She sensed that he really did admire how she'd handled her remarks—as if he didn't think he could have done better himself.

"Thanks," she said.

No longer feeling defensive, she knew she'd be more relaxed about asking for his input once in a while.

London brought the group to a stop in front of a stone pedestal with a grand statue of angels carrying a large chest by two long poles. On top of the chest was a golden lamb surrounded by sunlike rays.

"Can anybody guess what this is?" London asked.

Walter Shick spoke up.

"Why, it looks like the Hebrew Ark of the Covenant—the sacred chest that held the Ten Commandments."

"That's right," London said with a nod. "The sculpture was a gift to Gyor from the Hungarian King Charles III in 1731—an apology for doing damage to the city while apprehending a fugitive."

Walter's wife, Agnes, shook her head in admiration.

"The angels look like they're taking flight right in front of our eyes, carrying the Ark right along with them," she said.

London smiled at the observation. Indeed, the massive statue appeared to be both uncannily light and in motion. And she understood why. She looked at Emil, who of course understood such things better than she did. She thought it might be interesting to hear his explanation.

"Could you tell us something about the style of this statue?" she asked him.

Emil's eyes twinkled.

"Not just yet," he said. "I will in just a few moments, I expect."

London tilted her head in slight surprise.

Why not right now, while we're looking at the statue? she wondered.

She figured the *Nachtmusik*'s historian must have some good reason, so she nodded and moved her group toward their next destination—the Cathedral Basilica of the Assumption of Our Lady. London was a bit surprised to find the edifice not exactly stunning to look at—not nearly as large or decorative as St. Stephen's Basilica back in Budapest. She wondered—was this going to be a disappointment?

A well-dressed, somewhat potbellied doorkeeper stood watchfully next to the donation box, smiling in greeting at the new arrivals. In Hungarian, he said he was there to offer whatever assistance he could give during their visit to the basilica. London thanked him, and he opened the doors for them to enter as they put their donations into the box.

As London walked on inside, the sight that awaited her took her breath away. Those images she'd studied hadn't prepared her for the actual scene.

The interior of the basilica—its paintings, statues, and architectural features—seemed to be as wild with motion as the statue they'd just seen, and radiating with dazzling color. Though this cathedral was much smaller than the one in Budapest, it was every bit its equal as a feast to the eye.

London's mouth dropped open, and she looked at Emil.

He smiled at her, clearly understanding how she felt and why.

"Would you like me to …?" he asked tentatively.

"Yes, please," London said, again eager to hear what he had to say to the group.

Emil turned to the group and spoke.

"Ladies and gentlemen, you'll find that much of this city is decorated in the Baroque style—the statue you just saw, for example, and the interior of this basilica. The style originated in the seventeenth century and was meant to appeal to the senses and the emotions through movement, richness, detail, surprise, and vitality."

He chuckled at the wide-eyed tourists.

"And I can tell by your faces that this example of the Baroque has succeeded," he added.

The group laughed, and many nodded their heads in agreement.

London added, "You can *hear* the same energy and movement in the music of the period—the works of Handel, Vivaldi, and Bach. As for Gyor, much of the city as it exists now was built during the height of the Baroque era."

As London led the group among the dazzling sights of the basilica, she saw that even Mrs. Klimowski was looking about the space with apparent pleasure. It was the first time she'd seen anything other than a frown on the woman's features.

When London led her group into a small Gothic chapel on the south side of the basilica, they were greeted by a shining face with large, penetrating eyes. The crowned and bearded silver and gold head was mounted in a large glass case.

London said, "This is St. Ladislaus, a king of Hungary during the eleventh century, and one of the country's greatest heroes."

Agnes Shick peered through the glass with rapt fascination.

"Look at his eyes!" she said. "Why, I feel like he's peering right at me."

"In a way, he is," Emil said. "His actual skull is preserved as a relic inside this likeness."

"Oh, my!" Agnes gasped.

London herself felt a spasm of awe. Of course, she'd read about the St. Ladislaus reliquary last night, so it came as no surprise. But looking at it right now filled her with some of the same awe that she'd felt looking at St. Stephen's mummified "Holy Right" hand back in Budapest—a feeling that this city was under the watchful eyes of a kindly guardian.

She led the group back outside, where they continued their walking tour. Wonders seemed to leap out at them from around every corner of

Gyor's twisting streets. There were more wonderful statues, including one of the Archangel Michael defeating Satan in battle, and another of the Virgin Mary atop a column flanked by the four Christian Apostles. They passed on through the beautiful, spacious Vienna Gate Square with its Baroque Carmelite Church.

Finally they came to a pedestrian street marked by a startling sight—a bronze statue of a naked man paddling a boat over rocky waves.

"This is probably Gyor's most popular statue—or at least the most photographed," London explained to her group. "*The Boatman* was put here in 1997 in memory of how the city had been flooded in 1954. And I think it's a nice place to pause our tour for a little while. I'm sure some of you are tired, and I for one am getting hungry."

Some of the group murmured in agreement.

"As you can see, there are lots of cafés and restaurants around," London said. "I even saw a McDonald's on our way here, if any of you happen to be in the mood for it."

Some of the tourists laughed.

London looked at her watch and added, "Let's meet here again in an hour and a half to continue our tour. Meanwhile, please go and do as you like."

As the group started to disperse, Mr. and Mrs. Shick stepped toward her.

"Say, didn't that professor back in Budapest recommend a nice restaurant?" Walter asked.

"Yes, he did," Agnes said. "What did he say it was called?"

Other tourists who had been with London yesterday in Budapest seemed to share the Shicks' interest. London tried to remember. They had gone to the Duna Étterem for dinner and a friendly stranger … what had that professor's name been, anyway?

Oh, yes. Kallay—Vilmos Kallay.

He'd been a charming, eccentric sort of man, and he'd said he was a poet whose "day job" was in the "dismal science" of economics.

London now remembered the name of the restaurant that he had recommended in Gyor.

"It was called the Magyar Öröm," she said.

"That's right," Gus Jarrett said. "He said it was 'not to be missed.'"

"Well, then, let's not miss it," London said.

Emil already had his cell phone out and was searching for the place.

"We are in luck," he said. "Not only is the Magyar Öröm open, it is just a couple of blocks from here."

London reminded herself to call Amy during lunch to tell her the time and place of the rendezvous, so Amy could take over the tour from her. Then London and several others followed Emil toward the Magyar Öröm. They were pretty much the same small group of people who'd gone on London's little outing in Budapest yesterday. Among them were the Shicks, Gus and Honey Jarrett, and the rather peculiar and somewhat disagreeable Cyrus Bannister. Looking somewhat perkier than she had a while ago, Mrs. Klimowski decided to join them as well.

Definitely a mixed bag, London thought, not sure whether she was pleased or displeased with the group.

As Emil led them around a corner, London observed how the twisting, narrow streets made it hard to see very far in any direction. London remembered what Emil had said just a little while ago about the Baroque style—how it appealed to sense and emotion through *"movement, richness, detail, surprise, and vitality."*

And now it occurred to London that even the layout of Gyor's streets was Baroque in its way—filled with movement, vitality, and most of all …

Surprise.

She had to wonder what new surprises this ancient city had in store for them.

She felt a strange tingle inside.

Something tells me I can't even imagine what's coming next, she thought.

CHAPTER FOURTEEN

The Magyar Öröm proved to be a surprise, all right—and a charming surprise at that. As London and her group rounded a corner and approached their destination, they saw that most of the restaurant was in an outdoor patio. That seemed just right for a warm and sunny day like this.

Even better, they'd managed to arrive just before the afternoon rush, an especially busy time for Hungarian restaurants, so the host had no trouble putting several tables together for them. They were seated next to a low brick wall at the edge of the patio, overlooking a pedestrian street and giving them a delightful view of people's comings and goings in Old Town Gyor.

If the waiter, whose name was István, even noticed Mrs. Klimowski's dog he made no comment about it. Sir Reginald was especially well concealed in the handbag at the moment and apparently asleep.

István gave the group a few minutes to pore over their menus. A couple of people in the group were pleased to see the "Dracula dish," *paprikácsirke*, was on the menu. London herself decided she was in the mood for a lighter meal. Even though she couldn't quite pronounce the name, she managed to order the Hungarian-style stuffed crepes called *hortobágyi palacsinta*.

Soon István returned with their drinks and a soup appetizer. London sipped a spoonful of the soup and was startled by the tart, sweet taste. Sitting next to her and noticing her expression, Emil explained.

"It's a fruit-flavored soup called *gyümölcsleves*."

London tried another spoonful.

"It's cherry-flavored, isn't it?" she said.

"Probably. That's a popular flavor. Do you like it?"

"Oh, yes, very much. I've never tasted anything like it before."

Emil gave her a nudge.

"It might be nice to have some pictures, eh?" he suggested.

"Yes, I'm sure everyone would like that," London said.

As Emil got up and turned his cell phone toward the group, they were all startled by a strange and melancholy sound. On the other side of the wall, a strolling musician was playing a violin in the street right next to them. It was strange music, dissonant and harsh, but quite beautifully sad and touching all the same.

When he saw that he had their attention, the musician turned and played directly to the group. London noticed that he was rather shabbily dressed in a muslin shirt with puffy sleeves, a scarf around his head, a vest, and trousers with patches on the knees. He sported a wide handlebar mustache.

Although most of the group was listening in apparent enchantment, Mrs. Klimowski stirred restlessly. She reached into her bag, pulled out a smaller purse, and took out a handful of Hungarian paper money.

"Is fifteen hundred forint a lot of money?" she asked.

"It depends on what it's for," remarked Cyrus Bannister, who was sitting between the elderly woman and the low wall that separated them all from the street and the performer.

Mrs. Klimowski held the bills toward Cyrus.

"I want you to offer this money to that awful man," she said. "Tell him he can have it if he'll only stop it with that awful scraping and scratching and caterwauling."

Cyrus scowled sharply.

"I can't do that, ma'am," he said.

"Why? Isn't it enough money?"

"It's about five dollars," Cyrus said. "But my point is, he'd be deeply insulted."

Mrs. Klimowski let out a snort of annoyance.

"Would he, now? I think *I'm* the one who's being insulted, being forced to listen to such awful stuff. Give him the money, I tell you. Make him quit playing."

"I'll do no such thing," he said.

"Well, pay him to play some real *music*, then. Something traditionally Hungarian—a Liszt rhapsody, or one of those dances by Brahms."

Cyrus crossed his arms and glared straight ahead.

"I happen to know a few things about European folk music, madam," he said. "Liszt and Brahms aren't the least bit authentic when it comes to true Magyar music. What that gentleman is playing is as Magyar as you can get. It's the sort of music Bartok collected when he and his friend Zoltan Kodaly wandered around Eastern Europe in the early 1900s recording peasant songs."

"Bartok, eh?" Mrs. Klimowski huffed. "Such dreadful modern stuff. Him and that Schoenberg fellow."

Cyrus looked truly offended now, and it was easy for London to guess why. She remembered that he'd specifically chosen the Schoenberg Suite aboard the *Nachtmusik*.

"I'm sure I'm the only person who wanted it," he'd told London.

Cyrus said, "This man probably learned to play this music from his father, and his father probably learned it from his father, and ... who knows for how many generations this melody has been handed down? You should show some respect."

As they argued, the musician seemed to give up hope on getting any tips. As he wandered on down the street, Mrs. Klimowski turned her rage on Cyrus Bannister.

"And I think *you* should show some respect, young man! I'll have you know that mine has been a very tragic life! I deserve some consideration. But consideration is hard to come by nowadays."

Mrs. Klimowski reached into her bag for her colorful pillbox. She snapped it open, downed some pills with a glass of water, then dropped the box back in the bag.

Just as István the waiter started serving the main course of their meals, Mrs. Klimowski rose up from her chair. Sir Reginald Taft peeped over the top of the bouncing bag, then growled and settled back out of sight.

"I've quite lost my appetite, thank you very much," the elderly woman announced. "I really must get away from all this agitation and discourtesy."

She laid the forints she was still holding on the table and announced, "Someone else can enjoy my meal. I'm heading back to the boat. Perhaps after a good night's sleep, I'll be able to forget this whole unpleasant episode."

Alarmed, London got up from her chair as well.

"Why don't you stay?" she said.

"No. I won't endure another moment of this."

"At least let me see you back to the boat," London said.

"No!" Mrs. Klimowski snapped at her fiercely.

Then looking at the others, she raised her voice to a melodramatic pitch.

"And the same goes for the rest of you. I don't need your help, and

86

I certainly don't need your company. Mine has been a very tragic life. And merely to survive, I've developed an instinct to tell me who can be trusted and who can't be. And I can't trust any of you. I can feel it in my bones."

London saw that the others at the table were as startled and perplexed by this outburst as she was. Some of them—Agnes and Walter Shick—looked positively hurt by it.

"I'll leave here just the way I've gone through life—alone!" Mrs. Klimowski added.

With a wave her hand, she swept out of the patio and into the street.

London started to follow her, but Emil caught her by the arm.

"London, please do not go after her," he said. "She really does not wish for any of our company. You will only upset her further if you try to help."

London stammered, "But she's—she's—"

Loaded with furs and jewelry, London wanted to say.

"Don't worry about her," Gus Jarrett said. "It's only a short distance to the ship."

"She'll be all right," his wife, Honey, added.

London stood wavering for a moment.

"They are quite right, London," Emil said to her quietly. "She will be quite safe, I am sure."

London sat down, still trying to make up her mind.

Agnes Shick looked aghast at what had just happened.

"Was it something one of us said?" she said.

Cyrus Bannister chuckled snidely.

"Not at all," he said. "She just can't stand Magyar folk music—or Bartok or Schoenberg for that matter. It's nothing to do with any of us, I'm sure."

"Actually, I don't think she cares much for any of us either," Walter Shick muttered.

London realized that Gus was right—they really were quite close to the *Nachtmusik.* Their tour route had brought them circling around to within a handful of blocks of the boat. Besides, it was still a sunny afternoon, and the streets of Gyor hadn't seemed the least bit dangerous.

Surely she'll make it back OK, London told herself.

*

87

The group's meals soon arrived, and everybody seemed to enjoy their food—except for London herself. Her crepes were certainly delicious, but she kept picking at them listlessly, worrying about Mrs. Klimowski. But Gus and Honey Jarrett were especially hungry, so they shared Mrs. Klimowski's abandoned dish along with their own orders.

Finally István came around to take away their plates and asked if the group was ready for dessert. Everybody except London pored over the dessert menu eagerly. She didn't feel in the mood for something rich and sweet.

Before anyone could order, London heard a sharp noise from the street.

She turned and saw the tiny, mop-like Sir Reginald Taft standing among the pedestrians, looking agitated. Staring straight at London, the little dog barked again.

"Oh, my!" Agnes Shick said. "Mrs. Klimowski's dog must have gotten away from her!"

Cyrus Bannister chuckled.

"Can you blame him?" he said. "The poor animal must feel tremendously relieved."

But London didn't think Sir Reginald looked the least bit relieved. He kept yapping away as he darted about, avoiding pedestrians' feet.

Walter Shick looked as anxious as London felt.

"The poor woman must be beside herself with worry," he said. "We need to get this dog back to her."

Gus Jarrett let out a growling chuckle.

"Huh—I hope the old lady's dead!" he said.

His wife, Honey, looked at him with dismay.

"That's no way to talk!" she said.

"Well, it would be no great loss."

London agreed with Walter that the dog needed to be returned to Mrs. Klimowski, but wasn't sure how to go about it. She remembered the sly game of hide and seek Sir Reginald had played with Mrs. Klimowski yesterday. If the dog didn't want to be caught, what were they going to do about it?

"Maybe I can help," Honey said.

Her husband snarled in his wife's ear in an audible whisper.

"Don't you dare!" he said.

"I'll do whatever I like," Honey whispered back at him.

London recalled how the dog had eagerly jumped up into the woman's arms yesterday evening. But she also remembered how angry Gus had gotten about being contradicted. She didn't want there to be any trouble between Honey and Gus. But after all, it was really none of her concern.

"Please—let's try," she said to Honey.

"The rest of us should stay put," Cyrus said.

"That is right," Emil agreed. "If we all go after him, it might frighten him."

London and Honey went out into the street and cautiously approached the excited little animal. Just as she had yesterday, Honey walked to within a few feet of the dog, then crouched down in her precarious heels and tight skirt. She called out to him in the same warm and friendly voice as yesterday.

"Come here!"

But the dog didn't come to her this time. Instead, he turned around and trotted away into the crowd. London immediately hurried after him, weaving among the pedestrians as she went. For a few moments she could hear the clatter of Honey's heels, but the footsteps soon fell behind her. Honey simply wasn't practically dressed enough for this sort of pursuit.

Meanwhile, Sir Reginald made it very clear that he *wanted* London to follow her. He'd stop every now and then and look back to make sure she was still on his trail, then take off again.

London followed the dog past some of the landmarks they'd visited a little while ago, including the *Boatman* sculpture and the Vienna Gate Square, until at last they approached the Cathedral Basilica of the Assumption of Our Lady. London flashed back to what Mrs. Klimowski had said yesterday when she'd insisted upon a visit to St. Stephen's Basilica in Budapest.

"I have a greater need than most people for the comfort of prayer."

London felt a wave of relief.

This must where she came, she thought.

As they neared the entrance, London saw that the doorkeeper was the same man who had been there earlier, but now he wore a bright yellow flower in his lapel. The doorkeeper looked as if he might try to block the dog, but the little creature darted right past his big feet and on into the cathedral.

As the doorkeeper glared at London, she stammered in Hungarian.

"I'm very sorry. I'll go get him right away."

The doorkeeper nodded and stood aside, and London strode on into the cathedral.

Ahead of her, Sir Reginald stopped at the end of one of the pews and looked back at her. London felt a wave of relief as she saw a familiar figure sitting in that pew. The dog wasn't lost, after all. Mrs. Klimowski had returned to the cathedral instead of going back to the boat. She seemed to be the only person in the church at the moment.

But why was the dog so agitated?

Mrs. Klimowski's head was deeply bowed, and she looked like she was fast asleep. Followed by Sir Reginald, London slipped into the pew and sat down beside her.

"Mrs. Klimowski," she said in a soft voice.

The woman didn't move.

"Mrs. Klimowski, I'm glad I found you. We were all worried sick. It's time to wake up, though."

The woman still didn't move. London nudged her, to no effect. Then she noticed that there was a strange stillness about the elderly woman. Her mouth was hanging open, but she didn't seem to be breathing.

London reached out and touched the woman's hand.

Something was definitely wrong.

London gasped as she realized that the woman wasn't just sleeping.

Mrs. Klimowski was dead.

CHAPTER FIFTEEN

London found Alezredes (Lieutenant Colonel) Ferko Borsos to be an intimidating hulk of a man, with a head shaped like a bullet and a body shaped like a cannon barrel. His dark scowl made her wonder if he was about to arrest her.

Borsos was the *kapitánységvezető*—chief captain—of the Gyor Police. His iron-gray uniform with epaulets on its lapels as well as its shoulders added to his military bearing. He and his team had come to the basilica very promptly in answer to a call from the building's doorkeeper, who'd phoned for help as soon as London had rushed out calling for the police ... for an ambulance ... for any kind of help.

A medic who arrived with Borsos had confirmed that Mrs. Klimowski was indeed dead, fulfilling London's worst possible fears.

At the moment, London was sitting on a stone bench outside the church while Alezredes Borsos paced back and forth in front of her. Mrs. Klimowski's dog, Sir Reginald, crouched beside London's feet.

The alezredes didn't seem to be in a good mood as he asked London questions in faltering English.

"Tell me, please, why you think we're dealing with a case of—how do you say in English?— 'foul game'?"

Foul play, London thought, suppressing a sigh. But she didn't feel free to correct this man's English idioms the way she did with Emil.

"I didn't say she was murdered," London said.

"What are you saying, then?"

London hesitated. The truth was, she was still quite puzzled by what had happened—and also in something of a state of shock.

"I don't know how she died," London said. "But I do know she was robbed."

"And robbery—is that not 'foul game'?"

London choked down another sigh. It seemed futile to point out that the idiom "foul play" was normally used to refer to murder. It didn't surprise London that the alezredes spoke English, since he surely had to deal with English-speaking tourists. But his English was faulty, and London was worried about making herself clearly understood.

She wondered if maybe this conversation would go better in Hungarian.

Not that my Hungarian is anything to brag about, she thought.

She chose her words carefully and spoke very slowly in Hungarian.

"I noticed right away when I found her ... that way. Her pendant was missing. She'd been wearing it every time I saw her, all day yesterday and all day today."

"A pendant?"

"That's right," London said. "I'd warned her against wearing it—and also all the rest of her jewelry and her fur coat. I was afraid she'd be a target for thieves. I guess I was right."

Alezredes Borsos looked at her with a curious expression.

"Would you describe this pendant for me?" he asked.

"Certainly," London said. "It was a large gem—a ruby, I think—and it was set in gold among quite a few diamonds. I was worried about how she was practically flaunting it. And when I found her, it was gone. Someone must have taken it."

Borsos stood looking at her for a moment. Then he waved to one of his officers, who walked over to him. Borsos whispered something to the officer, who went away for a moment and came back with Mrs. Klimowski's leather bag, which of course no longer contained the dog.

With a gloved hand, Borsos reached into the bag and pulled out a pendant.

"Is this the pendant you mean?" he asked London.

London couldn't help but gasp at the sight of the familiar red jewel encrusted by diamonds.

"Yes, but ..."

"But what?" Borsos asked.

London didn't know what to say. All she knew was that she found this to be extremely odd. Mrs. Klimowski had seemed to be deliberately drawing attention to the pendant as well as the rest of her jewelry, keeping all of it as conspicuous as possible. Why had she decided to put it into her bag?

But one thing certainly seemed obvious. No one had stolen the pendant, and London hadn't noticed any other missing jewels—or any missing furs, for that matter.

Meanwhile, the coroner and his team were wheeling a gurney bearing Mrs. Klimowski's sheet-covered body out of the basilica and toward a waiting vehicle. Borsos walked over to the coroner and chatted with him quietly for a moment.

London watched as an officer questioned the doorkeeper closely. The poor man was obviously shaken by what had happened in the church that had been in his care. But for some reason, London found herself staring at the yellow flower in his lapel—the flower that he hadn't been wearing during her group's earlier visit to the basilica. She couldn't imagine why it mattered, except that it seemed out of character for the rather formal man.

Borsos walked back toward London as the coroner climbed into his van.

"Our coroner is going to do a complete examination," Borsos said to London, speaking in English again. "At the moment, he sees no reason to think there was any 'foul game.' The lady was quite elderly, and probably died of natural causes. We should know by sure tomorrow. Meanwhile ..."

He paused and scratched his chin.

London had a feeling she wasn't going to like whatever he had to say next.

"What did you say your job was aboard the tour boat?" he said. "Social, eh, dirigible?"

"Social director," London said.

"And when is your boat scheduled to leave Gyor?"

London gulped apprehensively.

"Tonight," she said.

"I'm afraid that is out of the question," Borsos said.

"But if you don't think she was murdered ..." London began.

"It makes no difference," Borsos said. "She died right here in Gyor, and we need to make perfectly sure we understand why and from what cause. If all goes well, you should be able to set sail tomorrow."

Tomorrow! London thought.

If all goes well!

Why did she have a feeling it wasn't going to be that simple?

But she wasn't in any position to argue.

"I'll talk to the captain about it," she said.

"Do that as soon as possible," Borsos said. "I will also have him officially notified. He held up the leather bag and peered at it thoughtfully. Then he reached inside and pulled out a smaller purse.

"This was inside," he said. "Did she carry anything else?"

"As far as I know, just the dog."

He opened a small purse. "She had money with her," he reported. "And of course the cards of credit. And her passport. All of that is still here."

Holding it open, he asked London, "Can you tell me if anything at all is missing?"

Glancing into it, she saw the items the Alezredes had mentioned, plus a lace handkerchief and a plastic pillbox.

"I never actually saw inside her bag," she replied with a shrug.

Borsos gave a sigh, then asked, "Do you know who the woman's property now belongs to?"

"I'm afraid not," London said.

"Well, then—we'll keep this bag and her other belongings until tomorrow. You may go."

Relieved that she didn't seem to be under suspicion, London stood up to go. Then she felt Sir Reginald rubbing against her ankle.

Borsos scowled at the animal.

"Meanwhile, we also have this dog to consider," he said. "Perhaps I should turn it over to animal services."

London shuddered at the thought of this tiny creature locked up in a cage in some kind of pound filled with stray animals.

"No, I'll take care of it," she said. "Until someone in her family tells us where to send it."

"That would be helpful," Borsos said with a nod. "You may go for now. But I must talk to you again tomorrow. I'm afraid there may be many formalities to deal with."

London picked up the dog, which settled comfortably against her shoulder. As she started to walk back toward the ship, she flashed back to all that had just happened. She had to steady herself from staggering at the thought of it all. And she realized that everything had happened so fast that she hadn't yet notified anyone else about it.

As she walked, she called Amy Blassingame and told her what had happened, and also asked her to notify Captain Hays. Then she cut Amy's queries short when she saw that she was getting a call from Emil.

"London!" Emil said when she answered the phone. "Where have you been? We were worried about you. Are you all right?"

"I'm fine, but …"

London hesitated, then said, "Emil, something has happened to Mrs. Klimowski. She's—she's dead."

"What? No! How did you find out?"

"Her dog led me back to the basilica. There she was, sitting in a pew. She must have died right there. The coroner seems to think it was from natural causes. I've been talking to the chief of police since then. He says that the *Nachtmusik* can't set sail tonight."

"That is understandable, I suppose."

"Where are you right now?"

"We finished eating and are back at the *Boatman* sculpture reuniting the rest of the group. What should we do now? Continue with the tour?"

"Yes, I suppose so," London said. "It's probably best to keep everybody occupied."

Then something else occurred to London.

"Oh, dear," she said to Emil. "Amy wanted to take over the tour from me this afternoon. I'd meant to call her and tell her about our rendezvous at the *Boatman* sculpture, but in all the confusion it slipped my mind."

"Do not worry, I will call her right now. What should I tell the group about Mrs. Klimowski?"

London thought hard for a moment.

"The truth, I suppose—that she passed away suddenly, and we don't know much more than that."

"I will tell them that."

"Thanks."

As they ended the call, London felt relieved that Sir Reginald Taft was still being so docile. He seemed quite comfortable curled up against her shoulder. She remembered Cyrus Bannister telling her that the dog really didn't like being stuck in Mrs. Klimowski's bag. She also remembered what he'd said when the dog had turned up at the restaurant a while ago.

"The poor animal must feel tremendously relieved."

London felt sad to think that it might have taken Mrs. Klimowski's death to ease the animal's discomfort.

But as they neared a street corner on their way back to the boat, Sir Reginald began to wiggle restlessly until he managed to scramble out of London's arms. London let out a gasp of alarm as the dog landed on the street.

What could she do if Sir Reginald simply decided to run away? She couldn't possibly catch him if he didn't want to be caught. Maybe

Alezredes Borsos had been right about putting Sir Reginald into the care of animal services. Had it been a mistake for London to try to take him back to the boat?

She quickly realized that Sir Reginald wasn't trying to escape. His attention had been caught by a vendor's stall on the street corner. But the stall was empty now, and London had no idea what was normally sold there.

Sir Reginald was certainly curious about the place. He walked around it a couple of times, as if to make sure someone wasn't hiding there. Then he trotted back over to London and when she leaned over he jumped back into her arms.

Scratching his head, she asked him, "What was bothering you, little guy?"

The dog gave her an odd look, as if he wished he could answer her question, but of course he couldn't talk. Then he snuggled quietly against her shoulder and let him carry her.

As they continued on their way to the boat, London felt all kinds of nagging worries.

She kept remembering how surprised she'd been when Borsos had pulled the pendant out of Mrs. Klimowski's bag. Until that very moment, she'd felt positive that the jewelry had been stolen.

But now she didn't know what to think.

Why had Mrs. Klimowski taken off the pendant?

Had she taken off the pendant, or had somebody else done it?

And why does it matter, anyway?

London knew that the truly hard work of dealing with Mrs. Klimowski's death was about to begin. There were already too many questions and too few answers.

But how could she possibly come up with any answers about a woman's death in a country where she had to struggle with the language?

She kept reminding herself of something Borsos had said.

"The lady was quite elderly, and probably died of natural causes."

London had absolutely no reason to think otherwise.

And yet ...

She sternly warned herself not to let her imagination run away with her.

Nobody was murdered.

But what was bothering her about the necklace *not* being stolen?

And why did she keep seeing that big yellow flower in her mind?

CHAPTER SIXTEEN

As she neared the boat again, London couldn't get the words *foul game* out of her mind. The alezredes had worded the idea clumsily, and even he had said that Mrs. Klimowski's death was "probably natural causes." The elderly woman had been frail and apparently in ill health. Nothing had been stolen.

But for some reason, the terrible idea kept nagging at her …

Foul game.

Her thoughts were interrupted by the sight of the portly, walrus-mustachioed Captain Hays, who was waiting for her at the far end of the gangway. The captain looked positively despondent as London walked toward him.

The news of Mrs. Klimowski's death had obviously hit him very hard. However, as they stepped into the reception area, Captain Hays's first concern seemed to be with London herself.

"Amy told me you found the poor woman," he said. "And in a cathedral, no less! What a terrible shock that must have been. How are you bearing up?"

"OK, I guess," London said.

But really, she felt too numb to know for sure just how she was "bearing up."

"Do you have any other news?" the captain asked.

"Not much, I'm afraid," London said. "The police chief told me it looks like Mrs. Klimowski died from natural causes. They expect to know more tomorrow."

"Well, I suppose we should at least be relieved it wasn't foul play," the captain said. "I've been trying to take care of things here as best we can. Before Amy left for the tour just now, she found Mrs. Klimowski's emergency contact number for me. It was her lawyer in New York City."

"A lawyer?" London asked with surprise.

"Yes, I found that odd. She didn't list friend or a relative or anyone like that. Just her lawyer. I tried to call him, but of course there's a huge time difference. I left a message, so I hope I can speak with him

98

tomorrow."

Captain Hays shook his head sadly.

"It's going to be a very difficult process, I fear. And I don't look forward to telling Mr. Lapham that our voyage has been disrupted."

London was startled to realize that the CEO really did have to be informed—and it wasn't likely to be a pleasant conversation. She remembered what Lapham had said to her over the phone.

There's a lot at stake in this new venture. I want to get things off to the best possible start.

A dead passenger and at least one night's delay in Gyor surely weren't what Lapham had in mind as "the best possible start." London herself felt terrible about disappointing the man who had made her feel so proud of her new job. She was sure that the captain felt the same kind of dread about that.

Captain Hays shook his head sadly and added, "I'm counting on you to help maintain some sense of order through this crisis."

"I'll do my best, sir," London replied.

The captain squinted curiously at Sir Reginald, who was still nestled against London's shoulder. Sir Reginald peered back at him intently.

"But tell me please—where did this animal come from?" Captain Hays asked.

London realized that the captain hadn't seen the dog before.

"This is—was—Mrs. Klimowski's dog," London said. "Sir Reginald Taft."

"My! Such a long name for such a small creature!"

"He led me right to Mrs. Klimowski's body," London said. "If he hadn't, we still might not know what had happened to her."

"A fine dog, then," Captain Hays said with a nod of approval. "Perhaps the lawyer will give us instructions as to his care. Or I suppose one of the other passengers might give him a new home."

"I hope so," London said.

London's head reeled from all that she had to do right now—and had to do fast. But first, she knew she had to take Sir Reginald back to Mrs. Klimowski's stateroom, which was right there on the Menuetto deck.

She used her master keycard to open the grand suite. As she had when Elsie had shown her this room yesterday, she heard soft and lovely piano music—Beethoven's *"Für Elise"*—and she saw

99

Beethoven's portrait scowling down from above the bed.

She was struck again by the size and luxury of the stateroom, with its balcony and separate seating area. A few of Mrs. Klimowski's belongings were placed tidily here and there. London felt a sudden pang of sadness for the unhappy woman who'd said that her life had been so tragic. Surely she'd come on this cruise of the Danube to make herself feel better.

But she only got to spend one night here, London thought. *And all this didn't seem to have helped her feel any better.*

London hadn't liked Mrs. Klimowski very much, and as far as she knew, no one else aboard the *Nachtmusik* had liked her either. But even so ...

She didn't deserve to die like this. All alone in a foreign country.

But again she wondered—just how and why had she died?

She still couldn't shake off the feeling that someone had done something terrible to her. But how could she know for sure?

Maybe the answer is right here in this room, she thought.

As she started to look around, she noticed something on the side table next to her bed. It was a piece of *Nachtmusik* stationery with Mrs. Klimowski's handwriting on it. It was the start of a message addressed to Mr. Lapham himself.

"I regret to inform you that I am most displeased by conditions and service aboard the Nachtmusik so far. I'm lucky (if that's quite the right word) to have gotten aboard at all, there was such an uncalled-for fuss about Sir Reginald Taft, my show champion dog and most trusted companion. It was quite traumatic. Mine has been a tragic life, and I'm a deeply sensitive person, and I require more kindness and consideration than most people, and ..."

The note ended there. Apparently Mrs. Klimowski had planned to finish it later. London couldn't imagine how much longer the woman might have gone on complaining about one thing or another. It certainly reminded her that she hardly missed this disagreeable person. But nor did anybody else aboard the *Nachtmusik* that she knew of.

Could the woman's nasty disposition alone be enough to drive someone to murder?

Next she saw that the closet door was partially open. She found it to be fairly crammed with expensive clothes, shoes, and furs. It looked as though Mrs. Klimowski could have spent months aboard the *Nachtmusik* without wearing the same outfit for more than one day.

London walked over to the chest and pulled a drawer open, then recoiled at the jumble of gold, silver, and precious gems scattered inside.

There were necklaces, bracelets, brooches, a tiara, and elegant hair fasteners. Some rings and earrings were displayed on black felt stands; others had been tossed casually inside.

London's mind boggled at how much this trove must be worth. Mrs. Klimowski must have been very rich. It wasn't hard to imagine that someone might have killed her for just some of these treasures.

And yet, nothing had been stolen from Mrs. Klimowski's person when she'd died. The heavy diamond and ruby pendant that she'd been flaunting hadn't been taken, although it still seemed strange to London that it had wound up in her purse when her body was found. And these precious items were just loose in a drawer in her stateroom.

London wandered into the bathroom. She gasped to see that the countertop was practically covered with containers of prescription medicine. She found it hard to believe her eyes.

Were all these for her? she wondered.

Mrs. Klimowski had been such a little woman. What use could she have possibly had for such a huge hoard of medications?

She was also startled by how tidily they were arranged—row after row, like an army. Most noticeable were three bottles lined up in front of the rest, as if leading some imaginary battle.

Meanwhile, Sir Reginald began wriggling in her grasp, so she leaned over and put him down gently. She followed him out of the bathroom into the bedroom, and he trotted straight to a flat, rectangular pad, then relieved himself right there. When the little dog stepped off the pad, it made a slight whirring sound, and the soiled area disappeared into a cylindrical shape on one end of the pad's plastic frame. A fresh clean pad appeared from a similar shape on the other end of the contraption.

A dog potty, London realized. And Sir Reginald was obviously accustomed to using it.

London had never seen such a thing before, and she'd given no thought to the niceties of keeping a dog in a stateroom. She was happy to realize that the cleverly designed conveyor belt left no odor behind.

"I'm glad that's taken care of for you," she told the dog. "Now how about food and water?"

She found bowls of both nearby, and spare food handy in a dresser drawer. The dog began drinking thirstily, so when he finished she added more water. There was plenty of food in his dinner dish.

"I'll have someone check in on you later," she told Sir Reginald.

She remembered how Cyrus Bannister had described Mrs. Klimowski as "high maintenance." With sad irony, it occurred to London that Sir Reginald probably wouldn't be nearly as "high maintenance" as his owner. It looked like he was going to be quite easy for someone to take care of.

Meanwhile, I've got work to do.

But she heard a whine as she walked toward the door to leave. She turned and saw the little mop of a dog staring up at her sadly.

For the first time since Mrs. Klimowski's death, London really felt like crying.

She wondered—how often had this little animal ever had to be alone?

He might not have enjoyed getting toted around in Mrs. Klimowski's handbag, but at least he was used to it—and he was used to *her.*

"I'm sorry," she said. "I really have to go."

The dog whined again.

"Okay, I'll check back on you myself," London promised. "I'll be back as soon as I can."

Sir Reginald whined some more.

"I'll make sure you're well taken care of," London said.

His little ears drooped but he didn't whine again.

London was tempted to pick up the dog and take him with her. But she had to get back to work, and the animal would be too much of a distraction, both for her and the people she had to deal with.

With painful determination, London closed the door.

Surely Mrs. Klimowski would have made arrangements for someone to take care of her dog.

I'll just have to fill in until the proper person is identified, she told herself as she hurried off to deal with the awful event of the day.

She had to find a way of sharing this terrible news with all the passengers.

CHAPTER SEVENTEEN

As she handed out printed letters to the passengers she met, London became uncomfortably aware that she was getting strange looks from at least some of them. Did they think she was somehow responsible for Mrs. Klimowski's death?

In any case, London had figured the best way to get the word out was via a dignified printed note. She'd written a short statement that began ...

Dear Epoch Voyager:
The staff and crew of the Nachtmusik *deeply regret to report the untimely passing of Mrs. Lillis Klimowski earlier today.*

There hadn't been much more for London to write at this point, except to assure the passengers that they'd be informed of any new developments and information as soon as possible. She signed the note:

London Rose, Social Director.

She'd saved the message on a thumb drive, taken it to the lobby, and given it to the receptionist with instructions to print copies of it on the *Nachtmusik's* letterhead and put the notices in the passengers' mailboxes and to distribute them to the crew.

Of course, she knew it was best to deliver such news personally and face-to-face whenever it was possible. Since both Emil and Amy were leading a tour group through Gyor, and other passengers were also out in town, she was passing the notes out to whomever she happened to meet, and also answering people's questions.

Meanwhile, some of them were looking at her suspiciously.

I shouldn't be surprised, she told herself.

She'd been the only one there when the poor woman was found. She'd been the first one to talk with the police. A few of the passengers were bound to at least wonder if she'd been negligent somehow.

She shook off the unpleasant thoughts and turned her attention to already-scheduled activities, which included swimming lessons, games of shuffleboard, table tennis, bridge, and a movie to be shown in the Amadeus Lounge.

When London arrived in the lounge just before the movie was about to start, Elsie was stunned about the news.

"The poor woman!" Elsie exclaimed. "But what about you? You've had such a shock. Are you sure you should try to keep working like this? Maybe you should take the rest of the day off. Surely somebody else on the staff ..."

"Everybody's already hard at work," London said. "And I need to stay hard at work too. It's the best thing for my nerves."

"I guess I can understand that," Elsie said. "Just let me know if there's anything I can do."

London thanked her and went back to her duties. The sight of the dead woman in the basilica kept flashing through her mind, and she really was glad to keep herself occupied.

Meanwhile, passengers were trickling back aboard from their ventures ashore and got the news either from the notice or from London directly. When Emil and Amy finally returned with their large tour group, London was relieved that Emil had already broken the terrible news to them, and judging from everybody's composure, he'd obviously handled it with grace and tact.

After asking London how she was doing, he got to another pressing issue.

"What about the dog?" he asked.

"I don't know," London said. "Maybe there's somebody back in the States who will want him, and we can find some way to send him back. In the meantime ... you wouldn't be interested in taking care of him, would you?"

Emil seemed to bristle at the very idea.

"I'm afraid not," he said with a touch of defensiveness in his voice. "I don't get along well with animals, especially dogs. I was actually thinking of some kind of makeshift kennel, perhaps in the cargo hold."

London was a little startled by his brusque words.

"I'd like to come up with something ... a little easier on the dog," London said. "Tell me if you get any ideas."

"I will," Emil said, as he walked stiffly away toward his stateroom.

London spent the rest of the waning day making sure that the passengers were both well-informed and well-occupied. She barely nibbled at a delicious dinner and then made her rounds of the evening activities. She was sure those occasional glances still came her way, but she was too tired to worry about any of that now. The remaining social events went smoothly, although somewhat subdued. A lot of passengers seemed to have turned in early.

Finally London assigned Amy to keep check on the remaining social events. She knew that she needed to get some rest, but when she headed for her stateroom, she remembered what she'd promised the dog.

"I'll check back on you myself."

She sighed and went to Mrs. Klimowski's stateroom instead. As soon as she approached the door, she heard the dog yapping as though he knew she was out there.

When she opened the door and walked inside, Sir Reginald ran in eager circles around her feet, yapping until she picked him up into her arms. Again, London felt a deep pang of sympathy.

"I'm sorry I had to leave you alone," she told the dog. "But I won't have any choice until …"

Her voice faded as she asked herself …

Until what?

Until someone else took responsibility for the dog?

As London scratched Sir Reginald's ears, she realized that she hadn't really begun to process her emotions over Mrs. Klimowski's death. All she knew was that a vague feeling of guilt was rising up inside her. She tried to convince herself that she couldn't have helped what had happened to the woman.

And yet …

She remembered that moment at the restaurant when the irate Mrs. Klimowski had gotten up from her chair to say that she was heading back to the boat. She remembered, too, how she had offered to go with her.

"No!" Mrs. Klimowski had snapped.

Then she had unleashed her ire toward everyone else at the table.

"I can't trust any of you," she'd said. *"I can feel it in my bones."*

And now London felt a surge of pity as she remembered the last thing she'd heard Mrs. Klimowski say.

"I'll leave here just the way I've gone through life—alone!"

London couldn't imagine how awful it must have been for the poor woman to die without feeling as though she could trust anyone around her. She couldn't help thinking she should have left that restaurant with Mrs. Klimowski, even if she hadn't wanted her company.

Maybe I could have done something.

Maybe I could have ...

But could she really have done anything at all? If Mrs. Klimowski really had died from natural causes, was there anything anybody could have done to save her?

And what if someone had really done the woman harm, as London couldn't help but suspect?

She had no idea what she could have done.

She did feel sure of one thing, though. She would have to take care of Mrs. Klimowski's dog until a place was found for it.

It has to be me.

She called for a steward to help her lug the portable potty and the food and bowls to her own stateroom down on the Allegro deck. Then she looked through an assortment of fancy leashes and collars lying on a table. She selected a fairly modest pair that weren't jewel-studded and put them on the dog.

Sir Reginald Taft wagged his tail, instantly delighted.

London escorted him out of the suite to the elevator and down to her own stateroom, where the steward had already deposited the dog's supplies. When she let him off the leash, Sir Reginald darted around looking keenly and enthusiastically at his new surroundings. He checked out his food and water bowls and his potty, and then looked up at London as though it all met with his approval.

Exhaustion from today's ordeal was catching up with London. She wanted to get a shower and a lot of sleep before she faced whatever tomorrow might bring. As she headed toward the bathroom, she heard a telltale plop. She looked around and saw that Sir Reginald had jumped up onto the bed and was curling up to make himself comfortable.

"Oh, no, you don't!" she said.

She picked up a cushion from one of the chairs and set it on the floor. Then she gently scooped up the dog and placed him on the cushion.

Sir Reginald let out a sound of discontent—more of a grumble than a growl.

London wagged her finger at him.

"None of that attitude," she said. "If we're going to be roommates even for a short while, you've got to be nice about it."

Sir Reginald stopped grumbling. London almost thought she saw him nod slightly in agreement.

She took a welcome shower and dressed for bed. Then she came out of the bathroom, only to find Sir Reginald curled up on the bed again.

Again, she picked up the animal, who felt limp and sleepy, and deposited him back on the cushion on the floor. He made another sound, which was more like a sigh this time.

London lay down on the bed and dozed. In just a few moments, she was wakened by the sound of soft snoring. She opened her eyes and saw that Sir Reginald was lying on the bed a couple of feet away from her, fast asleep. It was London's turn to sigh with resignation. There was obviously no way to make the dog change his mind about his place for the night.

Well, at least it's a queen-size bed, she thought.

With some luck, she wouldn't roll over and squash him.

As she began to doze again, she found herself wondering about what had happened to Mrs. Klimowski. Conflicting words kept echoing through her mind.

Natural causes, not foul game.

Why did she find herself doubting that explanation for Mrs. Klimowski's death?

One seemingly insignificant detail kept nagging at her—the fact that Mrs. Klimowski's pendant had turned up in her purse, not hanging around her neck.

After flaunting the object so brazenly, why had she taken it off?

Had she done so out of respect for her sacred surroundings?

Or …

Did she take it off at all?

Had some would-be thief removed the object, perhaps when the lady was unconscious or dead?

If so, why hadn't the thief stolen it?

Why put it in the purse?

London remembered how empty the sanctuary had been when she'd arrived.

She'd seen no one else except Mrs. Klimowski.

So who had been there when she'd died?

The dog, perhaps?

London reached over and petted the dog lightly.

"I wish you could talk," she whispered.

The dog made what sounded like a murmur of agreement.

Maybe he'll still find some way to tell me, she thought as she drifted off to sleep.

CHAPTER EIGHTEEN

Early the next morning, London and Elsie were struggling with a roulette table when London's phone buzzed. A text message informed her:

Captain Hays wishes to see you in his quarters.

Checking out the message, Elsie muttered, "What do you think that's about?" With a sigh, she dropped the heavy table leg on the floor among the other oddly shaped pieces of wood that lay scattered there.

London put down her screwdriver and considered the question.

"It could mean that Alezredes Borsos is here," she said. "He said yesterday he wanted to talk to me this morning. Maybe he's ready to wrap things up."

"Wrap things up?"

"Yesterday the coroner told him Mrs. Klimowski probably died from natural causes. I have to admit, I've had my doubts—and my worries. But with some luck, maybe they've confirmed that once and for all. And if they have, we can set sail for Vienna today."

Elsie's expression brightened. "Better late than never, I guess," she said. "The passengers are getting pretty restless—starting to look like some kind of herd on the verge of a stampede."

London couldn't disagree. Nobody aboard was happy to have their cruise interrupted. A few took the delay as a personal inconvenience. Most were disturbed at the death of a fellow passenger, even though no one claimed to have known Mrs. Klimowski well.

That was why London and Elsie had decided to set up an unused roulette table. Turning the Amadeus Lounge into a makeshift casino would offer at least some of the passengers a new pastime. Unfortunately, the roulette wheel was brand new and awaiting assembly.

"I'm sorry I can't help you finish this," London said, gesturing at the clutter on the floor.

Elsie laughed. "Obviously, I should have gotten a steward to take care of it in the first place. I'll call for one now. Go. The captain calls."

As London hurried to go down to the captain's quarters, a suite-sized complex on the lower level, her own words rattled through her brain.

"With some luck ..."

She certainly hoped that the coroner had determined that there had been no "foul game," to use the alezredes's phrase, in Mrs. Klimowski's death. But her worry rose as she saw several police officers in the passageway.

Why would they be here if nothing was wrong? she wondered.

She knocked on the door to the captain's quarters. Captain Hays opened the door and welcomed her into a small suite that was similar to her own stateroom plus a sitting area outfitted as an office. The simple décor showed that the amiable captain wasn't inclined toward ostentation.

At the moment, he looked rather nervous.

Standing squarely in the center of the room was Alezredes Borsos himself. His chin and his barrel chest jutted ominously in his customary military bearing. He looked a lot larger and more intimidating than he had yesterday outside the basilica.

"Good morning, Miss Rose," he said in his stiff English. "I wish we were meeting again under better circumstances."

London stood staring at him, waiting for him to explain what he meant. He stared back with a strangely cunning smirk, as if he knew something about her that even she didn't know.

The captain stammered, "London, I—I'm afraid that the coroner has determined that Mrs. Klimowski's death was a case of ... well ..."

"Foul play," the Alezredes said, with an emphasis on the second word.

He seemed pleased with himself to have learned the proper expression at last. Perhaps the captain had said it correctly in the moments before London had arrived.

London's heart jumped up in her throat. She couldn't say she was entirely surprised. Still, it was terrible to have her worst suspicions confirmed.

"I'm—I'm awfully sorry to hear that," London said.

Of course, that was putting it mildly. London felt a rising panic as she wondered what kinds of trouble were about to ensue.

Meanwhile, Borsos was eyeing London silently.

"My I ask what was the cause of death?" London said.

Borsos's lips shaped into a slight smile.

"Hamarosan megtudjuk, asszonyom," he said.

With her imperfect Hungarian, it took London a couple of seconds to understand what he'd said.

"In good time, ma'am."

London felt mystified.

"What do you mean, 'in good time'?" she asked. "If you know that Mrs. Klimowski was, well, murdered, you must have some idea of *how* she was murdered. Well, don't you?"

Borsos's smile broadened ever so slightly.

"Hamarosan megtudjuk," he said again.

London squinted at the man, trying to understand what was going on.

He seems to be playing some kind of game with me, she thought.

Which hardly seemed fair to her, considering that she had no idea what sort of game it was.

Unless ...

London stifled a gasp of alarm.

Am I a murder suspect?

Alezredes Borsos held London's gaze for a long moment, as if he were trying to read her thoughts. Uncomfortable under the intense scrutiny, she glanced over at Captain Hays, who did his best to smile reassuringly.

"I'm sure if we all cooperate with the alezredes, we'll get to the bottom of this," the captain told her. "Just answer his questions as best you can."

London nodded silently.

Then Borsos began to walk in a circle around her, making her feel even more insecure.

"You were the one who found Mrs. Klimowski's body, were you not?" he asked gruffly.

London fought down an impulse to snap back at him, *I told you about it yesterday.*

But she didn't dare provoke his anger.

"I was," she replied instead.

"When was the last time you saw Mrs. Klimowski before you found her in the church?" Borsos asked.

"Like I told you yesterday, she was part of a group I took for an afternoon meal at the Magyar Öröm. But I'm afraid she left before she ate much of anything."

"And why was that?" Borsos asked.

London hesitated. She knew she'd better consider her answers very carefully.

"I'm not sure exactly," London said. "She got irritated by a street musician—a violinist. This led to a rather testy exchange with another passenger."

Borsos tilted his head as if he didn't quite understand.

"What does this mean, 'a testy exchange'?"

"Um, it means a slight quarrel," London said, explaining the idiom.

"Anything serious?"

London thought back to Cyrus Bannister's curt defense of the musician.

"You should show some respect."

"Not really," London said. "It was about a difference in musical taste. A silly thing. But Mrs. Klimowski overreacted, I'm afraid."

"Overreacted?" Borsos asked.

"She suddenly seemed to be angry with us all. That's when she left."

"Ah." Borsos closed his eyes and seemed to ruminate on her words for a moment. Then his eyes snapped open and he barked, "But you said she did eat something while she was there with you."

"I think she did," London stammered. "We all had soup, but she left before the main meal. And she drank a bit of water to take some pills."

Again Borsos closed his eyes for a moment. He scratched his chin thoughtfully.

"What were your own feelings toward Mrs. Klimowski?" he asked.

London swallowed hard.

"I—well, I barely knew her, sir," she said.

"But how did you *feel* about her?" Borsos demanded.

London knew that she needed to be perfectly honest.

"I can't say I liked her, sir," she said.

"No?"

"I suppose I did feel sorry for her, though. She seemed awfully lonely, and she kept talking about what a tragic life she'd had. But she had a disagreeable personality. She was difficult to get along with, and …"

"And?" Borsos prodded.

"Well, as far as I know, nobody aboard the *Nachtmusik* liked her very much."

"Ah," Borsos said, as if she'd said something highly significant.

She couldn't imagine what that something might be, though.

"Did you mean the victim any harm?" Borsos asked.

"Of course not," London said.

"Are you aware that anyone else aboard the boat might have wished her harm?"

"Not that I know of," she said.

Borsos let out a chuckle, as if he knew better.

"Be that as it may," he said, "I need for you to write down the names of all the people who were with the victim at the restaurant. Better yet, draw it for me. Show me exactly where everyone was seated. Specifically who was next to her. And put a mark by the person she had that, eh, 'tested change' with."

It was all London could do to keep from correcting him.

"Testy exchange."

But that would only make things worse than they already were. London took out a pad of paper and drew a rectangle to represent the table. Then she thought for a moment and drew little circles to represent the people sitting there. She jotted down a name beside each circle, showing all of the people who had eaten at the Magyar Öröm. And she put a check beside Cyrus Bannister's name to indicate that he'd been the one who had quarreled with Mrs. Klimowski.

Borsos turned toward the captain and said, "Meanwhile, I must order that the *Nachtmusik* remain in port. All your passengers, crew, and staff must remain aboard."

Captain Hays's face was red with anger.

"Now see here, Alezredes Borsos," he said. "If you suspect anyone in my employ—or any of my passengers, for that matter—of foul play, you'd better come right out and say so. And if you try to arrest anybody, I'll have no choice but to contact the U.S. Embassy in Budapest. I'm sure that no one wants this unfortunate incident to assume international proportions."

"Nor do I," Borsos said. "But ..."

After a pause he repeated those words, *"Hamarosan megtudjuk."*

London reminded herself of their meaning.

"In good time."

She had a sinking feeling she was going to be hearing those words a

113

lot before this awful ordeal was over.

Borsos nodded as she handed him the diagram she'd made.

"That will be all for now," he said. "You may go."

Trembling with agitation, London left the captain's stateroom.

I'm one of his suspects, she realized.

As she headed down the passageway toward her own stateroom, two crew members came storming down the circular staircase from the deck above.

"It's chaos up there," one proclaimed as they trotted past her.

"What do those cops expect to find, anyway?" the other replied as they disappeared in the direction of the crew quarters.

And indeed, the sound of shouting voices drifted down the stairs. She scrambled up the spiral stairs to the Romanze deck, where she saw a few more confused-looking crew members scrambling about.

She also found herself face to face with Cyrus Bannister, who was on his way either to or from his Schoenberg Suite.

He asked her sharply, "Does anybody have any idea what's going on?"

London simply didn't know what to say.

"Well, why *don't* you know?" Cyrus added. "You're the social director, aren't you?"

Before London could reply, a voice came over the intercom.

"Fellow Epoch voyagers, this is your captain speaking. As you already know, the *Nachtmusik* has been detained in Gyor due to the untimely passing of one of our passengers. Unfortunately, this delay must continue for a while longer."

As the captain continued, several of the passengers let out a murmur of disappointment.

"The chief captain of the Gyor Rendőrség—the local police—also insists that everybody remain aboard the *Nachtmusik* until further notice. I apologize for this inconvenience, and I assure you that we will set sail again as soon as we possibly can."

The passengers were looking at London now, as if she could explain everything. She started avoiding their eyes.

The captain added, "Meanwhile, Alezredes Borsos wishes to speak to several passengers, who should come to my quarters as I call their names. The first are … Walter and Agnes Shick."

"Do you have any idea what this all about?" Cyrus asked London with annoyance.

"He just wants to ask all of us some questions," London said.

Cyrus squinted at her suspiciously as he headed away.

London felt a pang of guilt. She wished Borsos hadn't insisted that she write down that list. Her heart sank as she imagined the ordeal the elderly Shicks were likely to endure under the onslaught of Borsos's questions.

She also wished she hadn't had to single Cyrus out as the person who had quarreled with Mrs. Klimowski. She couldn't imagine that Cyrus or anybody else who had been at the restaurant had anything to do with Mrs. Klimowski's death. She hated the thought of getting them into any kind of trouble, even if only fleetingly.

But it's not like I had any choice, she reminded herself.

London rode the elevator down to the Allegro deck and headed for her stateroom. When she opened the door, she was a bit startled to be eagerly greeted by a little mop of a dog. She'd almost forgotten that she was taking care of Sir Reginald Taft for the time being.

She picked up the dog and sat down on her bed. Setting Reginald beside her, she started to think over her situation.

"What's going on, exactly?" she asked herself aloud.

The dog let out a low rumbling sound, as if he was curious himself. She looked Sir Reginald in the eyes.

"The Alezredes says he suspects foul play—concerning Mrs. Klimowski's death, I mean."

The dog tilted his head as if he were considering whether he agreed or not.

"I actually got that feeling right after I found her," London said. "Somehow I couldn't quite believe she died of natural causes. I'm not sure why I felt that way. Maybe it had something to do with how that pendant wound up in her purse. But that doesn't really make any sense, does it? Why would anybody kill somebody in order to steal something, then leave it behind like that?"

Scratching Sir Reginald under the chin, London said, "Anyway, Borsos wouldn't say why *he* thought it was foul play. And he wouldn't say *how* Mrs. Klimowski was supposedly killed. Was she poisoned? If so, does he think she was poisoned in the restaurant? I don't see how that was possible. She might have had some soup, but we all had that. She just took some of her medicine pills with water, but others certainly drank water too. It's pretty ridiculous to think she might have poisoned herself."

London thought for a moment.

"And why is Borsos so suspicious of our group, anyway? Doesn't he suspect that it might be someone who lives right here in Gyor? Now that I think of it, couldn't it have been that waiter named István? Couldn't he have put something in Mrs. Klimowski's water or her soup? Maybe the Alezredes has already thought of him. Why do you think he's being so secretive, anyway?"

Sir Reginald let out a little yap as if the answer was obvious.

"Yes, it's procedure, I suppose," London said. "He's going to be asking some of us a lot of questions, and he'd rather not tip us off as to what kinds of answers he might be looking for. Still, I really don't like this situation."

She almost thought she saw Reginald nod in agreement.

"And I wouldn't want this to get around but ... I don't like Alezredes Borsos. I don't like him at all. He strikes me as arrogant and way too self-confident. I'm not even sure he knows what he's doing. You met him yesterday. What do think of him?"

The dog didn't react at all this time.

Of course not, London thought. *He doesn't have any idea what I'm talking about.*

Still, it felt good to have some kind of sentient being to share her thoughts with.

"*'Hamarosan megtudjuk,'* he keeps saying. 'In good time.' As if he's got the case solved already, and he'll tell us who the killer is when he's gathered up enough evidence and feels good and ready."

Before she could think through this dawning realization, her phone rang. To her alarm she saw that the call was from Jeremy Lapham himself.

Oh, no, she thought.

This is going to be very bad.

116

CHAPTER NINETEEN

London had never before heard her name spoken with such obvious vexation.

Even over the phone, "Hello, London Rose" sounded more like a rumble of annoyance than a greeting.

The CEO's displeasure came through loud and clear, all the way from New York City to the *Nachtmusik* docked in Hungary.

"Hello, sir," she replied nervously. "How—how are you?"

"Rather distressed, I'm afraid. And this is hardly a friendly social call. Captain Hays contacted me last night with some extremely upsetting news."

London swallowed hard.

"Yes, sir," she said. "I'm afraid I know what it was about, sir."

"So is it true? Did a client of ours die on your watch?"

The words *your watch* felt like a punch in London's gut.

"I—I suppose you could say that, sir."

"And was there nothing at all you could have done about it?"

"I'm afraid not, Mr. Lapham."

She heard the CEO let out a dissatisfied groan.

"Well, I suppose that might be the case," he said. "The captain seems to think you notified the appropriate authorities."

His voice trailed off. Then he muttered, as though making the case for London's competence, "After all, I understand that the poor woman was elderly and a bit frail. And it seems that she *did* die from natural causes."

London felt a wave of panic.

Things are about to get even worse, she realized.

As of last night, there had been good reason to believe that Mrs. Klimowski had died from natural causes. But the captain apparently hadn't had a chance to talk to Mr. Lapham again since the alezredes had come on board with direr news.

And now here he was on the phone, waiting for London's next words. So it was up to her to break that news to him.

"Mr. Lapham, I'm sorry to say …"

117

"Well?"

"Sir, the captain hasn't had a chance to inform you this morning …"

"Yes, yes, what now?"

"The Gyor police have just told us they don't think that Mrs. Klimowski died from natural causes. They think it was … foul play."

She heard the CEO gasp.

"You can't mean that our passenger was murdered?"

"I'm afraid so."

"London, I'm flabbergasted. And I'm terribly disappointed in you. It was one thing to allow the woman to die of her own volition, as it were. It is quite another that she may have died in such a—well, such an involuntary manner."

Involuntary struck London as an odd word to use for it. But then, she'd sensed before now that the CEO was an odd sort of man.

"Mr. Lapham, I don't know what you expected me to—"

"I don't expect you to act as our clients' bodyguard," he interrupted. "But I *do* expect you to assure them at least a modicum of safety. You're supposed to know your way around these exotic ports, to make our passengers aware of where it is safe to visit and where it is not. And in this particular case, you failed very badly."

She wanted to plead that Mr. Lapham wasn't being fair. After all, Mrs. Klimowski had chosen to go off on her own. And she had died in a cathedral, a building that was guarded by a doorkeeper.

But deep inside, she couldn't help feeling responsible for the terrible thing that had happened.

Maybe he's got a right to be angry, she thought.

"I'm sorry, sir," she said.

"The situation is quite unacceptable. The *Nachtmusik* is supposed to be in Vienna by now. The captain told me last night that you are not allowed to sail out of Gyor. Is that still the case?"

"As far as I know, sir."

"In addition to the pain caused to our passenger's family and friends, I'm sure you're aware that the voyage is horribly behind schedule. Every day's delay is financially disastrous for Epoch World Cruise Lines. When do you expect that situation to change?"

"Perhaps—when the case is solved," London said.

But she knew that was only a guess on her part.

"Well, then, the case must be solved expeditiously. You'd better get right to it, hadn't you?"

"Sir?"

"Do I need to spell it out to you? It's up to you to discover whatever is needed to get the ship on its way."

London felt suddenly dizzy.

"Sir, I'm not sure I understand. This really is a matter for the Gyor Rendőrség—the local police."

"Bosh. I've traveled round the world a dozen times. And there's one thing I've learned about the police in every town or city in every country on the planet. They don't know what they're doing. They never get to the bottom of anything. They always look for the laziest explanation—and right now, I imagine that means they'll assume the victim was murdered by someone on board the *Nachtmusik*. I'm sure we can agree that's utter nonsense."

London felt too overwhelmed to know for sure whether she did agree. Even if the police were right that Mrs. Klimowski was murdered, they weren't giving her any information about it.

"London, you know perfectly well why I hired you for this job. You've gotten an excellent seat-of-the-pants education in the hallowed halls of the School of Hard Knocks, you can land on your feet like a proverbial cat in any situation, and you're a keen judge of character. Most of all, you're smart as a tack. Now I expect you to make like Nancy Drew, so to speak. As of this moment, I'm awaiting word that you've solved this matter. Get to it—and don't waste another minute. This voyage must continue."

He ended the call without giving London a chance to say a word, let alone protest.

London sat staring at the phone for a moment.

Then she looked at Sir Reginald, who seemed to have been listening attentively.

"Nancy Drew?" she said.

London remembered the name, of course. She had vivid memories of Mom reading stories of the teenaged detective to her when she was little.

"This is weird, Sir Reginald," she said. "There's nothing in my job description about crime solving. I'm not Nancy Drew material. Hey, I couldn't even figure out where that baklava had come from a couple of nights back!"

The dog peered at her with what almost appeared to be critical manner.

"And don't tell me you agree with him," London said with a wag of her finger.

Sir Reginald let out a small yap.

Of course, London knew perfectly well that she was really arguing with herself and not the dog. She couldn't shake off the feeling that Mr. Lapham had good reason to be disappointed with her—and also that he had good reason to expect her to make things better.

Most of all, she knew Mr. Lapham had very good cause for worry. As he himself had admitted the first time they'd talked, Epoch World Cruise Lines was in rocky financial shape, and the company's very survival might depend on *Nachtmusik*'s Danube voyage.

While being a detective was hardly in her job description, maybe it was time to try her hand at it anyway. After all, the future of Epoch World Cruise Lines depended on solving this murder.

For that matter, so did London's job.

For that matter, so did a whole lot else in her life.

Although Alezredes Borsos seemed convinced that Mrs. Klimowski had been killed by somebody aboard the *Nachtmusik*, he clearly didn't think the murderer was just any random passenger.

No, he'd seemed most interested in the people who'd been with Mrs. Klimowski at the Magyar Öröm yesterday—the people whose names London had written down on that list for him.

And I'm at the top of that list.

"I may have to learn to be a detective just to clear my name," she said to Sir Reginald.

The dog let out a little growl of disapproval.

"Yes, you and I both know I'm innocent. I just wish Borsos knew it."

The captain called over the intercom for Cyrus Bannister to come to his quarters.

"And now Borsos is going to interview Cyrus Bannister," London said to the dog. "I'm afraid I might have given Borsos reason to suspect Cyrus instead of me, although I didn't mean to make him think that. Well, I'm sure Cyrus will say whatever it takes to deflect suspicion away from himself, and ..."

London gasped aloud as something occurred to her.

"Oh, Reginald," she said. "There's something I need to go do— *right now.*"

CHAPTER TWENTY

As London jumped up from the bed, the dog darted anxiously around her feet.

Looking down at him, she explained, "I think I know who Borsos is going to suspect next. And I want to check into it before he does."

Maneuvering around the little animal, London hurried to the door. But when she opened it and stepped outside, Sir Reginald let out a series of loud barks.

"Sir Reginald, stop that!" she told him sharply.

He barked again.

Hastily, London glanced up and down the passageway. Although she saw no one at the moment, she didn't want to attract the attention of the police who were aboard the ship.

She shut the door behind her, closing the dog up in her stateroom.

He only yapped louder from inside.

When she opened the door again, he stopped yapping. Then he just sat there and stared at her with an expression that she felt sure was judgmental.

London fought down a sigh of frustration.

"Sir Reginald, you've got to let me go do this."

The dog let out a yip of disapproval.

"If I take you with me, do you promise to behave?" London asked.

The dog blinked at her silently. London sensed that they had come to an agreement. She went back into her room and fetched the leash and collar she'd found in Mrs. Klimowski's quarters.

"Don't take this the wrong way," she said as she put the collar and leash on the dog. "But I can't take any chances of you running away from me."

She swept Sir Reginald up into her arms, then headed down the passageway toward the elevator. She pushed the button and the elevator doors opened. It was only a short distance to her destination—the Trapp Family Singers suite, where Gus and Honey Jarrett were staying.

She rapped sharply on the door and heard Honey's voice from inside.

"Who is it?"

"It's London Rose, your social director."

"What do you want?"

Honey sounded markedly suspicious and uneasy.

"I just want to talk," London said.

"Are the police with you?"

"No, it's just me. And, uh, the dog. Look, just let me in, OK? This is important."

The door opened, and Honey let London and Sir Reginald inside the room. London heard an Austrian folk song playing softly. The room was decorated in pastel colors with pictures of the Austrian alps and the smiling Trapp Family Singers.

In her silky pink robe with fake fur trim and high-heeled pink slippers, Honey looked right at home in the fantasy surroundings.

London's eyes darted around the room.

"Where's Gus?" London asked.

"He went out," Honey said.

"What do you mean, out?"

"I mean off the ship."

"But everybody's supposed to stay on the ship."

Honey shrugged with unconvincing nonchalance.

"What can I say? He left real early, before he heard that order. He said he just wanted another look around town."

London shook her head doubtfully.

"Lying's not your forte, Honey," she said. "Come on, just tell me where he is."

Before Honey could try to lie some more, Sir Reginald let out a low growl.

"What is it, boy?" London asked the dog.

The dog leaped out of her hands and dashed to the bathroom door, which was closed shut. He started barking insistently.

London pointed at the door and glared at Honey.

"He's in there, isn't he?" she said.

"No, really, he's not!"

But the dog was making it abundantly clear that he was.

London knocked on the door and heard Gus reply in a frightened voice.

"Go away."

"Gus, listen to me," London said. "There's a good chance the police

122

will be knocking on this door in a few minutes. You might want to talk to me first. I might even be able to help."

That is, if you're not a killer, she thought.

A silence fell. Then the door opened, and Gus stepped out, looking scared and shaken. The dog jumped back up into London's arms.

"Why were you hiding in there, anyway?" London asked.

"I think you know why," Gus said.

London nodded. In fact, that was the reason she'd come here just now.

"In the restaurant you said, 'I hope the old lady's dead,'" London said. "Everyone at the table heard you say it. And I'm pretty sure somebody's telling the police chief about it. And so are you. That's why you're so scared. And that's why I came here."

"But honest to God, I didn't mean anything by it!" Gus exclaimed. "Look, I was just spouting off. I'm a loudmouth and a blowhard. I admit it."

Honey let out a scoff.

"It's about time you admitted it," she said.

London put her hands on her hips.

"Gus, I need for you to look me in the eye and tell me whether you killed Mrs. Klimowski or not."

"Why would I have killed her?"

"That's not what I'm asking."

Gus stared at her with pleading eyes.

"I didn't kill her," he said in a stricken voice. "I swear to God I didn't."

Honey let out another scoff.

"He's telling the truth," she said. "If you think *I'm* a bad liar, believe me, he's a whole lot worse."

London stared hard at him, trying to read his expression. He certainly seemed sincere. She didn't *think* he was lying. But how could she really know?

Her mind clicked away, trying to make up her mind. She remembered Gus's anger toward Honey for helping London with the dog after Mrs. Klimowski had disappeared.

"You've got a lot of nerve, making a fool out of me like that."

At the time, he'd struck London as rather menacing.

But Honey apparently didn't feel that way—neither then nor now.

But how can I be sure ...?

She shook her head and muttered quietly.

"I'm no Nancy Drew."

"Huh?" Gus said.

Honey scoffed yet again.

"The famous girl detective," she said to Gus. "You should read a book sometime." Then she said to London, "Who says you have to be Nancy Drew, anyway?"

"My boss," London said.

"Oh," Honey said. "And here I thought you were just a social director."

I wish, London thought.

Gus sat down on the edge of the bed.

"The captain called for that Cyrus Bannister guy to come to his quarters," Gus said. "He's the one who's telling on me, isn't he? Now there's a weird guy for you. And he and the old lady got into an argument just before she went away. If any of us killed the woman, I'll bet he did."

Honey rolled her eyes.

"They were just arguing about music," she said. "It was nothing to kill anybody about."

"You never know," Gus said. "He might have been a ticking bomb, ready to blow up over the tiniest little thing."

London scratched her chin thoughtfully. Was it possible that Gus was right? She'd felt uneasy about Cyrus since she'd first met him, and he certainly hadn't liked Mrs. Klimowski—especially how she treated her dog. And he'd been sitting right next to her at lunch. Could he have slipped something into her soup or her glass of water?

Maybe, she thought. *But why? Because of music?*

She shook her head and muttered aloud.

"It doesn't make any sense. None of it makes any sense."

London was startled out of her thoughts by a loud knock at the door.

The police! she realized.

CHAPTER TWENTY ONE

There was a louder knock at the door, followed by a sharp, authoritative voice.

"Ez a rendőség. Nyissa ki az ajtót."

"Huh?" Honey yelled back.

"They want to come inside," London explained to her quietly.

Sure enough, one of the police repeated the orders in English.

"This is the police. Open the door."

Gus was pale and silent and shaking with fear. But Honey seemed as calm as she possibly could be.

"What do you want?" Honey called back.

"Alezredes Borsos wishes to speak with Mr. Gus Jarrett. We've come to take him to the captain's quarters for questioning."

Gus jumped up from the bed and took a few steps toward the bathroom, but Honey held up her hand to stop him.

"Huh-uh, baby," she said. "You can't hide now. We'll all get in in trouble if you try. You've just got to go to the captain's room and explain to the nice cops that you're not a bloodthirsty killer. Don't worry, I'm sure you can do it. Who'd take you for a killer, anyway?"

Opening the door, Honey said, "Come on in, boys."

London had to restrain her own giggles at the looks on the officers' faces as they encountered the pink-clad Honey Jarrett with her flaming red hair. One of them looked at London instead, apparently trying to conceal his embarrassment.

Finally one of the officers made his way past Honey and asked her husband, "Are you Gus Jarrett?"

"Uh-huh," Gus murmured almost inaudibly.

"He means yes," Honey said. "But really, you guys are wasting your time with him. Gus is the most harmless little soul on the face of the planet—and one of the most boring, too. He wouldn't even hurt an old lady—even though I guess that's exactly what you think he did. It's all some mistake. Your boss will know it the moment he sets eyes on him. Well, be as nice as you can to him. He won't give you any trouble."

The cops started leading Gus into the hallway. Before she shut the door behind them, Honey called out to them.

"And don't even think about torturing him! That'd really make me mad, and you wouldn't like me when I'm mad. You hear?"

"Yes, madam," the English-speaking officer replied.

They left, and Honey shut the door behind them.

"This whole situation's crazy," Honey said to London. "Maybe you'd better get back to your Nancy Drew gig and figure out who *did* kill Mrs. Klimowski."

London put the dog on the floor and sat down on the bed.

"If only I knew where to begin," she said.

"Well, do you have any hunches?" Honey asked, sitting beside her.

London thought hard for a moment.

"It's hard for me to believe it was anyone on the ship," she said.

"Maybe you just don't *want* to believe it," Honey said.

She's right, London thought with a sigh.

After all, if someone on the boat was a murderer, it made London's failure to protect Mrs. Klimowski seem all the worse.

She and Honey both fell silent for a moment.

Leaning over to scratch the dog's head, Honey muttered, "Such a sweetie."

London said, "You know, if anybody knows who killed Mrs. Klimowski, it's …"

London's voice faded.

"It's this adorable little dog," Honey said.

"That's right," London said. "He was right there in the church when she died."

"If only he could talk," Honey said.

London agreed and left the stateroom and headed for her own quarters. Sir Reginald seemed to have gotten a bit tired, so she set him on the bed, where he quickly dozed off.

What do I do now? she wondered yet again.

She figured she'd better explore the ship looking for clues. She left Sir Reginald asleep in the room and took the elevator back up to the Menuetto level. When she got off the elevator, she found a number passengers milling about the reception area and chattering in small, restless groups.

A woman spotted her and cried out, "Oh, look! It's the social director!"

126

"Maybe she can explain things!" said a man in her group.

A small cluster of passengers rushed anxiously toward her.

"Could you please tell us what's happening?" the woman begged.

"There are policemen on board!" said a man, who London remembered was the woman's husband.

Another passenger broke in, "Why do we have to stay on the boat?"

"Are we prisoners?" said another.

Yet another said, "Are these really police? Or are they terrorists disguised as police?"

Another passenger let out a gasp.

"My God! Are we in a hostage situation?"

London felt a twinge of alarm.

I've got to stop this idea from getting around.

Calling up her calmest demeanor, she told them, "I can absolutely assure everybody that these uniformed men really *are* police, and they're only doing their jobs, and this is definitely not a hostage situation. The police are here about Mrs. Klimowski's unfortunate passing."

"Unfortunate passing!" snapped one passenger. "I think you mean murder!"

A murmur of agitated agreement passed through the group.

London fought down a sigh.

It was no longer possible to evade the topic with more soothing terms like "unfortunate passing."

The group of people clustering around her was getting larger.

"Yes, the police do suspect foul play," London said. "And the more we cooperate with them, the sooner they'll solve this case."

Another woman let out a gasp.

"Are you saying there's a killer in our midst?" she said.

"Right here on the boat?" another said.

"A serial killer, maybe?" another asked.

"Maybe one of us will be the next victim!" yet another exclaimed.

London knew she had to stop the rumor mill from getting out of hand.

"There's no serial killer," she said. "And no one on the *Nachtmusik* is in any danger—not with these policemen on board."

More passengers had arrived and gathered around her, and the passageway was effectively blocked. She tried to gauge their reactions. At least some of them appeared reassured by her words.

But London felt a sharp flash of worry.

How do I know I'm telling them the truth? she thought.

How did she know that no one was danger?

How could she even know for absolute certain that there wasn't a serial killer aboard, getting ready to take another life right now?

She actually knew very little herself—and yet it was her job to inspire these people with confidence and assurance. And to do that, she had to appear a lot more sure of herself than she really felt.

She swallowed hard. She hadn't expected bluffing to ever be part of her job. But now she really had no choice.

"I wish I could tell you more," she said, "but everything will be all right as long as everybody cooperates and stays calm. Now—will you please make sure that none of the other passengers spread any rumors? If you hear any crazy theories, try to set people straight. You know all there is to know at this point. Try to make sure everybody understands that."

Somewhat to London's surprise, several people nodded in agreement. She seemed to have genuinely managed to calm at least some of them down. Putting out fires like this was part of her job, of course, and sometimes she forgot that she was really good at her job.

As the passengers began to go their separate ways, London found herself watching them closely, wondering what they might be thinking.

A frightening possibility occurred to her.

What if one of them is the killer?

She shuddered as something else dawned on her.

They might be wondering the same thing about each other.

They might even be wondering the same thing about me.

For that matter, it now occurred to her—how certain could she be that Gus wasn't the killer after all?

Or Honey?

Or both of them together?

They'd both seemed perfectly innocent back in their stateroom. But maybe they were just really good actors—and really bad people.

She inhaled slowly to settle her thoughts. She told herself that now was no time to get paranoid.

Suddenly, Walter Shick came charging into the reception area.

"Someone, come quick!" he called out. "It's my wife! She's … she's not well!"

Then he turned and ran out of the lounge.

London gasped aloud as she got to her feet and started to dash after him.

Something had happened to Agnes Shick—but what?

Has the murderer struck again? London wondered.

Might there be a serial killer aboard the *Nachtmusik* after all?

CHAPTER TWENTY TWO

As she ran out of the lounge after Walter Shick, London grabbed her cell phone to call Bryce Yeaton, the ship's medic. But her fingers were shaking too hard to punch in his number.

Then she saw Bryce coming out of the ship's elevator with his black bag in hand.

"Oh, I'm so glad you're here," she said. "Something has happened to—"

"Yes, I know," Bryce interrupted her. "Agnes Shick is unwell. Walter just called me, and I came straight from the infirmary."

London and Bryce followed Walter into the hallway and to one of the smaller suites—the Johann Strauss II—where he and Agnes were staying.

When they both went inside, London saw that this suite was slightly smaller than the one that Mrs. Klimowski had inhabited, but she thought that it was much more cheerful. Decorated as a tribute to Johann Strauss II—the famous nineteenth-century "waltz king"—it featured pictures of the composer at every age of his life, pages of musical scores, and lush paintings of glamorous balls and exquisitely dressed dancers.

Agnes Shick was sitting on the edge of the bed, sweating and crying and gasping for breath. Her husband sat down beside her and gently smoothed her hair with his hand.

"Brian … Brian … is the doctor here?" she gasped.

"Yes, he's here."

London was startled.

Why was Agnes calling her husband Walter by the name "Brian"?

"Oh, Brian, Brian," Agnes repeated.

Walter gave London a quick, anxious look, then turned back to his wife.

"Hush, dear," he whispered soothingly. "It's Walter. I'm here for you. And so is the medic. London is here too."

Then Walter turned toward London and Bryce and said, "A few minutes ago Agnes and I came back to our room after being questioned

130

by that awful police chief. The attack started just now."

Agnes looked around nervously as Bryce crouched beside her.

"Tell me how it feels," he said to her in a gentle voice.

"It hurts," she said.

"Where?"

"In my chest. And I … I can barely breathe."

London wondered whether Agnes was having a heart attack.

She also wondered—had Mrs. Klimowski suffered these same symptoms before she died? Had Agnes Shick been poisoned, too?

Bryce took out his stethoscope and blood pressure cuff and quickly checked Agnes's heartbeat and blood pressure.

"Has she had episodes like this before?" Bryce asked Walter.

"Yes, but not for years."

"How long have the attacks lasted?"

"Oh, usually just a few minutes. But that was long ago. And this one seemed worse, and I—well, it really frightened me."

"I can understand why," Bryce said. "But don't worry, everything will be all right."

London was taken by the quietly authoritative, reassuring tone in his Australian-accented voice.

For the first time she realized that he was really quite an impressive man.

And handsome too.

As if London needed any further cause to feel attracted to him, he looked directly at her with clear, sensitive blue eyes and smiled.

"London, could you get us a glass of water?" he asked.

London nodded and headed for the bathroom. As she turned on the faucet and poured water into a glass, she tried to shake off her sudden surge of interest in Bryce. It hardly seemed to suit the moment.

What am I, some schoolgirl?

Then she advised herself, *Focus.*

She needed to keep her wits about her and deal with whatever was happening. And whatever was happening seemed very strange.

It didn't sound like Agnes had been poisoned, after all. But something must have happened to set off an anxiety attack. Was it just the stress of being interrogated by the alezredes? And why had she gotten confused about her husband's name?

Agnes called Walter "Brian."

Why had she done that?

131

Had her attack caused her some sort of mental confusion?

Or was there some other reason?

As she walked back into the room with the water, Bryce was sitting on the bed next to Agnes speaking to Walter.

"This is the Strauss room, eh? Nice music comes with these rooms, I believe. A waltz or two might be rather helpful right now, eh?"

Walter smiled slightly in agreement. He got up from the bed and flipped on a wall switch, and sure enough, a familiar melody began to play.

It was "The Blue Danube" waltz by Johann Strauss II. It began slowly and softly, then grew faster and more cheerful. With its steady, regular, dance-like beat of 1-2-3, 1-2-3, 1-2-3, it was also soothing and calming and cheerful. Soon both Agnes and her husband were visibly more at ease.

This attractive medic and chef had been clever to recommend it.

Meanwhile, Bryce had taken a small medicine container out of his bag.

He spoke to Agnes, who was still breathing quickly but was noticeably calmer.

"You're having a panic attack," he said. "I know it's frightening, but you're not in any danger, believe me. It will soon pass—just like all the attacks you used to have. Do you have any idea what might have triggered it?"

Agnes closed her eyes tightly.

"It's the police," she said. "It's all these police all over the place, and—"

Walter gently but firmly interrupted her.

"And being confined to this boat, I think," he said to Bryce.

"Understandable," Bryce said. "It's getting on a lot of passengers' nerves, I'm sure. Agnes, are you allergic to any medications?"

"No."

"Are you taking any prescription medicines?"

"A couple," Agnes said. "I can't remember their names."

Walter said, "She takes amlodipine for her blood pressure and pravastatin for her cholesterol levels. That's all. She's really very healthy."

Bryce opened the medicine container and took out a pill.

"I'd like you to take one of these, then," he said.

"What is it?" Agnes asked.

"Oh, it's a commonly prescribed mild tranquilizer, and you may well have taken it at other times for one reason or another. It's got a lot of trade names, but clinically speaking, it's a variety of benzodiazepine."

Agnes swallowed the pill with some water.

"There, now," Bryce said, patting her hand. "I'll bet you feel better already."

"I do, actually," Agnes replied.

London couldn't help but smile. Of course the pill couldn't possibly have taken effect yet. But Bryce's kindly manner and even his suggestion of music were already producing positive results.

"You'll feel just fine shortly," Bryce said to Agnes. Handing the medicine bottle to Walter he added, "I'm giving your husband four more pills for you to use as needed. I don't imagine you will need all of them during the rest of this trip, but if you do and you need more, come to the infirmary or give me a call."

Walter and Agnes both warmly thanked Bryce, and he and London left the room.

"It's nothing unexpected," Bryce said to London in a reassuring voice. "Mrs. Klimowski's death naturally has everyone aboard on edge—me too, to be perfectly honest. And now we're all confined to this boat, which is swarming with police. Nerves are rattled. But we'll all get through it, I promise. Now if you'll excuse me, I'd better get back to the infirmary. I wouldn't be surprised if I'll be having similar cases in the next little while."

As Bryce headed toward the elevator, London was seized by a renewed wave of exhaustion. She felt herself jump nervously when the elevator doors opened and a pair of the roaming police officers marched off.

How much more of this would it take, she wondered, *for me to have my very own panic attack?*

She hurried into the elevator before the doors closed again and took it down to the Allegro deck. Maybe she could find a few moments of peace and quiet in her own stateroom.

When London opened her door, she found Sir Reginald sitting on the bed looking at her rather expectantly, as if he was curious to hear where she'd been and what she'd been doing. She sat down on the bed and stroked his silky coat.

"It's a long story," she said. "It would only bore you."

Sir Reginald let out what sounded like a grunt of disagreement.

London sighed.

Here I go, talking to the dog again.

But maybe talking to the dog would help put her own roiling thoughts in order.

"Things aboard this ship are crazy," she told him. "Everybody's upset. And poor Mrs. Shick just had an awful anxiety attack. Fortunately, Bryce came right away to take care of her. He seems like an excellent medic."

Sir Reginald let out a quizzical little growl.

"OK, so he's also good-looking. So sue me for sort of getting a crush on him. I'm only human."

Continuing to pet the dog, she thought back over all that had just happened.

"But I just don't know, Sir Reginald," she said. "I can't help feel like there was something odd about Agnes's attack. And she actually called her husband Brian. His name's Walter. What do you suppose that was all about?"

Sir Reginald whimpered noncommittally.

"Walter seemed anxious about her calling him that. And he also seemed anxious when she mentioned being upset by all the police on board. What does she find so upsetting about police? I feel like ... well, maybe they're hiding something."

London shook her head.

"But that's crazy. What am I even thinking? That they might have had something to do with Mrs. Klimowski's death? That's just ridiculous. Walter and Agnes are two of the nicest people aboard the *Nachtmusik.* They'd never hurt a soul ..."

She paused, then added, "Or at least I don't think so. But what do I know about them, really? They were right there at the table with Mrs. Klimowski yesterday. What if they're not who they seem to be?"

Sir Reginald was looking at her with seemingly rapt attention.

"And anyway, what about Gus?" she said. "He was sitting at that table too. And so was Honey. And so were ..."

London fell silent.

Then she scratched the dog's head.

"I've got to get back to being Nancy Drew," she said. "I've got to do my best to solve this case on my own."

She tilted her head and looked into the dog's eyes.

"Whatever happened, you saw it, didn't you?" she said.

Sir Reginald let out a whimper. London sighed.

"It's like Honey said a little while ago—if only you could talk."

But as she sat and studied the dog's face, an idea started to occur to her.

"Maybe you *can* talk, in your own way."

Before she could think her idea through, her phone rang. She saw that the call was from Elsie Sloan.

"London!" Elsie exclaimed when she took the call. "Do you have any idea what's going on?"

"Just that the Gyor police suspect somebody on the boat of killing Mrs. Klimowski."

"Huh! What a ridiculous idea!"

London wished she could feel so sure that the idea was so ridiculous.

"They questioned me a little in the captain's quarters," London said, "and now they're questioning other people. They seem to be questioning everybody who had lunch with her yesterday."

"What can we do?"

Before London could open her mouth to reply, Elsie added, "And don't tell me we can just let them do their job. There's a mystery to solve."

"I know," London said. "And I want to solve it. And Mr. Lapham says he wants me to solve it too."

"My goodness, Mr. Lapham! You've got your marching orders from on high, then. So what do you want to do?"

The plan London had been forming before Elsie's call now began to take shape in her mind.

"Elsie, I need to get off this boat without the cops or the alezredes knowing about it. Do you have any idea how I could do that?"

Elsie let out a gasp of enthusiasm.

"Do I ever!" she said. "Right now I'm on the Menuetto deck. I see just one policeman keeping watch at the gangway. I'll have no trouble distracting him and—"

"Elsie, wait. I don't want to get you in trouble."

"Since when have I ever cared about getting into trouble?"

London couldn't help but admire Elsie's pluck.

And that's what I need right now.

Some good old-fashioned pluck.

"Where are you right now?" Elsie asked.

"In my stateroom."

"OK, then. Come up to the Menuetto deck and the reception area. We'll get right to work."

Elsie ended the call without explaining her plan any further. London got off the bed and put the dog on its leash and picked up the animal.

London hoped she could figure out on the fly what Elsie had in mind.

I might need to do a little improvising, she thought.

London left her room and took the elevator to the Menuetto deck. When she got off the elevator, she found no one in the reception area.

I just need to stay out of sight.

And I need to stay lucky.

Then she did hear a couple of voices—a man's and a woman's. The woman's voice was definitely Elsie's.

She slipped behind the reception desk, then peered over the top of it. Sure enough, she saw Elsie and one of the uniformed police officers standing at the end of the gangway. She could also make out at least some of what Elsie was saying to the officer as she jabbered.

It sounded to London like a Hungarian-English word salad—the kind of babbling a tourist might use when lost in a foreign city and knowing nothing of the local language except what could be found in a phrasebook.

London smiled at Elsie's guile.

She didn't know how well Elsie really knew Hungarian, but she was sure she was faking a good bit of her ignorance. And her tactic was working perfectly. The officer was smiling broadly, obviously charmed by the efforts of this pretty, tall blond woman to communicate with him. And he obviously didn't know any English.

But he also still seemed to be intent on doing his job.

"Do you want to leave the ship?" he said in Hungarian. "Because you can't."

"I don't understand," Elsie said in English with a shrug. "I wish I knew Hungarian better."

Then she strung a crazy assortment of English and Hungarian words together.

"Something ... going on ... don't know ... things happening ... what or where ... I should be ... we ... you ... don't know ... this is all

136

so scary … I've never been this afraid …"

The police officer interrupted gently in Hungarian.

"Are you scared about the murder? You needn't be. You're safe aboard the ship. But you'd be safest in your own room."

"Huh?"

"Where you, eh, live on the boat. Your room."

"Oh. What do you mean about … my room?"

"You ought to go there."

"Oh."

But she didn't move from her spot.

The officer gestured broadly, trying to make his meaning clearer as he kept speaking in Hungarian.

"Where … is … your … room?"

Elsie looked at him as if she didn't understand why he was asking the question.

"It is … not here," she managed to say in Hungarian.

"Another deck, then?"

The officer made a ladder-like gesture with his hands.

Elsie's eyes opened wider.

"Oh, I see," she said in English.

Then she repeated "I see" in Hungarian.

Pointing downward, the officer said, "Is your deck below?"

"Yes, down," Elsie said in Hungarian.

"Which level? How far below?"

"Down."

The officer was chuckling heartily, quite amused by the situation, and obviously more than a little smitten by Elsie.

"Come on," he said. "Let's get you where you're supposed to be."

And sure enough, he started to escort Elsie toward the elevator. Elsie had created exactly the kind of distraction she had promised, and London knew she needed to seize her opportunity. Without looking back, she rushed out through the reception area doors, down the gangway, and across the little raft to the riverside.

Then she set the little dog on the ground and held onto him by the leash.

"OK, Sir Reginald," she said. "Let's get moving."

As if he understood, the dog broke into a trot, and London followed him.

CHAPTER TWENTY THREE

As she followed Sir Reginald Taft through the twisting streets of Old Town Gyor, London was beginning to feel that her quest was absurd. The dog was certainly enthusiastic, tugging so hard on the leash that she broke into a jog to keep up with him.

She certainly didn't expect him to lead her straight to the murderer—especially not if the murderer was someone aboard the *Nachtmusik.*

But maybe he could lead her to …

Something, she thought. *Some clue only he knows how to find.*

But they seemed to be headed nowhere in particular. First they passed the statue of the Archangel Michael defeating Satan in battle, then the Virgin Mary on a column flanked by four Apostles.

"Do you really know where you're going?" she asked Sir Reginald as they approached the Vienna Gate Square with its Baroque Carmelite Church.

Then she silently scolded herself.

A silly question.

How could she expect the dog to even understand the task she'd set for him? Sir Reginald Taft was just a little Yorkshire Terrier, not some bloodhound trained for police work. Maybe he just thought they were out for another tour of Gyor.

But the dog trotted on steadfastly, and she kept following him.

By the time they reached the *Boatman* sculpture, London was tired and discouraged. She sat down on the low marble wall surrounding the sculpture to catch her breath and organize her thoughts. The dog sat down at her feet.

Just what do you think you're doing? she asked herself.

As if in reply, Mr. Lapham's words echoed through her mind.

"As of this moment, I'm awaiting word that you've solved this matter."

A lot of moments had already passed since that phone call. She could easily imagine Mr. Lapham sitting by the phone awaiting word from her that she'd cracked the mystery, his patience waning by the second. He really had made clear that he thought it was her responsibility.

What was more, Mr. Lapham didn't have much confidence in the police.

I guess it really is up to me, she thought.

She looked at Sir Reginald, who was now up again and pacing and wagging his tail as if he wanted to get on their way.

"Where are you taking me?" London asked.

The dog let out a little yap.

"I'll bet you're not taking me anywhere," London grumbled. "You're just taking me on a wild goose chase. I might as well head back to the boat and see if I can sneak back onboard without getting into trouble. This whole idea was a mistake."

Then she spotted the uniforms on the other side of the plaza.

And a risky mistake at that.

A couple of police officers were strolling along not far away. It hadn't occurred to her until just this moment to be on the lookout for police.

But maybe the police are on the lookout for me.

By now Borsos may have realized that she was no longer aboard the *Nachtmusik.* If so, maybe he'd put out an APB to the local police to watch out for her. And if he had, she'd certainly be easy to spot in her Epoch World Cruise Lines uniform, with its distinctive dark blue slacks and a blouse and vest.

I'm like a sitting duck, she realized.

She scooped up Sir Reginald in her arms and walked quickly to the nearest side street. As she rounded the corner she glanced back and saw that the two police officers didn't seem to have noticed her yet. But then Reginald leaped to the ground with an excited yap.

As London turned toward the dog, she found herself face to face with someone else wearing an Epoch World uniform. The woman backed up a few steps and they stared at each other in flustered surprise.

"What are you doing here?" London and Amy Blassingame blurted, practically in unison.

London reminded herself that she was Amy's boss.

"You tell me first," London demanded.

Amy let out a whining sigh.

"OK, if you must know, I'm on my way to meet somebody. I was startled when the little mutt yapped at me."

"Meet somebody?" London snapped. "Why would you …"

"Sneak off the ship?" Amy countered. "Why would anybody do a thing like that? I guess we could both get arrested today."

Struck by the foolishness of their situation, London let out a brief laugh.

Amy grinned slightly in response and pointed to a man who was sitting alone at a table in a nearby sidewalk café.

"There's my reason," she said.

London recognized him at once. He was the man Amy had been flirting with early yesterday morning at the end of the gangway.

"Who is he?" London asked.

"His name is Sandor Füst."

"So what is this—a date?"

"Well, yes, I guess you could call it that. I met him yesterday morning when you were on your way out with your tour group. He told me he'd be here today if I could get away to meet him. Well, I told him we wouldn't be here today, of course having no way of knowing someone would be murdered and we would be stuck here. But he said he'd be here anyway just in case."

Amy shrugged and added, "But when the police came on board a little while ago and the captain said we all had to stay aboard …"

Amy rolled her eyes like a teenager.

"Oh, London, I thought I'd go crazy, knowing that Sandor was out here expecting me—sort of—to meet him. I went to the reception room to see if I could figure out how to get off the boat, and then…"

Her voice faded, but London knew what she meant.

"You saw what Elsie and I were doing," she said.

"That's right. I saw how Elsie distracted that policeman and you slipped away. Elsie seemed to be having a good time with him. He stayed distracted after you got clear of the boat, so I had plenty of time and …"

Amy shrugged.

"Well, I seized the moment, so to speak. I know, it's not like me to be so spontaneous and devil-may-care. But here I am. And London, I'm so happy I took the plunge! Sandor and I don't know each other at all, and I don't speak any Hungarian and he doesn't speak much English. But that just makes it all the more exciting. And we both felt a connection between us the very second our eyes met on the shore. Isn't

140

it romantic?"

London couldn't deny that it sounded like quite an adventure. She hadn't realized Amy had this kind of pluck—and apparently Amy hadn't either. The so-called "River Troll" had an unexpected taste for adventure.

"So now if you don't mind …" Amy said, starting to walk toward the man, who was still waving at her.

London stopped her.

"Wait a minute, Amy," she said. "This isn't a good idea."

Amy scoffed.

"Well, you should talk. What are *you* doing ashore, anyway?"

"I'm trying to find out who killed Mrs. Klimowski."

"Aren't the police doing that?"

London fought down a groan of frustration.

"Supposedly," she said.

"What do you mean, supposedly?"

"The police chief, Alezredes Borsos, questioned me a while ago in the captain's quarters. And I'm not so sure he knows what he's doing. To make things worse, he acts like he suspects *me*."

"You?"

"That's right. And there's one more thing. I got a call from Mr. Lapham. He told me I've got to solve the case myself."

Amy's eyes widened.

"He *ordered* you to solve it?"

London nodded.

"I guess you'd better get to work, then," Amy said.

"And you'd better get back to the boat," London said.

"London, *why*? You get to have your little adventure. Why don't I get to have one too?"

London could think of a dozen reasons, including the likelihood that it was against Epoch World Cruise Lines policy for employees to fraternize with foreign locals. But London was worried about a far more serious issue.

"Amy, listen to me. You saw how things are aboard the boat. It's chaos. Nobody knows what's going on. It's risky enough that I'm out and about. If the police notice you're gone too, it'll only make things worse. They might even suspect *you*."

"Oh, my!" Amy said with a gasp.

London could see by her expression that the fun had just gone out

141

of her romantic adventure.

"You'd better get back there," London said.

"OK," Amy said. "But what will I tell the policeman who's guarding the gangway when I come back aboard? What should I say I was out doing?"

London thought for a moment. She had half a mind to tell Amy to tell the guard he'd get in bad trouble if Borsos found out he'd let her slip off the boat, and he'd better let her come back aboard quietly. But she was quickly shocked at herself for even considering such a sleazy tactic.

"What about the truth?" she said. "That you sneaked out for a date?"

"Well, I don't have a *good* excuse," Amy said with a tilt of her head. "So I guess the truth will do as well as anything. It won't make things any worse, anyway. But—what should I say if anyone asks about you?"

London wished she could suggest that Amy lie and say she hadn't seen her. But lying wouldn't be the right thing to do—especially not when finding out the truth was so desperately important.

"Just tell them the truth," she said. "Say I'm out doing some detective work of my own. Borsos won't like it but … well, I can't say I really care. I just need some time to check out a few things."

"All right then," Amy said, looking both scared and disappointed. She pointed to the man in the nearby café and added, "Do you think it's OK if I just go tell Sandor I've got to go?"

London fidgeted as she tried to decide. It was dawning on her that she was losing precious time dealing with Amy. She needed to get back to whatever she was out here to do.

"Do you *promise* to make it quick?" London asked.

Amy nodded.

"And do you *promise* not to change your mind about going back to the boat?" London added.

Amy nodded again.

"OK, then. I'll see you later today."

"Be careful, London," Amy said as she started to walk toward the café.

"I will," London said.

Still restless, Reginald tugged at the leash as if he wanted to stay with Amy.

142

"Come on," London said, tugging him away. "Let's keep looking."

Seeming to pick up the trail again, Reginald scurried onward. London began trotting after him again.

Sir Reginald turned a corner, and London stayed on his trail. They were near the Magyar Öröm restaurant now, and the streets were all familiar. London wondered—had Mrs. Klimowski walked this way yesterday before she was killed? Her brain clicked away as she tried to guess what had happened.

On a street corner a few blocks away, a familiar sight caught her eye. It was the vendor's stall she'd seen yesterday—the one Sir Reginald had seemed interested in.

And now he seemed interested in it again. In fact, he was tugging on his leash in that direction.

The stand had been closed yesterday afternoon, but now an elderly woman was there selling flowers.

London's eyes widened as something amid the flowers caught her attention.

That could be the clue I've been looking for.

CHAPTER TWENTY FOUR

There it was, amid the profusion of violets, lilies, tulips, and other blossoms on the counter in front of the vendor.

A batch of big yellow flowers in a tall vase.

Sunflowers, London realized. *Small ones, but sunflowers all the same.*

Exactly like the one she'd seen yesterday in an unlikely location.

Sir Reginald was tugging at his leash emphatically, so London picked him up and walked toward the stout, white-haired woman tending the flower stall. When they reached her, Sir Reginald let out a friendly yap, and the woman let out a gasp of happy exclamation.

"Oh, it's *you* again!" she said in Hungarian to the dog. "It's nice to see you!"

Then she glared at London with a curious expression.

"I don't recognize you, though," the woman said.

She kept chattering away in Hungarian a little too fast for London to follow her words perfectly. But the gist of what she was saying was that somebody else had been there with this very dog yesterday.

"It was an unhappy lady," the woman said, slowing her speech so that London could understand her better. The vendor obviously dealt a lot with foreigners and knew how to speak with them. "She was actually crying when she came here. I gave her one of my sunflowers to make her feel better."

London felt a tug of emotion.

She knew she shouldn't be surprised to hear this, given how distraught Mrs. Klimowski had been when she'd left the Magyar Öröm.

Still, hearing this made Mrs. Klimowski's death seem all the sadder.

The vendor took out a sunflower and gave it to London.

"Sunflowers are my favorite this time of year," she said. "Later in the summer you'll see fields and fields of them out in the countryside. Big ones, not like these little greenhouse plants. Our sunflower seeds are a major Hungarian export."

She nodded proudly and added, "The lady's tears kept coming but

144

she seemed grateful for the flower. She let me pet her dog."

The vendor scratched Sir Reginald under the chin.

"Please tell me ... what else happened when she was here?" London said.

The woman looked a little surprised at the question.

"Well, she talked to me some, but it was in English, and I know only a little English, but I remember her telling me something like ..."

The woman paused, as if searching her mind for the English words.

"'I am in need of spiritual' ... spiritual something ... I can't remember ..."

"Solace?" London asked, remembering what Mrs. Klimowski had said back in Budapest before their visit to St. Stephen's Basilica.

"Why, yes. I believe 'solace' was the word. She said her life had been, eh, 'tragic.'"

Again, London felt a stab of sadness to hear Mrs. Klimowski's familiar refrain.

"What happened next?" she asked.

"She left."

"Did she say where she was going?"

"No."

A theory began to snap together in London's mind. She didn't need the flower vendor to tell her where Mrs. Klimowski was off to next. London knew perfectly well where she'd gone for "spiritual solace." And the doorkeeper outside the basilica yesterday had been wearing exactly this sort of sunflower in his lapel—an odd, outsized sort of decoration to wear with a formal suit.

It's not a coincidence, she thought.

It just can't be.

Before London could ask any more questions, Sir Reginald let out a small warning growl.

London glanced around. Farther down the street she saw four police officers huddled together looking at a cell phone. One of them pointed at the phone, and then at London.

London heart pounded with alarm.

She'd been right to worry that Borsos had put out a police APB on her. The information on the cell phone might well have included a picture of her, or at least her uniform. And sure enough, these police officers had spotted her.

If only I'd had time to change out of my uniform, she thought.

But there was no turning back the clock. She had to act fast. She reached into her purse and took out about four thousand forint and set them on the counter.

"Here," she said.

"What's this for?" the vendor asked with surprise.

"For the flower," London said. "And your help. And for being such a nice person."

"But this is too much!" the vendor said.

"Please take it. I've got to go now."

And London saw that she didn't have a second to lose. The four police officers were now walking briskly in her direction. She glanced around anxiously for an escape route and spotted a narrow alleyway.

Holding onto Sir Reginald and the sunflower, she darted into the alley.

This is no good, she thought as she broke into a run.

The officers had surely seen her duck into this alley. They'd catch up with her any second. Still, she had to lose them somehow. She climbed down a small stairwell behind a building and ducked out of sight.

Sure enough, she heard the clatter of footsteps and the officers talking in Hungarian. Then the footsteps and the words grew fainter as the police officers continued on down the alleyway. She peeked up out of the stairwell and saw that they were gone, then stepped cautiously back into the alley.

"We're OK—for now," she said to Sir Reginald.

The dog let out what sounded like a little growl of disagreement.

"They'll be back—I know that," she admitted to Sir Reginald. "And there will be others. We can't keep dodging all the police officers in Gyor all day long. We'll get caught soon, but if we can only get to the basilica before they do …"

She trotted down to the end of the alley, looked around the corner, and didn't see any officers in sight. Then she began to plot out a roundabout route to the basilica.

If only I can get there in time, she thought.

It suddenly seemed possible that Mrs. Klimowski hadn't been killed by somebody aboard the *Nachtmusik* after all. And if London's luck held out, she might soon confront her killer face to face.

CHAPTER TWENTY FIVE

By the time London emerged from the alley onto a short, unfamiliar side street, she could hear the wail of a police car siren somewhere close behind her.

The cops who had spotted her hadn't wasted any time calling for backup.

Still holding Sir Reginald in her arms, she struggled to remember the map of the city she'd studied in preparation for leading tours. She'd spent some time going over the map, memorizing as many streets and landmarks as she could. After all, there could be nothing as embarrassing to a tour guide as getting lost, and the twisting, labyrinthine streets of Gyor could be a challenge even under normal circumstances.

But these aren't normal circumstances, she thought.

She was being hunted, and she would have to be quick on her feet to keep clear of the police. Could she weave and dodge her way from here to the basilica without getting hopelessly lost?

She knew the way there from the flower stand at the far end of the alley, but she didn't dare go back that way now.

First she had to be sure she knew exactly where she was. She made her way to a street sign at the end of the block.

As she'd hoped, the street was called Hó köz. That meant she wasn't lost yet. She followed the street to a pedestrian lane that ran alongside one of the city's many public squares. If she followed this lane, she knew she'd at least be heading in the right direction.

But I've got to hurry, she told herself.

She felt painfully conspicuous as she trotted amid other pedestrians in her Epoch World Cruise Lines uniform, carrying the mop of a dog in her arms. Then she spotted a police officer up ahead. He was talking to someone and hadn't seen her yet, but she didn't want to run right past him. Instead, she veered into a street called Káposztás köz. Visualizing the map in her head, she figured she still must be angling in more or less the right direction.

Or am I?

Tall, antique buildings with plaster walls and tiled roofs seemed to lean and crowd in around her almost teasingly, blocking her ability to see in any direction. The view cleared a little as she emerged onto another walkway along another public square, and again she felt reasonably sure she was on the right course.

But she hadn't gone far when a pair of officers came into view. Engaged in conversation, they were walking right toward her. It would be only a matter of seconds before they saw her.

Where could she hide?

London darted into a small, busy storefront café. She stood there amid the crowded tables, knowing that she was scarcely less conspicuous through the window than she had been on the street.

Glancing around, she saw that the two officers she was trying to avoid had paused right in front of the café to continue their conversation. They were also looking up and down the street—for her, she felt sure. If either of them so much as turned his head in her direction, she'd be spotted for sure.

The café tables were crowded with customers, and she was grateful that they were paying no attention to her at all. Seeing just one empty chair, she moved quickly and plopped down there.

London found herself sitting across from a bulky, bearded man who looked surprised to see her. But then his features broke into a broad grin.

In the best Hungarian she could muster, she said, "Do you mind if I sit here for a moment?"

Leering across the table at her, the man replied, "You may sit here for much longer than a moment, my dear. You are as pretty as your flower—even prettier, I think."

He was referring, of course, to the sunflower London was still holding in her hand.

"Please be my guest," he added. "I'm in no hurry—and I hope you aren't either."

London swallowed anxiously as she settled Sir Reginald onto her lap. At least she was facing away from the café windows and might not be especially noticeable from outside. And there was a mirror behind the coffee bar, so she could see the window from where she was sitting. But she wondered how long she'd be stuck sitting with this flirtatious and unattractive gentleman.

She forced a smile and tried to think of something to say, but no easy explanation for her actions came to mind.

"American?" the man asked.

London nodded.

"Ah," the man said in English. "Then perhaps I can practice my skills. Conversation is the best way to learn."

London stopped herself from politely saying, "That would be nice." She didn't want to give this man any encouragement.

"My name is Taavi Muszca," he told her. Then he added with a chuckle, "I believe the name 'Taavi' means 'adored' in your language."

London forced herself to laugh a little, but it didn't come out well.

Muszca peered at the name pin on her jacket.

"And I see that you are London Rose. I am pleased to meet you, London Rose."

"Likewise—Taavi Muszca," London replied uneasily.

Nodding at Sir Reginald, the man said, "Dogs are not normally allowed in here. But no matter. I own the café. I make the rules. You may do as you wish."

Now he's trying to impress me, she thought.

He wasn't succeeding, of course. He was only making London feel more queasy and uncomfortable and anxious to get away. But as she looked at the mirror behind the bar, she saw that the two officers seemed to have settled down to watching out for her in front of the café, vigilantly looking in every direction except through the window. They didn't look like they were going anywhere at that moment.

"Perhaps you would like something to drink, London Rose," Muszca said, sounding rather stiff and pedantic. "I am drinking plain *fekete kávé*—'black coffee' in your language. I would recommend something tastier and more traditionally Hungarian. Perhaps you would like a cup of *bécsi kávé*—coffee served with ice cream and chocolate and whipped cream."

It sounded delicious. But right now, London was only concerned about one thing—getting out of here and continuing on to the basilica.

"I will order it for you—on the house, of course," the man said.

He raised a pudgy hand to snap his fingers to summon a waiter.

"Wait a moment," London said, stopping him.

"Well?" Muszca said.

Well what? London wondered.

She had to improvise her way out of this situation. But she wasn't sure how. And she could still see the cops in the mirror.

"Does this café have a kitchen?" she blurted.

"But of course," Muszca said. "We serve meals here all day long. Have you had breakfast? We stopped serving breakfast a short while ago, but I'm sure I can persuade my cooks to make an exception for such a lovely young lady."

London's stomach felt queasy now. But a plan was starting to come together in her head.

"We are known for our *rántotta,* scrambled eggs," Muszca added. "It is prepared with bacon and peppers and a sausage called *kolbász.*"

"Yes, that sounds delicious, but …"

"But what?"

"I would love to see how it's made. Your kitchen must be wonderful."

Muszca smiled proudly, his vanity obviously piqued.

"But of course, London Rose," he said. "I will make the *rántotta* myself."

He rose out of his chair and gallantly helped London out of hers. Then he offered her his arm, which she reluctantly took. The dog let out an annoyed grumble as she shifted him to one side and held him in the crook of her other arm. She was grateful that Sir Reginald was being so patient and not attracting attention by yapping his displeasure.

As Muszca escorted her through the café, London noticed that his waiters were leering at her and nodding approvingly. They seemed accustomed to seeing their boss behaving this way with women.

By the time he led her through a pair of swinging doors, she was starting to feel desperate to get this over with. The kitchen was small but well-equipped, with ovens, stoves, and stainless steel surfaces. Several white-clad men wearing chef's hats were hard at work. The air was hot and thick with delicious smells, and Sir Reginald's head swiveled around as he sniffed with interest.

Stay cool, Sir Reginald, she thought.

She'd be in a real jam if he sprang out of her arms right here and now.

"A special guest?" one of the cooks asked Muszca with a wink.

"To be sure," Muszca said, switching into Hungarian. "An American lady, new to our country and our cuisine—and also to our language. London Rose is her name. She would like to see me prepare a plate of *rántotta.*"

Behind her back she heard a couple of the other cooks chuckling knowingly.

"Fogadok, hogy," one murmured.

London knew what this meant: "I'll bet she would."

She cringed sharply, then heard the other cook whisper, *"Nagyon forró."*

She also knew what this meant: "Very hot."

Muszca scowled at his indiscreet employees, obviously aware from her offended expression that she'd understood what had been said.

He began speaking to London in English, "Pay no attention to these uncouth fellows ..."

But London tuned out his words. She saw exactly what she'd been hoping to see. Far back in the preparation area next to an electric slicer was a door that looked like it might lead outside.

Or was it the door to a restroom or an office or ...?

She hesitated for only a moment, then shook off Muszca's arm. Clasping the little dog tightly, she charged toward the door, threw it open, and dashed on through it.

As the heavy door slammed behind her, London was relieved to see that she was in fact outside, standing in another alleyway, with no police in sight. And although she didn't know exactly where the alley might lead, she knew approximately where the basilica was from here.

As she broke into a run, she spoke to Sir Reginald.

"You were a very good boy back there. I'm starting to think we make a good team."

Behind her she heard the back door to the café fly open. She could hear Muszca shouting at her in Hungarian. She couldn't make out his words from this distance, but he sounded more confused and hurt than angry.

Tough luck, she thought.

She continued breathlessly on her way to the end of the alley. It opened onto a broad street marked *Káptalandomb.* She knew that was the name of a district rather than a street. Even so, she thought she remembered from the map that this street led in exactly the right direction.

She glanced both ways and saw no police officers in sight. As she stepped cautiously out of the alley, she was relieved to see a familiar sight directly in front of her—the central spire of the Cathedral Basilica of the Assumption of Our Lady.

It was still about a block away, though, and London felt more

151

exposed and visible than ever. She doubted very much that she could get all the way there without being spotted by the police. But it might not matter if she could accomplish what she hoped to do very quickly.

As she neared the basilica, she was pleased to see the same well-dressed, somewhat potbellied doorkeeper stationed outside the front entrance. He wasn't wearing a flower today, but she remembered vividly the one he'd been wearing yesterday.

And now she knew who must have given him that sunflower. So he'd definitely noticed the rich lady who had come to the basilica. He'd given Mrs. Klimowski a drink of water or something like that, then tried to take the necklace. He'd been interrupted in some way, and had to abandon the jewels.

As London ran toward him, the doorkeeper was looking at her with keen interest.

She slowed to a walk as she approached him.

Now that she came face to face with him, she felt at a loss for words.

What do you say to a killer?

CHAPTER TWENTY SIX

The siren of an approaching police car alerted London that she had very little time. With Sir Reginald still tucked under her arm, she stopped in front of the doorkeeper.

"I want to talk to you," she said to him in Hungarian.

He smiled at her in a hospitable manner.

"I'll be glad to assist you in any way," the doorman replied.

A clatter of footsteps across the pavement behind London announced that the police had caught up with her.

She was about to be arrested.

In a matter of moments, she'd be dragged away from here—possibly to jail.

The doorman looked puzzled as he glanced past London, then peered more closely at her.

"Oh, I recognize you," he said. "You were here yesterday. You were the one who ..."

"Yes, I was the one who came and told you that the elderly lady was dead."

"It was so terrible," the doorkeeper said, shaking his head. "And now I hear that she was murdered. But—what do all these policemen want?"

London couldn't ignore them any longer. She looked around and saw a semicircle of police officers standing around her and the doorkeeper. Worse still, Alezredes Borsos himself was climbing out of the police car that had just pulled up.

"Please don't arrest me yet," London pleaded with the officers. "Please let me talk to this man. Give me just a moment. That's all I need."

The uniformed officers looked at Borsos.

"Yes, give her a moment," he told them with a nod, sounding quite willing to indulge London in her request. More than that, he sounded rather amused at what she'd gotten herself into, and eager to see what would happen next.

What does he know that I don't know? she wondered.

153

London stared hard at the doorkeeper.

"What did you do to the lady?" she demanded. "And why? Did you intend to steal the necklace? Did you get interrupted? What happened?"

"I don't understand," the doorman sputtered. "I told the alezredes everything I knew."

"And now I want you to tell *me* everything," London said.

She put Sir Reginald on the ground and held on to the leash. The little dog stood there, glaring at the surrounding officers.

London held out her sunflower to the doorman.

"You were wearing one of these in your lapel yesterday," she said. "Where did you get it?"

"That lady gave it to me," he said. "On her way into the church. I told the alezredes—"

"She just gave it to you?" London interrupted. "What did she say to you?"

"Something about needing 'spiritual solace,' I think. She was sad, she said, and someone had given her the flower out of kindness, and now giving it to somebody else made her feel better. Then she went on inside the cathedral."

"And you didn't go inside with her? You didn't give her something … something to eat or drink?"

"I did not go inside," the doorman said firmly. "I always stay at my post."

"You didn't poison her?"

The man's eyes widened with alarm.

"No, of course not! I would never harm anybody."

London's certainty wavered as she began to see a problem with her assumption. If the doorman had killed Mrs. Klimowski, he probably wouldn't have been wearing her flower. The flower was a sign that she had interacted with him, nothing more.

Still, the man must know something.

"Who *was* with her, then?" she demanded.

"She came alone," the doorkeeper said. "But there was a tour group going in at the same time as she did—just like now."

Sure enough, London saw a group of about ten or twelve tourists following their guide into the church.

The doorkeeper continued, "The group left, and I thought she'd stayed alone inside to pray, as people sometimes do. That was when you came along and …"

His words faded again.

London was struggling with her thoughts now.

She also noticed that Sir Reginald was just sitting quietly, watching the cops but showing no interest in the doorman at all.

Surely, she thought, *the dog would show some sign if the doorkeeper was actually Mrs. Klimowski's murderer.*

Then London nearly scoffed at her own unrealistic expectation.

He's just a dog, she reminded herself.

Alezredes Borsos strode forward and spoke to London in his rather awkward English.

"Are you quite satisfied?" he asked her. "I wasn't sure you'd believe me, so I thought I'd let you ask him face to face."

The alezredes looked smug now, obviously pleased with himself for letting her make a fool of herself.

"The man is telling the truth," he added. "We have spoken to witnesses who confirm that he stood right here at his post the whole time the lady was inside. He never went inside. The tourists came and went. Those that we have found and interviewed said that they took no notice of the lady at all, let alone who might have been with her. Small wonder. People sit down to pray in the sanctuary all the time."

London swallowed hard.

It suddenly seemed very likely that she really had made a terrible error.

"And now," Borsos said to her, "would you kindly accompany me to the car? I'd rather not have to … well, become insistent, I suppose you could say."

London realized she had no choice. If she didn't cooperate, she'd probably be put in handcuffs right here in front of Cathedral Basilica of the Assumption of Our Lady. Would someone from the ship come and bail her out, or would she become an international incident?

More likely, she thought with a sigh, *I'll just be locked away and forgotten.*

With Sir Reginald following on the leash, she walked with Borsos to the car. The two of them got into the back seat and the dog hopped in with them.

"I half suspected all along you'd leave the ship," the alezredes said to her with a rather snide smile. "It is true what they say about you Yankees—that you love your liberty."

London knew that he was making a joke. Under different

circumstances, she might actually find it rather droll. But now was not one of those times.

Borsos stroked his chin sagely.

"I find it most interesting," he said, "that you would go to so much trouble to find someone to blame."

"'To blame'?" London echoed with a gasp. "I wasn't looking for anyone to blame. I'm trying to find whoever killed Mrs. Klimowski."

"So you say," Borsos said with a purr of suspicion.

London was starting to feel angry right now.

"OK, I made a mistake," she said. "But it wasn't entirely my fault. If you weren't so—so *secretive* about everything, this might never have happened. I had no idea that you'd confirmed the doorkeeper's alibi. In fact, you've told me next to nothing. I don't even know how Mrs. Klimowski was murdered."

"So you say," Borsos repeated.

London fell silent. This wasn't exactly what she'd had in mind when she'd run away from the prospect of a boring, safe life. It was almost as though she could hear a distant voice reprimanding her.

Planning. Everything has to be planned.

She'd rejected Ian's offer of a merger, and here she was in a foreign country in police custody. Had Ian been right?

Then London realized that the car was on its way to the *Nachtmusik.*

"You're not going to arrest me, I take it," she said.

"Not yet," Borsos said.

"If you suspect me of something, I think you should come out and say it."

Borsos let out a sardonic chuckle.

"Hamarosan megtudjuk, asszonyom," he said.

London was exasperated at hearing these words yet again—"We'll find out soon, ma'am."

"Since your departure," Borsos said, "there have been, eh, developments in the case."

"Such as?"

"Captain Hays was finally able to speak to the lady's lawyer in New York. It seems that she has no family, no heirs. She was quite wealthy, though. Her fortune would seem to be—how do say in English?—'up for takes.'"

London couldn't stop herself from correcting him.

156

"'Up for grabs,' you mean."

"So you say."

"What are you suggesting? That I'm somehow trying to get my hands on Mrs. Klimowski's fortune?"

Borsos chuckled again.

"You already have your hands on her dog," he said.

London could hardly believe her ears.

"What's that got to do with anything?" she said.

"Yesterday I suggested turning the dog over to animal services," he said. "You chose instead to keep him."

"I didn't choose to *keep* him!" London said. "I'm just taking care of him until—"

"Yes, I remember. You said, until someone in her family said where to send it. And now it appears there is no such family. I find it all most curious."

London was aghast now.

"I'm taking care of her dog just to be nice," she said. "I don't even *want* a dog. And I certainly don't have any interest in her money."

"So you say," Borsos said yet again. *"Hamarosan megtudjuk."*

She fell silent as the police car parked at the end of the *Nachtmusik*'s gangway.

I'm still a murder suspect, she reminded herself.

Or at least a person of interest.

London realized that she definitely needed a better plan.

157

CHAPTER TWENTY SEVEN

As she climbed out of the police car, London's whole body felt heavy with exhaustion and discouragement. Even Sir Reginald felt droopy in her arms, as if he shared in her despair.

And small wonder, she thought.

Her wild, desperate run through Old Town Gyor had accomplished nothing.

Less than nothing.

All she'd managed to do was accuse an innocent man of murder before being dragged away by the police. Not only had she made a fool of herself, she may well have set back the search for the actual killer.

But what else was I supposed to do? she wondered.

Her reluctance to turn detective was now completely gone, and solving the case was becoming more and more of an obsession by the minute.

She glanced at Alezredes Borsos, who had also gotten out of the police car and was walking with her toward the ship.

"I suppose we're all still supposed to stay on the ship," she said to him.

"That's right," he replied. "I don't much care about who comes aboard—as long as they don't plan to get off."

He gave her a sharp stare and added, "My men will do better now about keeping everybody aboard the boat."

London opted to say nothing. She saw that four bulky police officers now stood guard at the bottom of the gangway. No one was going to pull the same trick that she, Elsie, and Amy had managed a while ago.

"You may find me in the captain's quarters," Borsos said to her as they headed through the reception area and got on the elevator. "As for you—well, just go about your work. But I expect you to report to the captain hourly…"

He looked at his watch and added, "Starting as of an hour from right now. If you fail to do so, we will find you, and you will be expected to account for your movements. And kindly don't go playing,

158

eh, Miss Marple again."

Miss Marple? London wondered as she and Borsos rode the elevator down to the Allegro deck.

Then she remembered.

Oh, yes. The elderly spinster detective in the Agatha Christie books.

She didn't exactly feel flattered by the reference. But then, she hadn't liked being compared to Nancy Drew either. Not that she felt worthy of being compared to any detective, not after the mistake she'd just made.

It's like the baklava all over again—only a lot worse.

She and Borsos got off the elevator. He stalked away toward the captain's quarters and she walked toward her own room. She realized that her arm was tired from carrying Sir Reginald. She set him down to walk on his leash, but he followed beside her very sluggishly.

"You're tired too, eh?" she said to him. "Well, I can understand why."

They went into her room, and Sir Reginald walked over to the bed and looked up at it wistfully. The poor thing seemed to be too worn out to jump up to his own favorite resting spot. London realized she was over any qualms about letting him onto the mattress.

"You deserve a rest," she said.

She lifted him up and set him down, and he went to sleep instantly.

London let out a sigh of envy. She wished she could do the same. But she was too agitated to sleep even if she wanted to. She also knew where she wanted to check next.

She took the elevator back up to the Menuetto deck.

London felt relieved and lucky to be alone in the passageway, at least for the moment. She headed straight toward her destination, the "Beethoven" grand suite where Mrs. Klimowski had been staying.

But by the time she stood in front of the doorway, a new worry nagged her. As a high-ranking staff member, she had a master keycard, and under normal circumstances she'd have every right to come and go anywhere in the boat, including staterooms. But these weren't normal circumstances. And the fact that there were no passengers around at the moment didn't mean nobody was watching her.

Security cameras, she realized, taking care not to look up at them.

Whoever was watching the video monitors in the security station might be looking at her right now. Then again, maybe no one was watching those monitors. Or at least not all of them all the time.

159

London simply didn't know for sure.

I just have to risk it, she thought as she slipped her keycard into the slot, opened the door, and stepped inside.

It was the first time she'd been inside Mrs. Klimowski's stateroom since yesterday, when she'd taken Sir Reginald away to stay in her room. She took a deep breath and gazed around the sumptuous suite.

What to look for? Where to begin?

With a sudden chill, London got the feeling that someone was watching her right now. She shuddered, then giggled when she saw that it was the face of Ludwig van Beethoven himself, frowning down on her as if in stern disapproval.

London frowned back at the portrait above the bed.

"Don't judge me, Ludwig," she muttered. "I'm here for a good reason."

She wanted to have a more thorough look around than she'd had yesterday. The room had been quite neat at the time, but it was now in some disarray. The police had obviously taken a thorough look around themselves. London guessed that they might have snapped quite a few pictures, though they probably hadn't removed much if anything.

The drawer with her jewels was now sitting open. She remembered something Borsos had said during the drive back to the boat.

"It seems that she has no family, no heirs."

Which of course meant her whole fortune was, as Alezredes Borsos had worded it, "up for takes."

But no one seemed to be intent on taking this part of it.

As London thought back over the events of the last days, an unsettling feeling nagged at her.

I'm missing something, she thought. *I'm overlooking something.*

And it was something that surely even a capable amateur detective wouldn't overlook.

If so, at least she doubted that the police were faring much better. Alezredes Borsos didn't inspire her as a master investigator. London scoffed to herself as she remembered him insinuating that she herself wanted to get her hands on Mrs. Klimowski's fortune.

"You already have your hands on her dog," he'd said.

"Ridiculous!" London muttered aloud.

She picked up an especially lavish necklace clustered with diamonds. She felt a surge of sadness as she looked at the object. She wondered—had belongings like this made poor Mrs. Klimowski any happier? Did they give her any comfort from the "tragic life" she claimed to have lived?

Holding the necklace, London walked all around the room. For the first time she noticed that there were no pictures of friends, family, or loved ones anywhere. She felt sure that she could dig around through all her belongings and not find anything of that sort.

She really was alone in the world, London thought.

Looking again at the necklace in her hand, London supposed it wasn't surprising that Mrs. Klimowski was so alone. She'd made herself impossible to get along with, much less to like, and perhaps even to love. Even so, the woman's apparently empty life struck London as terribly sad.

Suddenly she was startled by a nearby sound—from the door, she realized.

It was someone using a keycard to enter.

Oh, no, London thought. *The police.*

Of course she knew better than to be surprised. She'd known she was taking a risk just by coming in here. But it wasn't going to look good for her to get caught clutching this necklace in her hand.

Before she could do anything about that, the door swung open and a figure stepped inside.

CHAPTER TWENTY EIGHT

"Amy!" London cried out in surprise. "What are you doing here?"

Amy pointed an accusing finger at the necklace in London's hand.

"Oh, my God!" Amy squealed. "I knew you were up to something. You're stealing that, aren't you?"

Then she backed away from London with alarm.

"Why, that must mean that you're the killer!"

"Don't be ridiculous," London replied, trying to sound calm.

"Well, how else do you explain—all *this*?"

"It's like I told you back in Old Town. I'm trying to solve the case. I'm trying to find Mrs. Klimowski's killer."

"Why should I believe you?" Amy asked.

London rolled her eyes and put the necklace back in the drawer.

"Amy, do you seriously believe I'm the killer? I'd be pretty stupid to try to steal anything out of this room right now, with police aboard the ship and everybody under suspicion. Besides, what about you? At least I've got a reason for coming here. I'm looking for clues. What are *you* doing here?"

Amy crossed her arms.

"Well, if you must know, I'm here to find out what you're doing. I glimpsed you coming off the elevator, then looked around the corner and saw you sneaking in here."

"I wasn't sneaking," London objected. "Well, not really. Anyhow, why didn't you just knock if you wanted to come in and check up on me?"

"Because I wanted to catch you in the act … of … whatever you were doing …" Amy's voice trailed off, then she added. "I actually got a little scared. I paced the passageway for a few minutes before I got the nerve to open the door."

"Well, you weren't very stealthy about it," London said. "Anyway, you don't seriously think I'm the killer, do you?"

Amy shrugged.

"No, I don't suppose I do," she said.

"That's a relief. Now that you're here, maybe you can help me look for clues."

London showed her the drawer full of jewels.

"She's got tons of valuables here that don't look like they've been touched, except maybe by the police," she explained. "At least I don't *think* they've been touched. I guess maybe it's possible that somebody stole a few small things. But nothing about this seems seem right to me. Why go to the trouble of killing somebody and leave so many valuables behind?"

"So what *was* the motive?" Amy asked.

"I wish I knew," London said, gesturing toward the jewels. "But the answer's not in this drawer."

"So where else should we look?"

"I'm going to try the bathroom," London said. "But you should get back to work."

Ignoring that suggestion, Amy followed London into the bathroom. Amy gasped at the sight of all the medicine bottles.

"She must have been in very poor health," Amy said.

London didn't doubt it. But she wondered whether all these medicines could possibly have been really helping her. Was it possible that they were making her much, much worse?

Suddenly she noticed something different about the containers. Like yesterday, they were arranged neatly in army-like rows. But yesterday, three containers had stood in a row in front of the others. Today there were only two of them there. The one in the middle was obviously missing.

She picked up the two bottles and looked at them closely.

"These are prednisone," she said.

"So?"

"It looks like the police took away the container between them. Judging from how the rest of the medicine was arranged, it was probably prednisone as well. The police must have thought it was important and took it in for analysis."

"What's it prescribed for?" Amy asked.

London read the label on one of the bottles.

"It says, 'Take as needed for stress, tiredness, anxiety, panic, depression, nervousness, lethargy, insomnia, poor appetite, or overeating.'"

Amy scoffed.

"Well, that pretty much covers everything, doesn't it?" she said.

"Way too much, it seems to me," London said. "There's something really wrong here. I guess the police thought so too."

"Who prescribed it for her?"

Reading from the bottle, London said, "Dr. Emory Bowen, a private physician in Port Mather, Long Island. That's where Mrs. Klimowski was from. It looks like most or maybe even all of the prescriptions were written by him."

London squinted at the bottle.

"Maybe we should ask Bryce what he thinks about it," she said. "He's surely had enough medical training to figure it out."

"I guess we could give him a call," Amy said.

Then London thought better of it.

"No, we'd better not," she said. "You and I will get into plenty of trouble if we get caught playing detective like this. It would be unfair to get Bryce into trouble as well."

Amy snapped her fingers.

"Hey, I've got it!" she said. "I know a pharmacist we can ask!"

"A pharmacist?"

"Sure. Sandor. You know … you remember …"

Her voice faded shyly.

Then London remembered the man sitting in the sidewalk café.

"The guy you went out to meet today," she said.

"Yeah. Like I said, we don't speak each other's languages very well. But he did manage to tell me what he did for a living. He's a pharmacist here in Gyor, with his own drugstore."

She took out her cell phone and added, "I've got his phone number. I could call him. Maybe he could at least tell us something about this medicine. What do you think?"

"Well, I guess there's no harm in giving him a call," London said with a shrug. "Helping us won't get *him* into any trouble, anyway."

Amy let out a squeal of delight.

"OK, I'll call him right now!" she said.

She snatched the medicine bottle out of London's hand and scampered out of the bathroom into the main room.

Picking up the remaining prednisone container, London stifled a groan of dismay. She now realized that Amy had been looking for any excuse she could think of to give her would-be boyfriend a call. And that was all this was, really—an excuse. Nothing was likely to come of it.

Well, I guess it's still up to me, then, she thought.

Looking at another container, she thought back to when Mrs. Klimowski had swallowed some pills with a glass of water at the Magyar Öröm. She'd done the same thing back in Budapest at the Duna Étterem restaurant. Was this the same medicine she'd taken those two times?

It seemed likely. Mrs. Klimowski been quite agitated on both occasions, and the prescription indicated its use for stress and anxiety, among all those other conditions. Might this particular medicine have been the cause of her death?

The police surely knew the answer to that question, even if they were keeping that answer to themselves. After all, the coroner had done a full autopsy, and he'd surely found what substances were in her system. But for some reason, the coroner and the police had decided that Mrs. Klimowski was murdered, not that she'd accidentally overdosed on some prescription medicine.

Why? London wondered.

Surely it was because they knew she'd died from some other cause.

London's thoughts were interrupted by the sound of Amy babbling over the phone in the next room, repeating certain words over and over.

"… Lots of prednisone … prednisone, I said … prednisone … We don't know what to … I said we don't … Could you repeat that for me? … What are you trying to say? … I don't understand …"

London shook her head in silent annoyance as she remembered something Amy had said when they'd run into each other in town.

"Sandor and I don't know each other at all, and I don't speak any Hungarian and he doesn't speak much English."

Obviously, the language gap between Amy and Sandor was pretty much insurmountable, at least over the phone.

She's just wasting her time, she thought.

But at least Amy was staying busy, giving London a moment to think things through. Despite all his secrecy, she believed Alezredes Borsos to be sure of at least one thing. Mrs. Klimowski had been murdered by someone who had been near her at the Magyar Öröm—in fact, someone on that list London had made of the people sitting at the table.

If so, when and how had the murderer struck?

She sighed with despair. She wished she'd been paying better attention at the time. She wished she'd been watching what was going

165

on that table. But it was too late now.

Then an idea hit her like a flash out of the blue.

Maybe it's not too late, she realized.

Maybe I can still find out what happened.

Maybe I can actually see …

Before she could think her idea through, Amy bustled back into the bathroom.

"Good news!" she said with breathless excitement, setting the bottle back on the counter. "I think Sandor can explain it all!"

Taken aback, London asked, "What?"

"Well, we had a hard time communicating over the phone, but he seemed to recognize the word 'prednisone.' It seems that the word is very similar in Hungarian. And he was worried about it. He said he could explain why in person."

"You know we're really restricted to the boat now," London reminded her. "You can't go sneaking off to meet him again."

Amy looked like a disappointed child. "I think he wanted to take me out for drinks and dinner," she whined.

London felt an urge to just say, *"Too bad. I guess it's not going to work out."*

After all, it seemed more and more obvious that Amy was more interested in having a rendezvous with Sandor than in actually solving the case. Then she remembered what the alezredes had actually said.

"Well, Borsos did tell me a little while ago that he didn't much care who comes aboard the *Nachtmusik.* He just doesn't want anybody to get off."

Amy's eyes widened with excitement.

"Do you mean the guards might let Sandor aboard?"

"I believe they would."

"Then we could have dinner here. The ship won't leave until at least late tonight. I'll call him back and invite him."

"Problem solved," London told her. "Meanwhile, I have something to take care of right now. You need to be out there helping our passengers get settled in for our voyage to the next port."

"That doesn't sound like much fun. What are you going to do?"

"This is not fun time," London snapped. "Passengers are still roaming the decks like agitated chickens." Realizing that she needed to remind Amy again about who was the boss, she added, "I need you to get serious about your job right now."

Amy crossed her arms and scowled.

"And just when I thought we were starting to get along. I should have known better."

London sighed as Amy charged huffily through the stateroom and out into the passageway.

She's back to River Troll mode again, she thought.

Before Amy left the room, she called back, "I'll do my job, but I *will* phone Sandor."

When the door closed behind Amy, London suddenly felt able to breathe a little easier. Now she could clear her head and remind herself what she'd been thinking a few moments ago when Amy had been on the phone.

Oh, yes, she remembered.

Maybe I can actually see *what happened to Mrs. Klimowski!*

She put the container of prednisone in her pocket. Then she dashed out of the stateroom and headed for her next destination.

CHAPTER TWENTY NINE

London rushed through the reception area and toward the lounge. The ship's library was tucked between the two, and she hurried to the door. With relief she saw that the person she hoped to see was there, sitting comfortably at a large table.

"London, what a nice surprise!" Emil said, looking up from a book with a German title. "I was getting a bit lonely here, with nothing except books to keep me company. Welcome to the least popular room on the *Nachtmusik*."

London had only glanced into the library before now. The walls were completely covered with shelves full of books of all kinds, popular paperbacks, tour guides, language dictionaries, with history and nonfiction sections. A selection of computer tablets surely must access an even wider range of e-books. A computer with a large screen and a cluster of folding chairs indicated that this could serve as a little lecture room from time to time.

Emil was sitting near a section of books that were all hardbacks, some of them looking very old. He showed her the one he was reading.

"As you can see," he said, "I am catching up on my Austrian history in preparation for our arrival in Vienna."

Then he added with a chuckle, "That is, if we ever get to Vienna. What are the chances, do you think? The police are keeping us here until they have solved Mrs. Klimowski's murder, is that correct?"

"Yes, that's right," London said, sitting next to him at the table. "But I don't know if they're making any progress."

"Then it appears that our entire tour could be in danger of cancellation."

"That's why I'm here."

Emil looked surprised, and London went on to explain.

"You've been taking pictures, haven't you? I mean of the tour groups and the places we visited."

Emil nodded.

"And you took some of our group at the restaurant in Budapest, and also here in Gyor, right?"

"Yes, I did," Emil said. "Why do you ask?"

"I wondered if I could have a look at them."

Emil gave her a strange, skeptical look.

"May I ask why?" he said.

London swallowed hard. How much of what she was doing did she want to explain to Emil? She'd avoided calling Bryce about Mrs. Klimowski's medications for fear of getting him mixed up in her illicit investigation. She didn't want to get Emil into trouble either.

"I'm just curious," she said.

Emil frowned. His darkening expression reminded London of a couple of other moments when he'd seemed haughty, condescending, or prickly.

"You are not telling me everything, are you?" Emil said.

London shrugged, trying to decide what to say.

Emil leaned toward her.

"I could not help but notice something a while ago," he said. "When the captain called several passengers to come to his quarters to be interviewed by the police, the people he called had all been with Mrs. Klimowski at both restaurants. One of those people was me."

His frown sharpened.

"Should I be concerned, London?"

London felt herself stiffen uneasily. True, Emil had been right there at both of those restaurants. But so had Mr. and Mrs. Shick, Honey and Gus Jarrett, Cyrus Bannister—and of course London herself.

Did she actually suspect Emil?

She didn't want to suspect anybody, particularly not a man she liked and even felt somewhat attracted to.

But how can I be sure?

She decided she had to be at least partially truthful.

"The alezredes won't tell me a lot," she said. "He won't even say the exact cause of Mrs. Klimowski's death. But he *does* seem to suspect our group. After all, we were close to Mrs. Klimowski shortly before she died. We had an opportunity to … well, poison her, maybe."

"That does make sense," Emil said with a tilt of his head.

"Actually, I seem to be at the top of Borsos's suspect list. After all, not only was I at the restaurant, but I found her body. But I'm not the killer, please believe me."

Emil's lips curled in a slight hint of a smirk.

"I should certainly hope not," he said.

169

Emil leaned back in his chair and steepled his fingers together.

"I take it you're conducting your own little investigation," he said. "One that the alezredes does not exactly approve of."

That's putting it mildly, London thought.

Emil continued, "And of course, you want to see exactly what happened when our group was all together—not just at the Magyar Öröm here in Gyor, but at the Duna Étterem back in Budapest. And I just happen to have a visual record of sorts."

"That's right," London said.

Emil gazed at her intently for a moment. London couldn't read his expression.

"Well," he finally said, "I suppose it is only reasonable for me to help you. After all, you are very anxious to clear yourself of suspicion. And I am anxious to clear myself as well. So let us get to work, shall we? I have moved the images onto the computer, so we can see them on the larger screen."

London breathed a little easier as Emil moved the computer screen so they could both view it.

He brought up a picture that showed the spacious, candlelit Duna Étterem with its low arching ceilings. Of all the people who had gone there to eat, that ones who most concerned London were sitting near the end of the table in close proximity to Mrs. Klimowski—the Jarretts, the Shicks, Cyrus Bannister, Emil, and herself.

This first picture captured a rather tense moment before the group had ordered.

Emil pointed at the picture and said, "Here we see Mrs. Klimowski sitting with that disagreeable little dog of hers in her handbag. And standing right next to her is the waiter—I can't remember his name."

"It was János," London said.

"That is right, János. He told her no dogs were allowed in the restaurant. She was stubborn about it. She stood her ground, so to speak."

London remembered the moment well.

"Wherever I go, he goes too," Mrs. Klimowski had said. *"If he leaves, I leave."*

It had seemed like a standoff for a few long seconds.

Emil brought up another picture that included a man with a push-broom mustache and thick wavy hair.

"That was when this fellow came along," Emil said.

"His name was Vilmos Kallay," London said. *"Professor* Vilmos Kallay. A nice man."

"Yes, I chatted with him briefly," Emil said. "He talked János into letting Mrs. Klimowski's dog stay with us at the table. He also recommended that we eat at the Magyar Öröm when we got here in Gyor."

Emil shrugged and added, "Well, there is probably not much else to see in these Budapest pictures. I do not know much about toxicology, but I find it hard to imagine Mrs. Klimowski was poisoned some twenty-four hours before she died. Even if such a thing were possible, surely a murderer would have preferred a faster-acting means of killing her."

"I agree," London said. "And even though Mrs. Klimowski exchanged some sharp words with János the waiter, he had no serious motive to kill her, or at least none that we know of. Especially if she wound up dying in another city."

"Well, then, let us skip to the pictures I took in Gyor yesterday," Emil said. "They are surely more pertinent."

He brought up a photo of the same group clustered together in the sunny sidewalk patio of the Magyar Öröm restaurant. London took note of exactly where the people had been seated at that table. She herself had been sitting directly to Mrs. Klimowski's left. She felt a slight chill when she noticed who was sitting on her right.

Cyrus Bannister.

While Mrs. Klimowski apparently hadn't inspired warm feelings from anybody aboard the *Nachtmusik*, the mysterious Cyrus Bannister seemed to have taken a special dislike to her almost from the moment they met.

"Show me another picture," London said to Emil.

The next photo brought back a vivid memory. It showed the strolling violinist playing his instrument in the street just beyond the low patio wall. She remembered how bitterly Mrs. Klimowski had complained about his dissonant music.

She pointed to Cyrus Bannister.

"He and Mrs. Klimowski had a bit of a tiff about that musician," she said.

"A bit of a tiff? Is that a motive for murder?"

"I suppose not," London said with a sigh. "Show me the next picture."

171

The next photo showed the group again. It caught the moment right after Mrs. Klimowski's tiff with Cyrus Bannister, when she took some pills with a glass of water. But something unexpected captured London's attention.

London felt a surge of excitement.

She stared again at the image on the screen.

That's it! That's what I've been trying to remember.

CHAPTER THIRTY

The object that London was staring at on the screen was small, flat, and brightly colored. Because it was cupped in Mrs. Klimowski's hand, only part of it was visible. But that part gleamed with an intricate design.

That's why I felt like I was missing something, she realized.

Apparently noticing London's interest, Emil peered at her over his black-rimmed glasses.

"Does something catch your attention?" he asked.

"Yes, yes, I think so," London said with excitement.

She pointed to the image on the screen.

"That's the pillbox she had at the restaurant," London said. "But it's definitely not the pillbox I saw in her purse after she was killed. The one in her purse was a cheap-looking thing made out of plastic."

"Interesting," Emil said. "I do not believe I noticed her pillbox. Of course, I was doing the best I could to avoid her when we were dining."

"I glimpsed it several times without thinking anything about it," London said. She pointed to the ruby pendant hanging conspicuously from Mrs. Klimowski's neck and added, "I was a lot more worried about this pendant and all the rest of her jewelry. She seemed determined to flaunt it, and I was afraid it would attract thieves."

"And you say she had a different one in her purse? It is not possible that she owned more than one pillbox?"

"Of course. But I didn't see any at all in her room. Just medications in their containers."

Emil peered at her more closely. "In her room?" he asked.

London felt herself blush.

"Well, it was my responsibility to check her room. To see if anything else was obviously missing. I wasn't thinking about pillboxes at the time, but I am certain that nothing like this was there."

"We must take a closer look," Emil said.

He zoomed into the image. The edge of the box appeared to be decorated with a floral pattern worked in gold. The top looked like it might be an enameled portrait, but most of that was hidden from view.

"That is no ordinary pillbox," Emil said.

"What is it, then?" London asked.

"I would rather not speculate just yet," he said.

London felt a twinge of impatience.

Why not? she wondered.

She had the feeling they were on the verge of solving some remarkable problem. She didn't understand why Emil couldn't be more upfront about it.

"I believe we have a bit of research to do," Emil said. "Can you access the *Nachtmusik*'s manifest? I would like to know a little more about Mrs. Klimowski."

Emil moved aside and London scooted her chair in front of the computer.

"I remember that she had a long name," London remarked.

She quickly brought up the passenger list. Sure enough, Mrs. Klimowski's name really stood out from the others. London spoke it aloud.

"Lillis Petrovna Ostrovsky Klimowski," she said. "That's a real mouthful, isn't it? It sounds like something a lady like her might make up to impress people. Do you suppose it's even real?"

Emil let out a slight gasp.

"It might very well be real," he said. "If so ..."

His voice faded.

"If so, what?" London asked.

"'Petrovna' is a patronymic," Emil said, pointing to the screen. "That means it identifies her father. In other words, the 'ovna' means that she is the daughter of Peter. Ostrovsky is her family name, and if I am right ..."

To London's frustration, his voice faded again.

"Perhaps I can find some genealogical information about Mrs. Klimowski," he said.

Emil's fingers rattled over the keyboard.

Soon he found the information he was looking for.

"Yes, it is just as I suspected," he said. "Lillis Petrovna Ostrovsky was born in New York City in 1930. She married Boris Klimowski, a millionaire industrialist, in 1954. But Klimowski died two years later. My guess is she inherited quite a fortune from him, which would explain how she came by her expensive furs and jewelry."

He peered closely at the screen, as if he didn't quite believe his eyes.

"But here is what becomes really interesting," he said. "Her father was none other than Baron Peter Vasílevich Kirsánov."

London's brow crinkled.

"Should I find that name familiar?" she asked.

"Probably not," Emil said. "But to a, uh, toughcore historian like me ..."

London smiled.

"I think the idiom you're looking for is 'hardcore,'" she said.

"Yes, hardcore historian. As such, it means a great deal to me. You see, Baron Peter Kirsánov was a hereditary Russian aristocrat, and a personal favorite of Tsar Nicholas II."

London's interest quickened.

"The last Emperor of the Russian Empire," she said.

"That is right. Of course, Tsar Nicholas and his family were assassinated during the Russian Revolution of 1917. But Baron Kirsánov escaped to America. He was then still a bachelor, and penniless, because the Bolsheviks had confiscated his fortune. He settled in New York and got married there. And it appears ..."

London's eyes widened.

"That he had a daughter," she said, finishing Emil's thought. "Lillis Kirsánov."

"Correct," Emil said.

London could hear Mrs. Klimowski's words echoing through her mind.

"Mine has been a tragic life."

Now London knew why she kept bringing up that theme. She'd been born into poverty, the daughter of an exiled Russian nobleman, and although she'd married into money, her husband had died after only two years of marriage, leaving her a bitter, unhappy, and lonely woman.

And perhaps, London thought, this explained why she'd found no sentimental mementoes or pictures among Mrs. Klimowski's belongings.

She had tried to bury her past under furs and jewelry.

"But what does any of this have to do with this box?" London asked.

Emil scratched his chin.

"I do not believe it was originally made as a pillbox. I believe it to be an antique snuffbox. And I have a, well, somewhat scholarly obsession with antique snuffboxes. I have collected quite a few myself. And I have studied their history, and I pay close attention to the market for them."

"Are they valuable?"

"Yes, old custom-made snuffboxes can rather valuable. Quite a few of them are worth, oh, at least five hundred dollars, sometimes even a few thousand."

London squinted skeptically.

"I'm no expert on jewelry," she said. "But my guess is that the pendant she wore is alone worth more than that. But the thief didn't take it."

"I believe this is no ordinary antique," Emil said, tracing the design on the edge of the box with his fingers. "I'm familiar with that motif. It is seen on snuffboxes that were made by Ilyich Kuragin during the late nineteenth century."

London's mouth fell slightly open.

"You mean of the House of Kuragin?" London said.

"That's right. The firm's founder, actually. This might be the craftsmanship of Ilyich himself."

London knew the name well. The House of Kuragin was world famous for its extremely valuable decorative objects, especially its starfish. Not many people could afford such precious things.

Emil leaned back in his chair.

"According to antique lore, Tsar Nicholas II once gave Baron Kirsánov a special gift—a Kuragin snuffbox with a portrait of his father, Tsar Alexander III, on its lid. The box is the stuff of legend among antiques dealers—especially because it was believed to have vanished along with the rest of Baron Kirsánov's fortune. But now it appears to have remained in his daughter's possession."

London exhaled sharply.

"If so," she said, "this snuffbox must be worth …"

"Oh, hundreds of thousands of dollars," London said. "Almost priceless."

Enough to kill for, maybe, London thought.

She fell speechless for a moment.

"Show us the whole group again," London said to Emil, pointing to the computer screen.

Emil zoomed away from the box to show the diners sitting around the table. London began to study their faces carefully.

Emil said, "It is interesting that Mrs. Klimowski made casual use of such an antique—as a pillbox. She ought to have taken much better care of it. It is entirely possible that she had no idea of its true value."

"But somebody *did* know its value," London said. "Somebody drugged her and took that box from her yesterday afternoon."

She added with determination. "And I think I know how to find out who that somebody was."

CHAPTER THIRTY ONE

London had to fight down a surge of doubt about what she had decided to do. She had had enlisted Emil and Elsie to help her move some tables and chairs in the Amadeus Lounge, but as she viewed the arrangement taking shape, she asked herself ...

Do you really think you're a real detective?

Her failure to solve the mystery of the baklava on her own still nagged at her. But it was too late to back out.

"Are you going to tell me what you're up to?" Elsie asked.

"Yes, I would like to know that myself," Emil said.

"Not yet," London said as she and Elsie pushed one table against another.

She had good reasons not to share her plan. For one thing, it was hardly even a plan just yet, only the bare bones hint of one. She suspected there were some surprises in store for her, and she was going to have to think quickly on her feet.

Be ready to improvise, she told herself.

Soon she and her two helpers had the tables and chairs exactly where she wanted them, in a corner of the lounge apart from other customers. They had even wheeled a couple of potted plants into position to separate their setting from the larger area.

"When are the others supposed to arrive?" Elsie asked. She had appointed one of her junior bartenders to take care of regular customers so she could stay with London.

London looked at her watch and said, "In ten minutes."

After she and Emil had identified the snuffbox in the library, London sent texts to a certain group of people. Along with Emil, they were the ones most likely to have had opportunities to both poison Mrs. Klimowski and take her snuffbox. She'd asked them to come to the Amadeus Lounge at a precise, designated time.

And that time was fast approaching.

For the moment, she didn't want any of those people to know why she wanted to see them—although from Emil's rather dark expression, it seemed likely that he'd guessed what she was up to.

He clearly wasn't pleased.

She couldn't blame him. She didn't want to think that the historian had been helpful only as a ruse, but she couldn't discount that possibility. It seemed to her a rather striking coincidence that he just happened to be an aficionado of snuffboxes. Had he only pretended to be surprised that Mrs. Klimowski used an incredibly valuable snuffbox to contain her pills?

One way or the other, she expected to soon find out.

Now that they were finished with the furniture, she was ready for her guests to arrive.

She was glad to see the first smiling face. It was Bryce Yeaton.

"Am I on time?" he asked.

London returned his smile. She couldn't really consider him to be a suspect, but as a chef and a medic he had to be included among those under consideration.

"Actually, you're a few minutes early, but that's OK," London said. "I was hoping you could help me with a medical question."

She reached into her pocket for the medicine vial she'd taken from Mrs. Klimowski's bathroom. But before she could ask Bryce anything about it, she heard a pair of voices approaching from the reception area. She sighed as she recognized one of those voices.

Amy Blassingame swept into the lounge with a man on her arm—the same fellow London had seen her with on two earlier occasions. Seeing who was already present, Amy smiled broadly.

"Hi, everybody! I want to introduce you to Sandor Füst. I met him yesterday, and ..."

Amy leaned toward Elsie and spoke in a semi-confidential whisper. "Isn't he *just* ... ?"

Sandor looked more than a little flustered and confused.

"I thought Sandor could help solve the case," Amy said.

"The case?" Bryce asked.

London's frustration grew. Of course Bryce had no idea what Amy was talking about. And this was hardly the way she wanted him to find out.

"You know, the murder case—who killed Mrs. Klimowski," Amy told him. "Sandor's a pharmacist. He's got special expertise that I'm sure will crack the mystery wide open."

Looking rather embarrassed, Sandor spoke to Amy in clumsy English.

179

"I am, eh, not sure I should be involved. It is really none of my—"

"Nonsense," Amy interrupted. "You're exactly who we need right now."

Remembering what Amy had said in Mrs. Klimowski's stateroom, she started to wonder.

Maybe he could be helpful after all.

Speaking to him in Hungarian, she said, "Amy says you are a pharmacist."

He looked downward shyly.

"Well, I prefer to think of myself as painter. But being a pharmacist is what I do during the day. You might say that I make a *living* as a druggist, but I really *live* for—"

"I'm London Rose," she gently interrupted him in Hungarian. She didn't have time to hear him chatter on and on about his hobby right now.

He said with a nod, "Amy told me about you—or tried to. My English is not so good and her Hungarian is, well …"

London searched her mind for the right word in Hungarian.

"Nonexistent?" she said.

"Yes, I'm afraid so," Sandor said.

Looking annoyed now, Amy murmured to London, "I think it's rude of you to talk in Hungarian like this. I can't understand a word you're saying."

That might just be a good thing, London thought.

At least it might keep Amy from interfering.

Sandor continued, "On the phone Amy told me something worrisome—I couldn't follow her words over the phone exactly. Something about a medication we Hungarians call *prednizolon.*"

She held up the medicine vial for him to see.

"I think this is what you mean. In English it's prednisone."

Bryce stepped toward them at the sound of the medicine's name.

"May I see that bottle?" he asked.

London handed it to Bryce, who read the label.

"Good God!" he exclaimed. "This prescription is outrageous!"

"What's the matter with it?" London asked.

Bryce looked at the bottle as if he couldn't believe his eyes.

"Well, there's nothing wrong with prednisone as a drug, per se," he said. "I prescribe it myself from time to time. It's useful for treating rheumatism and allergies, and also more serious conditions such as

180

leukemia. But these instructions …"

He read the prescription text aloud.

"'Take as needed for stress, tiredness, anxiety, panic, depression, nervousness, lethargy, insomnia, poor appetite, or overeating.'"

Bryce shuddered.

"Why, that's simply insane," he said. "The poor woman must have been taking the stuff almost constantly, for all the wrong reasons. If she's been doing this for long, I'm sure that her adrenal glands must have atrophied and stopped functioning altogether. I'm even a bit surprised she didn't die sooner."

London's mouth dropped open. She knew she ought to have been expecting surprises.

But this …

It was the sort of surprise she couldn't have anticipated.

She said to Bryce, "Are you saying she was murdered by her doctor back on Long Island?"

"Oh, surely not that," Bryce said with a scoff. "There are certainly more efficient ways to kill someone. But he's definitely a dangerous quack who was taking advantage of a rich and credulous woman. He ought to have his license taken away. In fact, he ought to be in jail, as far as I'm concerned. I'll get in touch with the authorities myself."

"Then … then … maybe she wasn't murdered at all," London said.

"Probably not," Bryce said. "She was almost certain to die sooner rather than later. Unfortunately, she happened to die during this voyage."

London felt stymied. Then she spoke to Bryce again.

"So you're *sure* she wasn't poisoned?"

Bryce shrugged.

"I'm probably not the right person to ask," Bryce said, nodding toward Sandor. "Surely the pharmacist can give you a better answer. Unfortunately, I don't speak any Hungarian."

Maybe Sandor can tell me, she thought.

If only I can ask the right questions.

She began to speak to Sandor in the best Hungarian she could muster.

"You understand the effects of prednisone, don't you?"

"Oh, yes."

"Then suppose a thief who knew nothing of her medications intended to rob her of something—a piece of jewelry perhaps. Maybe

181

he used something to sedate her—what in English we call a 'knockout drug.' He would have had no intention of killing her. Her death might well have been an awful accident."

"It makes sense," Sandor said, looking quite interested now.

"How soon before her death might she have been drugged?"

"It's impossible to say," Sandor said. "The interaction between the knockout drug and the *prednizolon* would have been utterly unpredictable. The drug might have been administered a few minutes before her death—or it might have been hours. I don't think there is any way to know."

London's spirits sank. The whole mystery seemed to have suddenly gotten much larger, covering a greater period of time.

"What kind of drug might a thief have used to knock her out?" London asked Sandor.

"Oh, something very common, I imagine," Sandor said.

At this point, London knew she was only putting together some pieces of the puzzle that the official autopsy had surely revealed, but which Alezredes Borsos had refused to tell her.

One, Mrs. Klimowski was probably taking too much of a drug called prednisone.

Two, there was a second drug in her system—possibly a knockout drug.

Three, intended or not, the interaction was fatal.

Then Sandor added, "I've heard of thieves using certain types of benzodiazepine for that purpose."

London was startled. The possible knockout drug's name in Hungarian was almost identical to a word she had heard just recently.

And she remembered all too well who had said it, and to whom.

Bryce had said it while offering a pill to Agnes Shick.

"Clinically speaking, it's a variety of benzodiazepine."

London turned to look at Bryce. So far, he'd seemed unable to understand the conversation. But did London note a telltale change in his expression since Sandor had said that that word—benzodiazepine?

No, it can't be, she thought.

But she couldn't help but shudder at the possibility.

She remembered the busy scene this morning in the Habsburg Restaurant, when both she and Bryce had been dashing around taking care of breakfast diners. Mrs. Klimowski had been there for breakfast. Bryce could have slipped her the drug then. Since it hadn't had an immediate effect, he could have left the boat and followed her until …

She stood there staring at him, trying to decide whether to confront him about this grim hypothesis.

But before she could make up her mind, the other people she'd been expecting started to arrive.

Walter and Agnes Shick were the first to come into the lounge. London felt an unexpected pang of relief to see that Agnes was quite alive and even seemed to be feeling better, even after the dose of benzodiazepine Bryce had given her.

Then Honey and Gus Jarrett arrived, followed by Cyrus Bannister.

She welcomed them, then asked them to sit in specific seats where the tables had been moved together.

"Would you mind telling us what this is all about?" Cyrus asked crossly.

London hesitated.

She had no idea how any of them might react if she told them the truth.

But at that moment, a deep, Hungarian-accented voice boomed from the entrance.

"I believe the lady is about to accuse one of you of murder."

CHAPTER THIRTY TWO

London spun around and saw Alezredes Borsos himself standing in the doorway, his arms crossed and with a smirk on his lips. Two of his officers were with him. They all appeared to be alert and ready for action.

"You look surprised to see me, London Rose," Borsos said. "Did you imagine I haven't been following your movements ever since you and I came on board? My men have been watching all the security monitors."

He walked toward her with a jaunty gait.

"Yes," he continued, "I know that you and this other lady here went into the victim's stateroom. I could have taken you into custody right then and there, but I thought I would give you 'more leash,' I believe is the English expression. I was curious as to what you might do next. I thought you might give yourself away. And now I find you right here, surrounded by the very people you listed for me earlier—the people who had been sitting with the murder victim at the Magyar Öröm, along with a few others."

Don't let him intimidate you, London told herself.

She crossed her arms and glared back at him.

"I've found out something that you and your men didn't find," she said.

"And what is that?"

"The victim *was* robbed," she replied.

"Of what?" Borsos asked, looking startled.

London had to stop herself from laughing and blurting out the truth about the snuffbox. She hoped that that bit of information might yet turn out to be a winning card.

Instead she said, "Now you know what it's like when people keep secrets from you, eh, Alezredes Borsos?"

Borsos's eyebrows narrowed.

"I'm warning you ..." he began.

"Yes, well, anyway—I suppose you have to cross *me* off your suspect list. After all, why would I be rounding up suspects if I'm actually the killer?"

The alezredes wagged his finger at her with a low chuckle.

"You are clever, London Rose," he said. "I shall not underestimate you. But as I like to say ..."

"Yes, I know," London interrupted, echoing his words. "*Hamarosan megtudjuk*—we'll soon see."

"That is right," Borsos said. "For all I really know, what you are doing now is really just a charade to help conceal your own guilt."

Now London couldn't help but laugh.

"Oh, come on, sir," she said. "Surely you don't really believe that."

"*Hamarosan megtudjuk,*" Borsos repeated with a grin.

Meanwhile, London could see that the people seated at the table were looking quite alarmed, and some of them appeared to be angry. Even Emil appeared to be annoyed with her.

"So we're here because we're murder suspects?" Gus asked London.

"And you expect to find the killer right now?" Honey said.

"This is outrageous," Cyrus Bannister said, rising from his chair. "I refuse to take any part in this travesty."

"Stay seated, Mr. Bannister," Borsos said. "I for one would like to see how this plays out. London Rose is suggesting, and I agree, that Mrs. Klimowski might have been poisoned by someone who was at the Magyar Öröm yesterday—someone who is here with us right now."

Possibly, London thought.

Although after finding out about the unpredictable timing of the knockout drug, now she couldn't be sure. Nevertheless, this was the only tactic she had going, and she needed to see it through.

"I'm actually quite intrigued," Borsos continued. "Miss London Rose has set up a scene worthy of, eh, Miss Marple, I think."

London bristled at hearing that name again.

Nobody had better mention Nancy Drew, she thought.

But she realized that Borsos's presence had really raised the stakes for her. What if she couldn't get the killer to reveal himself or herself? Where would that leave her? Surely Borsos could arrest her for, say, obstructing his investigation. She sensed that she needed help from someone else.

But who could help me now? she wondered.

Then she reminded herself—there *was* someone who might well know the identity of the killer, even if he hadn't yet said so.

She tugged Elsie aside and handed her the key card to her room.

She whispered, "Go down to my quarters and fetch Sir Reginald."

"Why?"

"Just do it, please."

Looking a bit surprised, Elsie nodded and left the lounge.

London walked around the table and spoke to the people already seated there.

"As you've probably noticed, you're sitting in the same positions where you were sitting at Magyar Öröm yesterday."

Cyrus Bannister scoffed noisily.

"All of us except Mrs. Klimowski," he said. "Apparently she couldn't make it. Too bad."

Patting the empty chair right next to his, he added, "I see you saved her place, though."

"That's right," London said.

Then, looking at Amy, she said, "Could you be Mrs. Klimowski for us, please?"

Looking distinctly uneasy and maybe a little frightened, Amy sat in the empty chair.

London took a look around the lounge. In addition to Borsos and his team, three people were still standing—Sandor, Bryce, and herself. She saw that Borsos had taken out his handcuffs and was fingering them eagerly, as if he expected to make an arrest at any moment.

I hope I don't disappoint him, she thought.

She decided to take care of the most distasteful part of her questioning right away and get it done with. Walter and Agnes Shick were sitting farthest away from where Mrs. Klimowski would have been. Even so, London knew that it wasn't entirely impossible for one of them to have found some way to slip Mrs. Klimowski a dose of something.

As London approached the couple, she saw that Borsos stepped a few steps toward them as well, his handcuffs very much at the ready.

Something was still troubling London about the couple—the way Agnes had called Walter "Brian" back in their stateroom. It had to have been more than a casual slip of the tongue. Was it possible that these two kindly, elderly people weren't who or what they seemed to be?

London searched for the words to ask them about it delicately.

In a gentle voice, she said, "Mr. and Mrs. Shick, I have to ask …"

Walter Shick raised his hand to stop her from saying more.

"Yes, yes, I know," he said, almost in a whisper. "You are concerned about what Agnes said a while ago. Please don't speak about it in front of these others. Let me explain in my own way."

He took a small notepad out of his pocket and jotted something down on it, concealing whatever he was writing with his cupped left hand. Then he folded the paper and handed it to London. She unfolded it and read it silently.

Agnes and I have been in a witness protection program for 30 years now. Sometimes we get confused and call each other by our original given names. I can't explain further. But I must trust you to believe me, and not to tell this to another living soul. Our lives might still be in danger.

London felt a chill as she read those words. She remembered what Agnes had told Bryce when he'd asked her what might have triggered her panic attack.

"It's all these police all over the place all the time ..."

Of course, London realized.

Whatever had been the reason for the couple going into witness protection, it was no wonder that a murder and the presence of the police were enough to trigger terrifying memories.

As she folded the paper, she heard the alezredes's handcuffs rattle in his hand. She looked at him sternly and shook her head no. Feigning a casual composure, Borsos stepped back and fingered the cuffs as if he was only using them as a stress toy.

London slipped the note into her pocket and nodded at Walter reassuringly. He looked back at her with an expression of deep gratitude.

Then London stepped toward Emil, who was seated on the opposite side of the table from the Shicks. For a moment, words failed her.

Then she said, "Emil, I'm afraid I have to ask ..."

Emil nodded at her with a slight smirk on his lips.

"Yes, of course," he said. "You remember when I complained about Mrs. Klimowski. 'High maintenance' was the phrase we agreed upon, I believe. Well, it is pretty scant as motives for murder go. And I don't believe I have the manners of a common thief. But I would be rather disappointed in your intellectual prowess if you did not include me among your roster of suspects."

London felt truly taken aback by his vaguely cynical tone.

Borsos had moved closer to Emil. Now he shuffled indecisively, the handcuffs rattling in his hand.

Emil continued, "I did not kill her. But I do not expect you to take my word for it. By all means, proceed with your inquiry. 'Murder will out,' I believe is the English expression, am I correct?"

London nodded at him silently.

Then she shook her head at Borsos—not so much to suggest that Emil was innocent, which she felt surprisingly unsure of, but to indicate that his guilt was anything but certain.

"I guess we're next," Gus said with grunt of annoyance as London stepped toward him and Honey.

Borsos also stepped closer to the couple, the handcuffs swinging freely in his hand.

Honey sighed. "Oh, London, surely you don't believe ..."

London didn't reply.

I'm not sure what to believe, she thought to herself.

But she didn't know what to ask the couple at the moment.

Again she heard the rattle of Borsos's handcuffs.

And again, she shook her head slightly. Looking disappointed, the alezredes resumed his would-be casual air.

Finally she came to Cyrus Bannister, who was sitting next to Amy, just as he had been sitting next to Mrs. Klimowski at the restaurant.

Borsos again followed London's lead, dangling the handcuffs just behind Bannister.

"Don't even start," Bannister said in a sullen voice. "I know what you're going to say. The woman and I argued before she went away. Can I help it if she had a hopelessly backward taste in music? She didn't appreciate the wonderful gift of folk culture that sidewalk violinist had to offer. And she actually wanted me to pay him not to play. And the way she treated that dog! The nerve of that woman! It still irritates me to think about it. And to be perfectly honest, I can't say I miss her."

London was irritated by his tone of voice.

But that was all she felt, just irritated.

Her gut told her that this was a quarrelsome man, but probably not a murderer.

But how can I know?

When she heard Borsos's cuffs rattling again, she shook her head again. And again Borsos fingered the cuffs awkwardly.

London's spirits sank as she realized she'd addressed everybody at the table.

But what did I learn? she wondered.

She closed her eyes for a moment, then remembered something her dad used to tell her when they'd been playing chess.

"Look at the whole board. But look at more than that. Look at everything else."

It had seemed like puzzling advice, and she'd never quite known how it applied to chess.

But now she realized …

It's exactly what I need to do right now.

Her brain clicked away as she replayed all the events that had led to this moment, starting from when she'd first arrived at the *Nachtmusik* and Elsie had greeted her. It all came back to her like a video on fast-forward.

The whole board.

More than the board.

More than just the people who were at this table.

I mustn't leave anything out.

Then something in her mind popped into place.

She spoke to Sandor Füst in Hungarian, pointing to a spot on the floor.

"I wonder if you could help us, please, Mr. Füst. A sidewalk violinist was standing right over there. Could you take his place, please?"

Looking perplexed all over again, Sandor moved to that position.

And now something about his face struck him that hadn't before—something about his nose.

Everything seemed to be coming together now.

Without pausing to think things through, she turned toward Amy.

Holding out her hand, she said, "I believe you have something quite interesting with you right now—a pretty little box."

Amy looked back at her with a curious expression.

"Do you mean—this?" she asked.

She reached into her handbag and held out a small box decorated with floral gold patterns, with the enameled portrait of a nobleman on the top.

There it is, London thought.

And now I know the truth.

CHAPTER THIRTY THREE

With a guileless expression, Amy sat at the table holding the stolen snuffbox toward London.

London heard Borsos's handcuffs rattle once again. And again, London turned to him with shake of her head.

"No, Amy's not the killer," she said. "She's not a thief, either. In fact, Amy is perfectly innocent. She has no idea what this is all about."

Borsos stammered as he handled the handcuffs awkwardly.

"But—but—she has—right in her hand—"

London was about to point out the real culprit when she heard a growling sound behind her. She turned and saw that Elsie had returned to the lounge with Sir Reginald in her arms. And sure enough, Sir Reginald was confirming her own conclusions, growling at the man who called himself Sandor Füst.

The man looked at the dog with mock disappointment. When he spoke, it was no longer in Hungarian but in English, with a suave, articulate, upper-class British accent.

"*Et tu,* my canine friend? It appears that I've been identified."

London was amazed. He suddenly seemed like an entirely different person now. Merely by changing his posture, voice, and facial expression, he'd transformed himself unrecognizably, the same way she now knew he had into Professor Kallay and the sidewalk violinist. Also, his calmness and self-confidence seemed utterly uncanny to London—and utterly out of place.

But most of all, he had assumed a daunting and imposing presence. Even Borsos looked puzzled and intimidated and made no motion with his handcuffs.

"You figured it out, then?" the man said to London.

She nodded. Indeed she had. During her mental replay, she'd remembered Professor Kallay back in Budapest, with his push-broom mustache and thick wavy hair. Then she'd pictured the violinist in his peasant garb with his wide, handlebar mustache. Finally she'd remembered something that had been said just a few moments before …

191

"What gave me away?" the man asked. "Nothing about my face, I hope."

"Only barely," London said. "It wouldn't have been enough. I noticed something more important."

"Well, perhaps you'll tell me someday," he said with a rakish grin. "This is the end of the road, as they say. But before I'm arrested, I'd like to say for the record that I did *not* intend to kill the unfortunate lady. Homicide is not my style in the least. It was a regrettable accident. I would never harm a lady for a mere piece of jewelry. All I wanted was the snuffbox."

London nodded in agreement.

"So," she said, "when you removed the unconscious woman's pendant and put it into her purse, you were making a sort of statement."

The man tilted his head with appreciation.

"Quite right. I was showing my contempt for petty ostentation. I was hoping somebody would notice that touch. You are quite an exceptional person, London Rose. But I am no ordinary thief, if I may say so myself."

No ordinary thief, indeed, London thought.

He was obviously a master of disguise—and a master of many other sorts of cunning, London felt sure.

Looking rather dazed, Borsos stepped toward him with his handcuffs. The man fairly glided out of his grasp and walked over to Amy. Borsos seemed too perplexed to know exactly what to do.

"Thank you for looking after this for me, Amy," the man said, taking the box out of her hand. "I do apologize for my duplicity earlier today. But when I saw the policemen approaching you at the café, I was afraid I might get searched myself. So I offered it to you as a gift to get it off my hands. I came aboard just now with no intention other than to retrieve it—a bit too confidently, it seems."

Borsos looked utterly aghast as the man slipped the box into his pocket.

"How dare you, sir!" Borsos said.

The man chuckled lightheartedly.

"Now, now, sir. I believe you're overreacting. We both know I'm not going to get out of here with my intended quarry. You're going to arrest me, of course. And I do intend to come along quietly."

Putting his hands behind his back, he added, "You've been itching to use those handcuffs for the last few minutes. Now is your opportunity."

Borsos glared at him uneasily, then stepped behind him. London heard the rattling of handcuffs as Borsos snapped them open. The man looked over his shoulder at Borsos and spoke in a helpful-sounding voice.

"You'd best make them tight."

Then the master thief stepped away from the alezredes and added, "I'm told that I can be rather—well, slippery, shall we say."

Borsos looked down at his own hands with a horrified expression. Sure enough, it was *he* who was suddenly wearing the handcuffs. London's mind boggled at how the man called Sandor had achieved such a swift, deft sleight-of-hand.

Borsos roared like a trapped animal and lunged at the thief. The man eluded the alezredes's manacled grip with incredible agility, leaping up onto the tables where the other astonished onlookers were still seated. He dashed across the tabletops and took a huge leap toward the entrance to the lounge.

The two other police officers ran toward him and tried to tackle him. But the man made another uncanny maneuver, slipping away from them. The two officers' heads cracked together instead.

As the man disappeared from the lounge, Sir Reginald leaped out of Elsie's arms and charged after him.

"Oh no," London cried, running after the dog who was following the fleeing man.

They all raced through the reception area to the top of the gangway.

With Sir Reginald snapping at his heels, the thief charged straight toward the two officers now guarding the far end of the gangway. London had no doubt he would make his way past them too.

Just then, the little dog managed to get his teeth into the man's pants leg, throwing him off balance. The thief kicked out sharply as he fell, sending poor Sir Reginald flying into the water.

Meanwhile, the two police officers took advantage of the man's momentary awkwardness and piled onto him before he could get back on his feet. London heard Borsos's voice booming at his men from the top of the gangway in Hungarian.

"Arrest that man!"

As the officers both sat on their captive, holding him down, London dashed past them and on down the gangway.

She looked into the water but could see no sign of the dog.

She reached the shore and called out over the water, "Sir Reginald, where are you?"

The little animal was nowhere in sight.

CHAPTER THIRTY FOUR

London plunged into the water, slipping and sliding as she searched for Sir Reginald Taft.

Has he already drowned?

She struggled to contain her panic. She just couldn't let the brave little dog die.

As she splashed farther from the shore, the steep bottom gave out from under her, and the water closed over her head. Managing to regain her footing, she straightened up and gasped for air.

London was up to her neck in the water, and the mud under her feet was oozy and sticky. She kicked off her shoes and began to swim frantically, first one way and then another. Finally she felt her fingers brush against a wet, hairy object. She glimpsed what looked like a floating wig half-submerged in the water.

It didn't seem like it was moving.

She managed to catch hold of the long hair, but then she stumbled and was submerged all over again. This time she swallowed some water, then coughed and choked violently when she bobbed back up into the air.

She was clutching the furry bundle in both hands now, but she couldn't regain her footing.

Suddenly London felt a strong arm reach around her shoulders from behind and lift her up, so that her head was well above water. Still holding onto the limp animal, she coughed all the water out of her throat and let her unseen rescuer drag her up onto the shore.

Grateful to be on solid dry ground, London collapsed and lay there catching her breath for a few moments.

Then she looked up and saw a familiar pair of sensitive blue eyes looking down at her.

She heard a familiar Australian-accented voice.

"Are you all right?" Bryce Yeaton asked.

"Yes, I think so," London gasped. "But what about …?"

"I don't know," Bryce said. "Let's check."

London pulled herself up, and she and Bryce stooped over the motionless dog. London was horrified to see how lifeless he appeared to be, lying on his back with his little feet in the air.

Bryce pressed on the dog's tiny chest, and the creature spewed up some water.

Sir Reginald turned over and scrambled to his feet, coughing and yapping.

"Oh, thank goodness!" London exclaimed with almost unimaginable relief. "I just *couldn't* let him drown!"

"I couldn't let either of you drown," Bryce said, putting a strong, comforting arm around her shoulder.

Now Sir Reginald seemed quite irritated at his undignified state. He shook violently, throwing mud and water all over Bryce and London.

"Oh, well," London said. "We weren't looking our best, anyway."

She and Bryce looked at each other and laughed. Suddenly it felt just fine to London to be all wet and muddy and sitting there on the ground with these two companions.

*

London took Sir Reginald to her room and rinsed him off in the bathroom sink, but he was still a tangled mass of wet hair. Too tired to deal with that problem now, she patted him partly dry, then took a shower herself and fell fast asleep on her bed for a little while.

When she woke up, she saw a text message on her phone. It was from Captain Hays, asking her to come at once to his stateroom. She put on a clean uniform and went straight there.

She knocked, and the relieved-looking captain opened the door for her.

"I am very glad to see you safe and sound," Captain Hays said. "I'm told that you've had quite an adventure."

As she came inside, she saw Alezredes Borsos rise from a chair.

"Quite an adventure indeed," the alezredes said to her in an amiable tone than she'd never heard from him before. "My men and I owe you quite a debt of thanks."

With uncharacteristic gallantry, Borsos offered her a seat.

"So what about that man you arrested?" London asked. "Did you find out who he was?"

"We certainly did," Borsos replied. "I checked with INTERPOL and found out that he is none other than Swain Warrington."

"That name isn't familiar to me," London said.

"No? Well, it is familiar to those of us in European law enforcement. He is a criminal genius—a nefarious master jewel thief who has been wanted all over the continent for years, but he has always managed to avoid capture until now. Thanks in no small part to yourself, he has at last been apprehended by the Gyor Rendőrség—our fine local police."

London smiled at how Borsos's chest swelled with pride. His present courtesy to her notwithstanding, London didn't doubt that he was going to take a great deal of credit for the capture of Swain Warrington. And the truth was, she didn't hold it against him one small bit.

It's really as it should be.

After all, she wasn't looking for fame and renown for her prowess as a detective.

"Has he confessed?" London asked.

"Oh, he's been quite talkative—and even rather charming, I must say. It's rather hard not to like the fellow. He's a true gentleman thief, you see, and he's quite apologetic that Mrs. Klimowski died on account of the mistake he made in drugging her. He says he doesn't practice his 'trade,' as he puts it, out of malice or greed, but rather for the challenge and the sport of it."

He chuckled and added, "He also told us the secret of the snuffbox. What an amazing story!"

Borsos leaned back in his chair and grinned at London.

"He also suggested that I find out more about him by asking—and these were his exact words—'that delightful and brilliant lady detective.'"

It took London a moment to realize that Warrington had meant herself.

"I'm not sure I understand," she said.

"Well, perhaps you can offer me your own account of his recent movements and methods."

London realized that she'd actually figured out a great deal about Warrington.

"He's a master of disguise, obviously," she said. "And that means quick-change disguise, I'm sure. I'll bet he can walk around a street corner dressed as one character, then appear on the other side looking like someone else altogether. Sometimes he might not even need makeup. Look at how he transformed himself right in front of our eyes from a shy pharmacist into a suave mastermind. He's also got an encyclopedic intelligence, and he's adept at many skills—including the violin."

"That is his reputation, yes," Borsos said.

London continued, "When my group dined at the Duna Étterem back in Budapest, our table was visited by a kindly economics professor named Vilmos Kallay—actually Warrington in disguise, of course."

"Of course," Borsos said.

"My guess is Warrington travels around Europe, covertly scouting groups of tourists and wealthy people, looking for especially rare and precious items to steal. Not many people would have known the true value of Mrs. Klimowski's snuffbox. But due to his expertise, he knew exactly what it was the moment he first glimpsed it in her hand at the Duna Étterem."

"Go on," Borsos said with another nod.

"Then he started planning his long game. When he found out the *Nachtmusik*'s next stop was Gyor, he eagerly recommended that we eat at the Magyar Öröm. Then he traveled here himself, changing disguises as he closed in on his quarry. He charmed himself into Amy's heart in the guise of a pharmacist, then showed up at the restaurant as a gypsy violinist."

London paused to think.

"When he saw Mrs. Klimowski leave the restaurant, he hurried after her, changing disguises as he went. He followed a crowd of tourists into the basilica and sat down in the pew beside her, feigning sympathy for her obvious distress. She was grateful and trusting. And then … well, he must have drugged her."

"And how did he do that?" Borsos asked.

"By offering her a drink, I suppose, to make her feel better," London said. "Perhaps out of a flask."

"Very good!" Borsos replied. "Our coroner found brandy in her stomach as well as the traces of prednisone and benzodiazepine in her bloodstream."

London tried to picture what must have happened next.

"She dozed off right there," London said. "He relieved her of her snuffbox, then stealthily removed her necklace and slipped it in her handbag—to show his contempt for 'petty ostentation,' as he put it. He also took the pills out of the snuffbox and put them into a cheap plastic pillbox, which he put in her handbag. That must have been when Mrs. Klimowski's dog got free and came back to the restaurant looking for help."

London scratched her chin, and continued, "Warrington had no idea that her life was in any danger. He didn't find out about it until the next morning, when he was presumably getting ready to leave Gyor. He felt guilty and alarmed, and took advantage of Amy's attraction to his 'pharmacist' persona to try to get a better idea of what had happened. Then, just as he said, he'd slipped the box to her out of fear of police who came too close, and ..."

London shrugged. "Well, I guess that's pretty much the whole story."

"Except for one thing," Borsos said. "How did you discover him?"

"Well, there was something about his face," London said. "But that alone wouldn't have been enough. He's such a master of disguise, I'm sure he's seldom ever recognized. That's why he's so daring and brazen."

"So what was it, then?"

"When he introduced himself as Sandor, he told me he liked to be thought of as a painter, but that he had to work as a pharmacist 'during the day.' That was strikingly similar to something Professor Kallay had told us—that he was a poet, but he worked as an economist in his 'day job.'"

Borsos squinted as if he didn't quite understand.

"Don't you see?" London said. "The characters Warrington plays have something in common—a certain 'theme,' if you will. Or as gamblers might put it, a 'tell.' They have personal passions aside from their daily work. If we'd talked to him in violinist guise, he might have admitted that he too had some sort of a 'day job.' Those characters actually reflect an aspect of Warrington's own personality—his passion for the sheer sport of thievery. Of course, the dog recognized him by smell, which sealed the case for me."

Borsos actually applauded.

"Bravo, Miss Rose. Brilliantly deduced, with a keen sense of psychology. I doubt that Swain Warrington himself could give a more precise and detailed account of his own activities. And I must say, he speaks very highly of you as an adversary. 'I look forward to the day when London Rose and I match wits again,' he says."

Borsos slapped his knee, laughing.

"A perfectly ridiculous notion, of course, now that we've caught him. He's going to be in prison for many years, I'm sure. I doubt that he'll ever practice his so-called 'trade' again."

London couldn't help but smile.

Somehow, she wondered whether Swain Warrington didn't have his own plans for the near future.

If so, maybe they don't involve staying in prison.

Borsos got to his feet and bowed to both London and the captain.

"And now, if you'll kindly excuse me, I must take my leave. I wish all of you a fine voyage to Vienna and beyond."

*

Night had fallen by the time the *Nachtmusik* began to navigate its way through the narrow waterways of Small Danube back to the main river. London and Bryce stood at the rail of the Rondo deck watching the lights of Gyor slip behind them. Soon Elsie came trotting up to join them.

"I'm glad I found you two!" she said. "And I must say, it's good to see both of you safe and sound. No more adventures since this afternoon, eh?"

London smiled and crossed her fingers.

"No, and we'll try to keep it that way, won't we, Bryce?"

"Absolutely," Bryce said.

Elsie petted the clean and well-trimmed little dog that London was holding in her arms.

"Goodness, I don't believe I've seen this adorable puppy before," she said.

London and Bryce laughed.

"Yes, you have," London said. "It's Mrs. Klimowski's dog. But I'm not surprised that you don't recognize him. He was such a mess when we dragged him out of the water, as soon as I got the chance I took him to the *Nachtmusik*'s beautician. She gave him a shampoo, and then we looked up how to take care of a Yorkshire Terrier's coat. Most people who keep them as pets rather than show dogs keep their coats trimmed short, like his is now."

"Aw, now he looks like a teddy bear," Elsie said, scratching the dog under the chin.

"He looks like a real dog, if you ask me," Bryce said. "An authentic scrappy little terrier, ready and eager to tangle with international jewel thieves. And the change was long overdue."

A worried look crossed Elsie's face.

"But who's going to keep him now that Mrs. Klimowski is gone?" she said.

"Well, I talked to Captain Hays about that a while ago," London said. "I guess you've heard that Mrs. Klimowski didn't have any heirs. And it seems that she's leaving her whole fortune to some semi-secret society called the Sisters of Mnemosyne. She didn't leave any instructions for this little guy's care, and no money either. So ..."

London's heart warmed as she finished her sentence.

"... it looks like I get to keep him."

She also felt a lump form in her throat. It had never occurred to her until today that she might really love having a dog of her very own. Especially this little dog.

She added, "I don't think he was very happy with Mrs. Klimowski, getting carried around in a bag like that. I want to give him a whole new life. And no more calling him Sir Reginald Taft. From now on it's just Sir Reggie—isn't it, buddy?"

The newly renamed dog let out a yap of approval. As London and her two friends laughed again, her phone rang.

"Oh, dear," she said as she saw who was calling. "I've really got to take this."

"Don't tell me," Elsie said. "It's Jeremy Lapham."

"That's right," London said. "After I talk to him, I'll probably turn in for the night. I'll see you both in Vienna when we get there!"

London walked toward the elevator as she took the call.

"Well done, London Rose!" Mr. Lapham exclaimed. "The captain told me all about your superb detective work! Congratulations and cheers and kudos are definitely in order. You've not only solved the mystery of our unfortunate passenger's death, but you've put the *Nachtmusik* back en route to her next destination. With a little bit of luck, Epoch World Cruise Lines is likely to survive after all! And all thanks to you! Brava, my dear!"

"Thank you, sir," London said as the elevator took her down to the Allegro deck.

"Now I suppose you'll be happy to get back to your regular duties."

"I think so, sir."

But London felt an odd pang as she said so. At first she'd been reluctant to try her hand at crime solving, but something had changed. Was it possible that she was going to miss the mental challenge and adrenaline rush of being an amateur detective? Without meaning to, she'd been developing a taste for it.

Well, I might wind up doing it again someday, she thought. *Who knows?*

She also remembered what Borsos had said Swain Warrington said about her.

"I look forward to the day when London Rose and I match wits again."

Was her path destined to cross his again one of these days?

London had no idea how she felt about that possibility.

"Where are you right now?" Mr. Lapham asked.

"On my way back to my room," London said.

"Excellent! You'll find a little surprise waiting for you there!"

And without another word, Mr. Lapham ended the call.

What on earth ... ? London wondered.

She walked inside her room, set Sir Reggie down, and turned on the light. As the little dog clambered tiredly up onto the bed, London saw a startling and familiar sight. A silver compote cover was right in the center of her little table. She lifted the shiny lid, and sure enough, a golden piece of baklava was underneath. In front of it was a card that read:

With compliments and gratitude from Jeremy Lapham—
a favorite of yours, I believe!

London let out a gasp of surprised delight.

How did he know? she wondered.

She sat down and took a taste of the delicately layered, almost unbelievably rich and tasty dessert.

I guess that's another mystery, she thought with a smile.

At least it didn't involve anybody's murder. And now she had the delicious pastries of Vienna to look forward to—and a pleasant, uncomplicated visit.

Or so she hoped.

Who knows what the future holds? she wondered.

NOW AVAILABLE!

DEATH (AND APPLE STRUDEL)
(A European Voyage Cozy Mystery—Book 2)

"When you think that life cannot get better, Blake Pierce comes up with another masterpiece of thriller and mystery! This book is full of twists, and the end brings a surprising revelation. Strongly recommended for the permanent library of any reader who enjoys a very well-written thriller."
--Books and Movie Reviews (re *Almost Gone*)

DEATH (AND APPLE STRUDEL) is book two in a charming new cozy mystery series by #1 bestselling author Blake Pierce, whose *Once Gone* has over 1,500 five-star reviews. The series begins with MURDER (AND BAKLAVA)—BOOK #1.

When London Rose, 33, is proposed to by her long-time boyfriend, she realizes she is facing a stable, predictable, pre-determined (and passionless) life. She freaks out and runs the other way—accepting instead a job across the Atlantic, as a tour-guide on a high-end European cruise line that travels through a country a day. London is searching for a more romantic, unscripted and exciting life that she feels sure exists out there somewhere.

London is elated: the European river towns are small, historic and charming. She gets to see a new port every night, gets to sample an endless array of new cuisine and meet a stream of interesting people. It is a traveler's dream, and it is anything but predictable.

In Book 2, DEATH (AND APPLE STRUDEL), the cruise takes them into Vienna and Salzburg, home of Mozart and the birthplace of music, and all seems picture-perfect. Until, that its, their tour guide turns up dead after giving the passengers a tour of Mozart's theatre. Suspicion falls on them. Who could have killed her? And why?

Laugh-out-loud funny, romantic, endearing, rife with new sights, culture and food, DEATH (AND APPLE STRUDEL) offers a fun and suspenseful trip through the heart of Europe, anchored in an intriguing mystery that will keep you on the edge of your seat and guessing until the very last page.

Book #3 (CRIME AND LAGER) is now also available.

Blake Pierce

Blake Pierce is the USA Today bestselling author of the RILEY PAIGE mystery series, which includes seventeen books. Blake Pierce is also the author of the MACKENZIE WHITE mystery series, comprising fourteen books; of the AVERY BLACK mystery series, comprising six books; of the KERI LOCKE mystery series, comprising five books; of the MAKING OF RILEY PAIGE mystery series, comprising six books; of the KATE WISE mystery series, comprising seven books; of the CHLOE FINE psychological suspense mystery, comprising six books; of the JESSE HUNT psychological suspense thriller series, comprising fourteen books (and counting); of the AU PAIR psychological suspense thriller series, comprising three books; of the ZOE PRIME mystery series, comprising four books (and counting); of the new ADELE SHARP mystery series, comprising four six books (and counting); and of the new EUROPEAN VOYAGE cozy mystery series.

An avid reader and lifelong fan of the mystery and thriller genres, Blake loves to hear from you, so please feel free to visit www.blakepierceauthor.com to learn more and stay in touch.

BOOKS BY BLAKE PIERCE

EUROPEAN VOYAGE COZY MYSTERY SERIES
MURDER (AND BAKLAVA) (Book #1)
DEATH (AND APPLE STRUDEL) (Book #2)
CRIME (AND LAGER) (Book #3)

ADELE SHARP MYSTERY SERIES
LEFT TO DIE (Book #1)
LEFT TO RUN (Book #2)
LEFT TO HIDE (Book #3)
LEFT TO KILL (Book #4)
LEFT TO MURDER (Book #5)
LEFT TO ENVY (Book #6)
LEFT TO LAPSE (Book #7)

THE AU PAIR SERIES
ALMOST GONE (Book#1)
ALMOST LOST (Book #2)
ALMOST DEAD (Book #3)

ZOE PRIME MYSTERY SERIES
FACE OF DEATH (Book#1)
FACE OF MURDER (Book #2)
FACE OF FEAR (Book #3)
FACE OF MADNESS (Book #4)
FACE OF FURY (Book #5)
FACE OF DARKNESS (Book #6)

A JESSIE HUNT PSYCHOLOGICAL SUSPENSE SERIES
THE PERFECT WIFE (Book #1)
THE PERFECT BLOCK (Book #2)
THE PERFECT HOUSE (Book #3)
THE PERFECT SMILE (Book #4)
THE PERFECT LIE (Book #5)
THE PERFECT LOOK (Book #6)

THE PERFECT AFFAIR (Book #7)
THE PERFECT ALIBI (Book #8)
THE PERFECT NEIGHBOR (Book #9)
THE PERFECT DISGUISE (Book #10)
THE PERFECT SECRET (Book #11)
THE PERFECT FAÇADE (Book #12)
THE PERFECT IMPRESSION (Book #13)
THE PERFECT DECEIT (Book #14)
THE PERFECT MISTRESS (Book #15)

CHLOE FINE PSYCHOLOGICAL SUSPENSE SERIES
NEXT DOOR (Book #1)
A NEIGHBOR'S LIE (Book #2)
CUL DE SAC (Book #3)
SILENT NEIGHBOR (Book #4)
HOMECOMING (Book #5)
TINTED WINDOWS (Book #6)

KATE WISE MYSTERY SERIES
IF SHE KNEW (Book #1)
IF SHE SAW (Book #2)
IF SHE RAN (Book #3)
IF SHE HID (Book #4)
IF SHE FLED (Book #5)
IF SHE FEARED (Book #6)
IF SHE HEARD (Book #7)

THE MAKING OF RILEY PAIGE SERIES
WATCHING (Book #1)
WAITING (Book #2)
LURING (Book #3)
TAKING (Book #4)
STALKING (Book #5)
KILLING (Book #6)

RILEY PAIGE MYSTERY SERIES
ONCE GONE (Book #1)
ONCE TAKEN (Book #2)
ONCE CRAVED (Book #3)

ONCE LURED (Book #4)
ONCE HUNTED (Book #5)
ONCE PINED (Book #6)
ONCE FORSAKEN (Book #7)
ONCE COLD (Book #8)
ONCE STALKED (Book #9)
ONCE LOST (Book #10)
ONCE BURIED (Book #11)
ONCE BOUND (Book #12)
ONCE TRAPPED (Book #13)
ONCE DORMANT (Book #14)
ONCE SHUNNED (Book #15)
ONCE MISSED (Book #16)
ONCE CHOSEN (Book #17)

MACKENZIE WHITE MYSTERY SERIES
BEFORE HE KILLS (Book #1)
BEFORE HE SEES (Book #2)
BEFORE HE COVETS (Book #3)
BEFORE HE TAKES (Book #4)
BEFORE HE NEEDS (Book #5)
BEFORE HE FEELS (Book #6)
BEFORE HE SINS (Book #7)
BEFORE HE HUNTS (Book #8)
BEFORE HE PREYS (Book #9)
BEFORE HE LONGS (Book #10)
BEFORE HE LAPSES (Book #11)
BEFORE HE ENVIES (Book #12)
BEFORE HE STALKS (Book #13)
BEFORE HE HARMS (Book #14)

AVERY BLACK MYSTERY SERIES
CAUSE TO KILL (Book #1)
CAUSE TO RUN (Book #2)
CAUSE TO HIDE (Book #3)
CAUSE TO FEAR (Book #4)
CAUSE TO SAVE (Book #5)
CAUSE TO DREAD (Book #6)

KERI LOCKE MYSTERY SERIES
A TRACE OF DEATH (Book #1)
A TRACE OF MUDER (Book #2)
A TRACE OF VICE (Book #3)
A TRACE OF CRIME (Book #4)
A TRACE OF HOPE (Book #5)

Made in the USA
Las Vegas, NV
06 January 2022

40572405R00125